Charlie Kane
The Magic Writer

Charlie Kane
The Magic Writer
Book One of the Kane Saga

Frances,
    Write magic into your
world!
        Kelly Scidmore-Sievers

Kelly Scidmore-Sievers
Illustration by Emilia Kolarova

outskirtspress
DENVER, COLORADO

Charlie Kane the Magic Writer
Book One of the Kane Saga
All Rights Reserved.
Copyright © 2014 Kelly Scidmore-Sievers
v2.0

Cover Illustration by Emilia Kolarova

Outskirts Press, Inc.
http://www.outskirtspress.com

ISBN: 978-1-4787-2848-1

Library of Congress Control Number: 2014915435

Outskirts Press and the "OP" logo are trademarks belonging to Outskirts Press, Inc.

PRINTED IN THE UNITED STATES OF AMERICA

I dedicate this book to my children Charles, Cassandra and Jeff. It's been a privilege to be a part of your world all these years. You are my true heroes. And to my husband Daniel who pushes me outside my comfort zone to do things I never thought possible. Thank you for having faith in me and believing in me especially during the times when I lost faith in myself. Without you four I would never have accomplished this dream.

The only thing necessary for the triumph of evil is for good men to do nothing.

— Edmund Burke

Chapter One

The Uninvited Visitor

The sun peeked through a broken slit in Charlie's blinds and fell directly onto his sleeping face. The warmth of the light brought an unsuspecting smile to his peaceful features. Pulling the covers up to his chin he let out a small groan as the bed grew warmer and he became more awake to the coming of a new day. He turned towards the edge of the bed and let his leg hang out from the sheets to test the chilliness of his room. His long gangly leg dangled over, searching for the floor and found warmth he didn't expect to find on a cold winter day. The unexpected warmth prompted a quick hop out of bed to start another day.

What to do, what to do, Charlie pondered. Saturdays were his favorite day of the week. Of course Saturdays were probably all teenagers favorite day of the week, but Charlie's reasons for enjoying Saturday were different. Most teenagers were excited about being off school for the weekend and making plans for partying and social events. Charlie on the other hand enjoyed school. Well at least the learning part. He just didn't really enjoy the social part of it. He couldn't wait for Saturday because it was the one day he felt free to read and play chess and study up on topics he really enjoyed. He never went to parties and rarely socialized unless playing a game of chess with his one friend Amanda or telling his stories of a far-away land to his sister Kassie. Otherwise his time was spent quietly with family, books and computers.

Charlie was especially excited for this Saturday. He'd been playing with an idea all week for a story about a young boy's adventure into a strange land where he meets strange creatures he'd only read about in his fantasy books. Kassie loved stories about far away mystical lands, so he was going to write this one for her, certain she'd love all the creatures he was planning to create. But first Charlie needed brain food. Lucky Charms. That was another thing Charlie loved about Saturday. His mom insisted on the family eating oatmeal or eggs or fruit or yogurt all week since she felt they were a more acceptable brain food source, but on Saturdays they were allowed to eat anything they wanted for breakfast. Charlie's choice of Saturday breakfast food was Lucky Charms. And no matter what his mom proclaimed, Charlie insisted that Lucky Charms was better brain food then oatmeal or fruits. He always seemed to have the best ideas after a heaping bowl of Lucky Charms.

Charlie found his sister had already beaten him to the kitchen for breakfast and a small look of panic came and went from his face quickly as he saw Kassie was actually sitting with a bowl of fresh grapes and strawberries and a glass of milk in front of her. True, Kassie had better nutrition than her brother, but once in a great while she was known to indulge in a bowl of Lucky Charms. Since Charlie knew he'd only left enough Lucky Charms for one more bowl, he was relieved to see Kassie was staying true to her healthy eating on this Saturday. Charlie felt for certain he'd need a heaping bowl of cereal and not one morsel less this morning to get his creative brainwaves moving for his special laid book plans.

"Hey, Charlie," Kassie sang out before popping a beautiful bright red strawberry into her mouth.

"Hey sis," Charlie answered back while pouring his heaping bowl of Lucky Charms.

"You're so predictable," Kassie said. "Always head right for the Lucky Charms every Saturday, then up to your room and onto the computer you'll go. Maybe you should try doing something different. Mix it up."

"Why should I mix it up? If it's not broken, why fix it? Besides, a bowl of Lucky Charms can only bring luck thus the name *Lucky Charms*."

Kassie chuckled. "Sometimes you are so ridiculous yet so funny," she said as she popped the last strawberry into her mouth and gathered up the bowl and cup, went to the sink and then paused, turning to Charlie. "Mom said we're all going to Alzanos for dinner tonight and then to see The Hobbit."

The Hobbit! Charlie couldn't believe it. The day just kept getting better and better. "Awesome," Charlie exclaimed. "I've been waiting for that movie for months! It's finally here!"

"Yeah, I thought you'd be excited about that. Mom also said we can bring a friend if we want. I'm bringing Alison."

Charlie's smile faded a little with that news. He always looked forward to spending time with just family and was a little disappointed Alison would be joining them. Strange as it was, he so loved it when he and Kassie sat at the movies together, especially when it was a fantasy movie, which was their favorite to watch. Kassie picked up on the change of the mood quickly, even though Charlie covered it up by smiling broader again.

"Hey, you know, I'm planning a 'Just Dance' day tomorrow with Alison and some of the others, so I'm thinking maybe I'll skip asking her to go tonight. You know how it is, if you spend too much time together then they aren't special anymore. Unless you plan to bring Amanda or something tonight."

Charlie turned and faced Kassie, who was standing by the sink wiping down her last plate before putting it in the dishwasher. He silently watched her as she wiped the dish and then shook it off. Certainly she didn't think she was fooling him with this Just Dance thing. How could she believe that would fool him? Her heart was so huge and whether she knew it or not she wore it on her sleeve.

The silence brought her gaze towards Charlie and they stared at each other for a short while in silence both truly knowing what was behind the others stare. They knew each other so well. Charlie was the one to break the silence. "Amanda is out of town this weekend, so I won't be asking her, but don't feel you have to not ask Alison because of that."

"No, I'd rather not, really. Alison doesn't even really get stories like the Hobbit anyway. She'd only make me mad with her comments about it through the movie," she said before giving him a quick smile and leaving the room.

Charlie sat down at the computer, pulled up Word and started to write. He hadn't gotten more than a paragraph into the story when he heard his mother yell up the stairs. "Charlie, go downstairs and get the clothes out of the dryer for me please."

Well, there was one downfall to weekends...chores. "Sure Mom," he yelled back. Maybe he could get at least one more paragraph written before going downstairs.

Ten minutes later Charlie, once again absorbed in his story, heard his mother's voice. "Charlie, now please."

"I'm coming," he yelled back. He hadn't meant to get so caught up in the story to forget his mom's request. Well, maybe if he could just run downstairs and whip through those clothes he could get back upstairs before losing his place in this story. His mom just didn't get how easy it was to lose the rhythm of a story when you stop, and he knew if he told her she'd never understand.

Charlie took the stairs two at a time and made it down to the bottom of the steps only to hear his mom's voice once again, "Charlie, don't jump down the stairs. One of these times you're going to fall and break your neck." This statement from her was so predictable minus the neck part. That changed every time. Sometimes it was neck, sometimes leg, sometimes head, but all in all she said it often. Why couldn't she understand how he just wanted to get to the bottom as fast as he could so as not to waste so much time? "Sorry mom, I won't do it again," was his regular response, knowing all too well he probably would.

The laundry room was in the basement along with shelves filled with sealed boxes and Christmas decorations. An old couch sat in the middle of the basement along with an old sewing machine and then the washer and dryer. All in all it wasn't a place they ever really ventured much other than to use the laundry facilities. Charlie had always been curious what stayed hidden among all those sealed boxes. He'd asked his Dad once a long time ago only to get a two word response: "The past."

Charlie grabbed the laundry basket off the top of the dryer, placed it under the dryer door and scooped the warm soft clothes into the basket. As Charlie was grabbing a handful of warm clothes, he felt something move. Startled he yanked his hand away from the clothes, making a yelping sound. Charlie's imagination started going wild, wondering if a snake or a rat had made its way into the dryer, but his imagination would never have guessed what appeared next. Out from beneath his father's black work pants, black socks, shirts and underwear, a dull black eyeball peered out. Then another one peeked through a holey pair of dark grey underwear. Charlie knew instinctively he should back away from the strange creature creeping out of his father's clothes, but he rarely did what most people would naturally do. So Charlie inched forward, crouching lower to get a better glimpse at these strange dark eyeballs peering out from his father's underwear.

"Hey there," Charlie crooned soothingly to the eyes hoping to coax the creature out.

"Hey yourself," a grouchy voice answered back as it stuck out first one dark green hairy leg and then another, scooting out the dryer opening. "You think you can help or something you Knucklehead," came the gruff voice of this new creation to the Kane's dryer.

Charlie stood stunned as what appeared to be a mystical creature seen only in books or in his imagination managed to stumble the rest of the way out of the dryer, planting his feet down right in front of him. Charlie closed his eyes and shook his head. Opening his eyes, he saw the creature staring at him with a grimace on his face. He stood silently appraising the creature, starting from his fat toes up to his dark black cloth of an outfit strapped around his torso and further up to his hairy dark green face where a-top his head laid his father's grey holey underwear.

"Close your air hole, Knucklehead," the creature growled. "Haven't you ever seen a goblin before?"

Charlie hadn't realized he'd been staring open mouthed and quickly closed his mouth. He was sensitive to being told his mouth was hanging open. His grandfather pointed it out to him all the time. "Charlie, you're going to eat all the flies in here if you don't close it," he'd state. Or, "what are you, a baby bird waiting to be fed?" So the last thing Charlie needed was for this goblin thing to be lecturing him about his bad habit.

"Did you say goblin?"

"What are you deaf or something? Geez, Forerunner never told me I'd be bringing back a deaf and dumb human."

Bring back? Forerunner? What was going on here, Charlie wondered, pinching himself in the arm to see if it felt real and flinched when he realized he was really standing here looking at a goblin. "I don't understand. Take what human back where and how did you get in the dryer?" Charlie asked as he bent down to inspect it, to see if he might find other mystical creatures perching in there somewhere.

"Dryer? Oh, you mean the portal?" The goblin asked as he looked back towards the dryer Charlie was now peering into.

"Portal?" His dryer a portal? A portal to where? "How is it possible for this dryer to be a portal?" Charlie asked as he inspected it even closer looking for any holes and cracks anywhere that might explain a goblin emerging from it.

"Portals are rarely wide open for all to see, Knucklehead, so you might as well stop playing around there. You'll never find the opening."

Charlie still stuck his head into the dryer and took his hand and felt around in there as his curiosity got the better of him. The goblin rapped his fist on the top of the dryer causing Charlie to jump and bang his head. "Hey, Knucklehead! I don't have all day you know! Get your fat Knucklehead out of there already."

Charlie pulled his head out from the dryer, rubbing the bump on his scalp from where he had just hit it. "I don't understand. How is it I'm staring at a goblin wearing my father's underwear as a hat standing in my basement having just emerged from my dryer?"

The goblin's eyes looked up trying to see what was on his head and he grabbed the underwear off his scalp, tossing it to the floor, and for whatever reason this action brought a chuckle to Charlie's mouth. "I liked you better with the underwear. And my dad thinks I'm a butthead," and his chuckle turned into downright laughter. And for a single moment he was certain he saw a glimpse of a smile on the grouchy goblin's face. But no sooner had he seen the upward curve of the goblin's lip then it disappeared again.

The goblin rapped his fist this time on Charlie's head before speaking, "Get over yourself already, Knucklehead. We need to be heading out and I don't have time for such childish speechness. It's hard to believe you're the savior of Pulchritude Amity."

"Speechness?" Charlie laughed harder at the goblin's strange word choice. "You have...funny speechness." Charlie let out a rapid succession of laughter. Then Charlie received a harsher rap to the head from the fist.

"I don't have time for this stupidness, Knucklehead. We need to leave before we get discovered."

Charlie stopped laughing even though he almost had another surge of hilarity from the stupidness comment. "Leave? I'm not going anywhere, and why do you keep calling me Knucklehead. My name is Charlie."

"Charlie...Knucklehead...aren't they the same?" The goblin responded as he grabbed Charlie's arm and started to crawl into the dryer.

"Hey let go! I'm not getting into that deathtrap," Charlie stated as he tried to yank his arm free from the goblin's grasp only to fail. "Hey, you're pretty strong," he said as he struggled harder to try and break free.

"I'm not asking. I'm insistamating," the goblin growled to Charlie. The misuse of another word didn't fall flat on the boy's intelligence and a brand new session of laughter began. The laughter opened up a moment of weakness, which gave the goblin an opportunity to drag Charlie into the dryer with him. The laughter dissipated as quickly as it had begun as Charlie's head was banged here and there in order to fit him into the dryer along with a short plump goblin.

"Hey, stop! What are you doing...ouch!" Charlie tried putting his hands to his head to protect it from bumping the edges sticking out inside the dryer; however quarters were so tight that any movement by him caused him to collide into the goblin's plump body.

"Stop moving, Knucklehead. I *would* be the loser to get this crap job. It will be the last time I get some gruel while Forerunner decides who should bring back a snotty boy." Very slowly the goblin squirmed a bit until he was able to grasp a rock from a small pouch attached to his belt and placed it in a small hole in the far right hand corner of the dryer. Quarters became even tighter for Charlie as the goblin wrapped his arms around him in a rather awkward bear hug. Charlie squirmed more to try and free himself from this crazy creature before suffocating from the lack of room. Suddenly a humming vibration started pulsing through his body, and he felt the tight inner area of the dryer begin to expand.

"Leave...me...alone," Charlie spat out as he tried breaking free from the goblin's strong grip. Before the goblin could reply, a loud whirring sound encased the dryer, and Charlie and the goblin found themselves somersaulting around and around while their heads took turns banging against the dryer walls and each other's heads. Someone had turned the dryer on, or so Charlie thought, and his voice screamed out "Help" over and over in rhythm to the bumping of his head against the dryer wall and then the goblin's head. By the third help Charlie felt nauseous and a rather violent bump of his head against the dryer wall brought blackness. The last thing he remembered was the goblin pulling him closer and whispering "almost home."

Chapter Two
The Journey Through Mud Valley

Kassie sat at her desk in her room skimming over the contents displayed on her facebook wall and she laughed at a post Alison had written about running with her team in the forest preserve. Alison had been chatting with Katie about how she was certain bigfoot did not actually have big feet when 'bam!', her head collided into a low tree branch. She collapsed and felt woozy and when she looked up the whole team had circled back for her and was standing around her laughing. Sounds just like Alison to be so clumsy. Kassie posted on her wall "so true to you" and laughed as she wrote it.

"Kassie, your brother never brought the laundry up. Please go see what is taking him," her mother yelled up to her. Kassie sighed. So true of Charlie also. He gets so absorbed in other things like comic books, or video games or his writings that he forgets to do what he was asked. Likely he was letting curiosity about those taped boxes downstairs distract him and he forgot the laundry. Dad should never have told him that he had boxes from the past down there that only spurred on her brother's imagination. Charlie had wanted to look through them, but Dad said it would be too much work to dig through those boxes and promised him one day he would. One day still hadn't happened. That was Dad's favorite spiel, the 'one day' that never came. Charlie had probably gotten tired of waiting for that one day and was likely caught up unwrapping and digging through all those old boxes. Dad wouldn't be happy if that was the case.

"Okay mom. I'll go check."

The basement was void of Charlie but he must have been here, figured Kassie, since half of Dad's laundry was in the basket in front

CHARLIE KANE THE MAGIC WRITER

of the dryer. Great, he got halfway and obviously got caught up in some story idea or got a call from Amanda and disappeared and as usual she'd have to finish what he started. She sighed again. She sure did love Charlie, but he certainly didn't seem like the older of the two of them. He wasn't too far off from college and she could picture his dorm filled with half-done stuff and his roommate wondering where Charlie had wandered off to. Kassie smiled as she pictured it and opened the dryer door to scoop out the remaining laundry. The last item missed the basket as she scooped it out and landed on the floor with a 'plink'. Since when did underwear 'plink'? She picked the shorts off the floor and a small blue stone fell free. Kassie squatted down and gently picked up the stone. She brought it close to her face and examined it. She'd never seen such a shiny and glittery blue stone before. Where had this come from? Well she knew who could find that out, she thought to herself as she pocketed the stone.

Charlie started to move, first a flutter of his eyelids and then the wiggling of his fingers. An ache crept through his back up to his scalp. He didn't remember his bed feeling this hard and cold and where was the warmth that greeted him every day? His eyes fluttered again and he grimaced as the movement caused the aching in his head to feel worse.

"Wake up Knucklehead."

Charlie's eyes opened wide and he was greeted by the blackness of the goblin's gaze. At first he felt confused and then it all came back to him. He jumped up and backed away from the goblin, putting his hands out in front of him for protection. "What...what's going on?" He sputtered.

"We're home," the goblin answered nonchalantly, and turning from Charlie he leaned over and picked up a shiny blue stone. He placed the stone into his pouch and turned back to face Charlie. "And we need to be leaving."

A cool breeze blew across Charlie's face and brought a chill down his spine. For the first time he became aware he was no longer cramped in a dryer, though his head still felt the effects. He glanced around him but saw he was no longer home, even if the goblin claimed he was.

He stood among tall old trees that appeared to have a face of their own and were naked. The nude branches swayed as the cool breeze picked up and the movement created a haunting dance. Grey clouds scattered throughout the sky covered any hope that sunlight would peek through. The ground was void of anything green or alive as every inch seemed to be covered in dirt with patches of mud scattered around indicating rain had come recently. To Charlie's left was a strange boulder with blue rocks at its base, and at the top sprouted a strange-looking patch of glittery blue flowers. He had never seen flowers so bright blue before let alone with such a glint to them and he took a step forward in order to get a better look. A strong green arm barricaded his way.

"Whoa there Knucklehead. No one touches the indulgent blues. They're sacred here."

Here? Sacred here? Charlie glanced around and then abruptly turned and stared eye to eye with the goblin. "Here? You said here. Where is here?"

"Pulchritude Amity of course. We are wasting valuable daylight and need to make use of it." The hairy green Goblin took a firm grasp of Charlie's arm and tugged him into motion as the goblin started to trek forward. Charlie tugged downward as hard as he could to free himself of the goblin's grasp and surprising the hairy gremlin with his quick thrust, broke free. The problem with this plan was he surprised himself as well, and the rough thrust that tore the goblin's hand away from his arm caused Charlie to lose his balance and land butt first into a pile of mud. The boy sat stunned, staring up at the goblin as he felt the mud sticking to him.

"Get up," the goblin stated firmly.

Charlie didn't move an inch. "I'm not going anywhere until you explain what is going on." Charlie pulled his hands out of the mud, shook some mud off and crossed his arms, giving the goblin his most intimidating stare.

"You better get up now," the goblin growled as he stepped towards Charlie. The cold mud that the boy sat in started to warm, and mud bubbles started to develop around his thighs and buttocks. The bubbles started small then became bigger and bigger and white foam started exploding out of them. Charlie felt sudden heat searing through his legs, causing him to jump to his feet and yell in pain.

"I told you to get up, Knucklehead. Maybe next time you'll listen."

Charlie rubbed the back of his thighs as he still felt the burning pain eating into his skin. "What…what was that?" He asked.

"Mud Lava. It loves the warmth of human skin and since that is in short supply, I'm sure you awakened a surprised Mud Lava."

Charlie felt as if the goblin was speaking a totally new language. Mud Lava. And short supply of humans. He must be dreaming, but the burning on the back of his thighs felt so real. "Don't think I've forgotten you were stealing me away somewhere just because I'm standing. I'm still not going anywhere until you explain yourself."

The goblin's hard face softened a little as he watched Charlie rub his thighs again. "I suppose I owe you that much. But first we need to make a little distance before nightfall. This area of Mud Valley is not a safe place to make camp…lots of Mud Lava."

Charlie looked around again. So this was Mud Valley. And this was daytime, although it was hard to believe. With the gloominess all around them he couldn't imagine night could get much darker. "Okay, I'll go with you but only as far as we can go until night fall and then we camp and you explain all this," Charlie swept his hands around to indicate the land they stood in.

"Fine," the goblin grudgingly answered. "Stay close and stay out of those mud piles." The goblin needn't tell Charlie twice and he subconsciously rubbed his burning thighs. The boy took up behind the goblin and kept his face down watching for more Mud Lava as they moved forward. They zigged and zagged around mud puddles as they walked deeper and deeper into the woods. The landscape was drab and dark. Bare trees and black dirt with scattered mud piles could be seen all around them, and the one rare boulder topped with blue blossoms disappeared from sight.

The boy was such an annoyance. He would never understand how one stupid human could possibly make any difference to this world, but Forerunner insisted this boy was the key as his father, Daubier had been so many years ago. The goblin hadn't liked Daubier anymore than he cared for his son Charlie. Both had such an uppity attitude to them as though humans were so much better than his race. He turned and glanced back at his companion or as he liked to think of him, his captive. He watched as the boy was hopping around mud piles never glancing up to notice what was in front of him. He was so engrossed in what was beneath him; it would be easy to take him out. How could someone so clueless and helpless be of any use to them? And he's a human to boot! Forerunner claimed that the boy possessed all the traits required to find the remaining three humans still in Pulchritude Amity. Forerunner also claimed the boy was supposedly intelligent, disciplined, knowledgeable and strong minded. The goblin watched Charlie as he jumped over a mud pile, slid and almost fell into another mud pit in front of him but at the last minute righted himself. He looked up at the goblin and smiled a half smug smile as to seem so proud he hadn't fallen flat on his face. Yeah, not sure about Forerunner's judgment on this one, he thought.

"Stop jumping around or you'll fall and break your neck," he growled.

Charlie stopped abruptly and the smile disappeared from his face. He stared directly at the squat goblin. "What did you just say?"

"Real intelligent Forerunner," the goblin mumbled. "Just stop with the messing around. I don't have the skill to take care of an injured human." He turned and started stomping forward again.

"It's just my mom says that to me all the time. It's strange you'd say the same thing." Perhaps it was the gloominess that surrounded him, or perhaps it was that one small phrase, but he started thinking of home and the coziness of his computer chair and how much he already missed those things. "I want to know what is happening! I refuse to go even one more inch until you explain why I'm here and when I can go back home. It's cold here and so...dreary. I don't want to be here and I don't understand why I am. And...and you're a goblin!" Saying the words made it so real and so strange. The stress of the events of the day made him lose sight of the fact he was actually walking with and talking to a goblin. "Goblins are enemies of humans and yet here I am being strung along by one."

The goblin in question stopped in his tracks and turned to face Charlie. "So smart boy, how would you know that humans and goblins are enemies? Have you ever met a goblin before?"

"Well, uh...no, but I've read about it in books. It's common knowledge," Charlie stammered foolishly.

"Do you believe everything you read? If I remember right, in your world books are...what do they call it...fraction?"

Charlie cracked a smile at the goblin's obvious mistake. "Fiction," he corrected, "And not all books are fiction. And what did you say about my world? Are you saying we are no longer in my world...but a different...world?" Charlie glanced around again. The land had faded behind a darkness Charlie had never known before. Now he understood the difference between daylight and nighttime here. He would never have believed this world could be much darker than the gloomy daylight had been. He shivered and wrapped his arms tightly around himself to try and ignite some warmth. The night brought a chill, but he realized the eeriness the darkness of night brought with it was as much responsible for the shiver as was the cold.

The shiver did not go unnoticed by the goblin. "I forgot how human skin is so thin. I suppose this spot is as good as any for us to camp. Not too many creatures should find us in this part of Mud Valley. The lack of food source keeps them away," he commented as he began unpacking a few items from his backpack. Charlie watched as the hairy kobold took several sticks and started piling them into a pyramid shape on the ground in front of him.

"Normally I'd forgo a fire," the goblin stated as he scanned the air above them. "But I had forgotten that humans feel the chill in the air far before we do. Forerunner would never forgive me if I risked all to bring you here and then allowed you to freeze before we reached him." The green goblin took a red and yellow stone from his pack and tapped them together over the twigs and a fire ignited. Charlie stood fascinated by not only the color of the rocks, but by how easily the goblin had started up the fire by just striking them together. His green guide allowed a true smile to pass across his lips as he watched Charlie's fascination with the fire. It had been a long time since he had seen such intrigue with such a small piece of magic.

"How...how did you do that?" Charlie's curious nature took his mind off the chill in the air. The goblin handed the two rocks to Charlie to investigate. "It's a small bit of magic a human gave me long ago." He purposely left out the part that the human had been Charlie's father. Forerunner had warned him that he was not allowed to disclose that information to Charlie. And loyalty was one trait the hairy goblin had that he was proud of. Forerunner had his reasons to want that information kept quiet. The squat goblin respected him and would do whatever he was told. Otherwise he'd never have taken this job. Charlie wasn't too farfetched with his notion that goblins and humans were enemies. However, Pulchritude Amity was in dire straits and humans and magic were their last options to bring it back to what this world once was. The two went hand in hand. So the goblins realized they had to make some sort of truce with human kind if they wanted to fix this world once again and rid themselves of Czar Nefarious.

The fat hairy goblin watched intently as Charlie tapped the rocks and fire flew from them. It didn't take him long to bring fire from the stones. A red hue glowed around his hands as they brought magic to life. Magic lived in him. The goblin could see it now. With the right tools this boy could be strong in magic. For the first time since their meeting the squat goblin started to realize that Forerunner may be right. Charlie may be the answer. While the stones entertained the boy, the goblin pulled some dried food from his pack and tore a piece off and munched on it.

"I'm sort of hungry," Charlie stated and let his eyes look pleadingly at the goblin.

Charlie's hairy green captor humphed and grudgingly tore another piece from the dried food and tossed it to the boy. "I suppose I have to feed you if I expect you to keep up with me tomorrow. We have a long day ahead and likely not as safe as today. Eat that up quickly and get some sleep." He bent over and picked up the stones Charlie had dropped in order to catch the food that was tossed him, and then quickly placed them into his pack. It would be a long trip if they lost those. Fire would be essential to keeping the boy alive.

"I'm not going anywhere tomorrow unless you tell me what is going on," Charlie firmly stated in between bites of chewing. He choked and coughed a bit as he tried to swallow the tasteless morsel of food. "What is this stuff?" Charlie asked as his face twisted into a look of disgust.

"Food. Shut up and eat it Knucklehead."

"I already told you, my name is Charlie. Stop calling me that." The goblin sat down across from him and leaned up against the tree.

"You look more like a Knucklehead than a Charlie to me," the hairy gremlin proudly proclaimed as the two stubbornly stared at each other.

"Hey, it just dawned on me; I don't know your name."

"Dim," was Dim's single word answer.

"Dim?" Charlie smiled at the name. "Well, that seems to fit." Dim continued to stare at Charlie lost to the insult. "So, I'm waiting for my explanation."

Dim sighed as he realized how stubborn this boy was. He was exhausted just listening to him. "I suppose you'll keep bothering me until you find out what is going on," he sighed. "Pulchritude Amity is a world full of life." Charlie scrunched his face with disbelief at this news. "I see you. I know what you're thinking. This doesn't look like a place full of life. I suppose I should rephrase that. Pulchritude Amity used to be a place full of life. Now it is slowly dying. The first to go are humans and with them magic. So few humans are still alive here in Pulchritude Amity and honestly I don't think most races would care if humans disappeared for good." Charlie's face changed from disbelief to one of concern at this news.

"So, I'm right. Goblins and humans are enemies," Charlie exclaimed as he slowly scooted backwards to distance himself from Dim.

"I can't deny that goblins and humans have a...difficult past. But as humans disappear from our land, so does the magic. Czar Nefarious realized this himself and declared any remaining humans must be captured and imprisoned until he was able to extract the magic from them. As if it's that simple, but Nefarious doesn't understand magic and that it's not something you can just extract from someone. Forerunner understands the origins of magic thanks to... another human long gone from here now. But it didn't take long for Forerunner to discover a different human who would be able to bring back magic to this land. But in order to do that we must bury our... conflicts with humans to succeed...at least for now," Dim whispered this last bit. The last wasn't lost on Charlie, but he chose to ignore it for now and stay silent. The goblin was finally explaining himself and he didn't want to interrupt, afraid Dim would stop. Keeping his mouth closed was difficult since Charlie was itching with questions.

"Anyway, Czar Nefarious hasn't been able to locate any more humans, so he hasn't been able to extract magic from anyone, but he has his hunters searching every inch of this land. There aren't many left to be found. Forerunner calculates three in total. Four if we count you." Dim became silent as he tried to decide how much more was okay to reveal to this skinny, knowledge-soaking boy. His silence opened up room for Charlie's questions.

"Okay...I get the gist but I still don't understand why you needed to kidnap me and bring me to this...dreary place."

"You're the one Charlie. The one to bring magic back or so Forerunner assumes."

Charlie stared at Dim astonished. "Me? But I don't know magic."

"You'll be surprised how much you already know and how much you'll learn with the right teacher and the right tools." Dim picked up a twig that still held fire in its body and twirled it between his stubby fingers. "We...need you. Forerunner thinks we need you. He felt we needed to get to you before Nefarious does. And believe me if you think humans and goblins are enemies, you don't want to be found by Nefarious. You'll find we are one and the same if that happens."

Charlie felt so many more questions spring to his mind, but before he could ask them Dim stood up and extinguished the flame at the end of the twig with his hand signaling the end to the conversation. "It's late. There'll be more time later to explain things. For now you need to sleep."

"What about you? Aren't you going to sleep?"

"Someone needs to keep watch and since I'm assuming you don't have a weapon or the knowledge how to use one, that someone is me. I'll sleep later. There'll be plenty of time for that."

Charlie curled up on the hard cold ground and pulled his hoodie over his head and tried to make comfort where there wasn't any. Dim stood a short distance off leaning on a tree, arms crossed and staring into the dark. Within a few minutes Dim heard light snoring coming from near the fire. The boy was asleep.

Charlie woke slowly and moved his leg to dangle off his bed to test the temperature in the room only to realize there wasn't a bed to dangle a leg from. He moved his foot in a back and forth motion and felt a cold hard surface. He opened his eyes and was greeted by a foggy mist. It only took him a few seconds to remember the events of yesterday, and from the looks of things yesterday was not a dream. He sat up and glanced around him but the fog was so thick he wasn't able to see further than a few feet in front of himself. He wasn't certain what to do. He didn't see Dim sitting close by and the fresh memory of the Mud Lavas kept him from moving. "Dim?" He whispered.

Out of the fog a green form presented itself. "You're awake I see," Dim responded. He sat himself down across from Charlie. The fog danced around him giving a mystical feel to his presence. He handed Charlie another square chunk of dried food. Charlie took the food and started eating the dry substance. He tried hard this time not to gag as he swallowed. "Isn't there anything better to eat around here than this stuff?" Charlie asked as he lifted the food towards Dim's face to indicate what he was talking about.

"Trust me, if you ever end up wandering around out here very long, you'll be thankful for whatever food you can lay hands on," Dim gruffly retorted. "Now shut up and eat Knucklehead."

Dim shoved his remaining food into his mouth and stood. "We'll need to stay close this morning," he stated as he looked up and glanced around. "The fog should last a short while longer and seeing you don't know the land around here, I think it would be best for us to hook up." He pulled out a rope and started to tie one end to his belt and, stepping forward, connected the second end to Charlie's belt.

Charlie felt nerves spread through him at the thought of having to travel today among the fog and he started to feel a pang of homesickness. "You know I feel terrible about the...problems you are dealing with here in your land, but honestly, I don't think I want to go with you today. I just really want to go home."

Dim paused in the midst of tying the knot onto Charlie's belt. "Home? You want to go home? Don't you understand what is at stake here if you leave?"

"No, no, I don't," Charlie yelled "You don't tell me anything! So, I go home and magic leaves? Do you know how crazy that sounds? I don't know magic. You're putting all your hopes in me and magic? It's crazy! All for what? So some evil Czar thing doesn't take the magic from you?" Geez, listen to me, Charlie thought. I'm sounding crazy just like Dim. He couldn't help but let his thoughts fall back to sitting on his bed reading a book feeling warm and secure. But instead he was in some land where some crazy goblin was pinning the hopes of salvation on him.

The goblin took a deep breath to calm himself before speaking again. "I'm sure this does sound crazy to you. Believe me when I say this world needs humans to exist and keep the balance." The goblin scanned around him before continuing. "This land where it seems drab and dead was once vibrant and beautiful." Not that beauty meant anything to the goblin race, but Dim assumed playing to the loss of beauty might tug at the heart strings of this human boy. "Now it's dead. As dead as Czar Nefarious' black heart." Dim stopped for a moment and tried to read Charlie's thoughts on what he had just said, but he couldn't tell anything since Charlie had now let his head droop to stare at his feet which were playing in the dirt. "Listen, Charlie," Dim tried with a softer tone. "I'll make a deal with you. You go with me to meet Forerunner and after you've talked with him, you can determine whether or not you want to stay. And if you want to go back, I'll take you back. Deal?"

Charlie looked up and studied Dim's eyes to determine if he was being honest. And to his surprise it sure seemed like he was. "Okay... deal."

By late day the landscape began to change. No longer did Charlie need to dodge Mud Lavas. The haunting whisperings from the trees faded. Ahead of them lay tall brown grass that came to Charlie's waist and was sharp enough to cut skin. Charlie found himself walking with his hands stuffed into his pockets to hide his bare skin. They stopped briefly and the goblin untied the rope that connected them and stowed it away. To their left rocks and boulders climbed higher and higher and in the distance Charlie could see how they would eventually form into mountains. He sure hoped they would not have to climb those. His feet were sore even though he wore his newest shoes that were built for running. The thought of having to climb mountains seemed impossible.

The day wore on as the unlikely pair started to make headway traveling from Mud Valley into Majestic Caverns. Charlie saw he was right and those rocks and boulders grew bigger and bigger and eventually rose into huge mountains. The sharp brown grass disappeared and the ground they walked on was encased in pebbles and rocks. In the distance he heard flapping sounds and what he believed were cawing noises, deep and echoing through the air. It was the first sounds of any wildlife since Charlie had set foot in this strange land.

"Do I hear birds?" asked Charlie.

"Those are Raptor Soarers and Crownerts. We better pick it up and get to that cave up ahead before they appear above us, otherwise we could be dinner."

Charlie stopped and smirked at Dim, expecting to see a smile back. "Raptor Soarers and Cownerts? Are you joking me?"

Taking a step forward, Dim reached out and grabbed ahold of Charlie's shirt and pulled hard, starting towards the cave. "Stupid human. Why would I be joking over something that would end our existence? Dim doesn't joke." Somehow Charlie knew from the firm grip and growling voice that Dim was serious, so he started to hurry along with the goblin to reach the cave. As they ducked into the cave Charlie glimpsed a boulder sized creature floating above them and the cawing became louder. Dim shoved him up against the side of the cave and placed his grubby, hairy green palm over Charlie's mouth to hush him. "Now, Knucklehead, if you want to live, shut up, make no noise."

Chapter Three
The Trovac Skrbnik

C harlie could feel his heart beating in his throat and felt a bit of panic when he heard the *plumf* as whatever was outside landed on the ground near the cave. The cawing became almost unbearable and he brought his hands up to cover his ears. More *plumfs* followed and he became aware that there was more than one creature landing outside the cave. Charlie tried pressing up as close to the rock wall as possible and hoped he could meld into the stone and disappear. If the cawing was at first unbearable, Charlie was completely unnerved when the cawing stopped and silence filled the cave. He dropped his hands from his ears and glanced at Dim only to receive a steely cold stare back to indicate all was not over. They stood up against the wall of the cave for what seemed like hours to Charlie but in fact were only a few minutes when a broad sharp brown beak the size of Charlie's legs squeezed its way into the cave opening and cawed. The vibration left Charlie shaken and if it weren't for Dim's palm over his mouth he would have screamed in terror.

The beak bumped around inside the cave, scrabbling closer and closer, coming within inches of Charlie's foot. This was no ordinary bird. From the size of the beak, he imagined the bird had to be the size of a dinosaur. He could now understand how Dim's comment that they would be dinner finally made sense. The enormous beak would probably tear his limbs off in a matter of seconds. The beak stopped in front of him, not being able to reach any further into the cave, and it eventually withdrew.

Charlie wanted to say something to Dim, but took the hint that all was not clear since the goblin didn't move his hand from Charlie's mouth. The silence grew until he was certain Dim was being over cautious. Just when he had had enough and was about to pull Dim's hand from his mouth there was another sound that emanated from outside the cave. He thought he heard a whizzing and clashing sound and then a *smack*. He looked back into the goblin's eyes. What he found there frightened him more than what he had seen when the giant beak made its way into the cave. Dim's eyes searched around the small cave frantically looking for something. Before Charlie knew it the goblin's hand was gone from his mouth. For a small goblin, he was extremely strong and that became evident to Charlie when Dim hoisted him over his head and shoved him into a crevice above them. Charlie took the hint and grasped on to the edge of the crevice, squeezing his body as far into the crack as he could. He glanced back over the ledge to see what the goblin had in mind for himself since there was no other room in the crevice and even if there was the goblin's stout short body would never fit.

Realizing this, the hairy goblin began moving rapidly along the wall, looking for his own hiding place. Before Dim was able to secure a place of safety for himself, however, the whizz, clash and splat sound grew louder, and the author of the noise made its entrance into the cave. He felt a sinking feeling inside as his new found concern for this fat, big mouthed goblin caused an anxious feeling in the pit of his stomach. Charlie was not certain what to make of the creature that came through the front of the cave. It appeared to be a stick creature shaped to his mind like a giant walking slingshot, at least knee high to a man. As it entered the cave it flung something from its slingshot arms with a whizzing sound which crashed into the rock wall with a *splat* just a few feet from where Dim was searching the wall. The part of the wall where the projectile hit started to sizzle and an odorous smell came from the spot. Within seconds the sizzle stopped and left behind a dark, evil-looking stain.

Dim stayed completely still. Charlie wanted to yell for the goblin to run, but the fear of what that substance the stick figure threw could do to Dim if he was hit kept him silent. If that stuff could burn rock what would it do if it hit the goblin or even himself? It did not take him long to find out the answer to that question as the stick figure turned slightly and released another gooey missile. This time the stick man hit his target striking the goblin on his left arm. Charlie heard the splat as it struck, followed by a loud deep growl of pain from Dim. Charlie heard the sizzle, and he felt sick to his stomach, and only felt sicker when he detected the nasty, odorous smell. The squat goblin turned to face the stick man, but was only able to keep his feet for a few more seconds before he slumped to his knees on the cave floor. He grabbed his left arm and let another loud growl-moan permeate the air. Within seconds the odorous smell disappeared as did the sizzle and all that was left was an ugly wound burned into Dim's left arm.

Charlie stayed completely still from shock and uncertainty. Should he jump down and help the goblin? But what would he be able to do to help him? He'd likely just get himself shot by the evil stick man himself. But he couldn't just stay silent and do nothing. After all, without Dim he'd be pretty lost. And even though he sensed humans and goblins were not friends, he somehow had to admit he sort of liked Dim. Or at least he found him funny. Sure he didn't intend to be, but nonetheless, he was.

The stick figure moved again and now was situated below Charlie. If he were to get down and help Dim this was his chance. Perhaps he could jump down onto the stick figure and take it by surprise, but he had no idea if this stick figure truly was made of a stick or just looked like one. If he was like a stick, he should easily be able to handle it as long as he stayed away from the side that shot out the acid. But if he jumped down to fight this stick figure and it was solid or had other tricks up its sleeve other than the splat he could find himself in the same condition as Dim.

It only took Charlie a few seconds to come to the conclusion that he must take the chance with the walking stick. If he did nothing then Dim might die and leave Charlie alone holed up in this crevice and lost in a very strange world.

The goblin was moaning now and he was sinking lower towards the ground. Charlie needed to act quickly. The stick man was inching closer to Dim, and looked ready to strike again. Looking at the cave floor he spotted a rock not too far away. He felt certain if he could reach the rock quickly enough, he'd be able to use it as a weapon. If the stick monster was truly made out of a stick then the rock could be very useful. However, if he wasn't quick enough he'd be splatted. Charlie scooted out to the edge of the crevice and tried to aim his jump to land precisely next to the rock. Taking a silent breath he jumped. His accuracy was spot on as he landed next to the rock. However, he was now face to face with the evil stick monster, which had turned at the sound of Charlie landing on the cave floor. Up close Charlie could see that there was a hole in the stick where it spit out its odorous weapon.

Charlie quickly bent down to pick up the rock at the exact time that the stick creature fired out another sticky-looking rocket of goo. It was fortunate that he had leaned over since the splat was right on target and just barely soared over Charlie's head hitting a few pieces of hair he had sticking up before making a resounding *splat* against the cave's wall behind him. Charlie heard the sizzle over his head as the few pieces of hair that had been touched by the splat disintegrated. He knew he probably only had moments to get his aim right with the rock or else another splat was coming. This time he would not be so lucky to avoid it. With as much precision as he could summon, Charlie aimed and threw the rock at the stick monster. He said a quick prayer that the stick monster really was a stick! With horror he saw that the rock only grazed the stick man, causing it to wobble and stumble, and it misfired its next nasty splat into the floor of the cave. Now he was really desperate. No more rocks and no more time.

Without thinking Charlie charged the stick monster and grabbed it, lifting it off the ground with the firing hole facing away from him. The thing was heavier than it looked, and it struggled, at least as much as a stick could struggle, and started firing splats all over the place. It did feel like a stick though, and he did the only thing he could think of to do. He remembered his mom used to start campfires by breaking smaller sticks over her knee for kindling. So Charlie grabbed the bottom of the stick monster and closer to the middle and whacked the thing down on his right knee. He heard a crack and at the same time had to bite his lip to keep from shouting out in pain. Well that hurt! Nevertheless, he brought the stick monster up and then down on his knee again, and was rewarded with a resounding crack as the thing split into two pieces in his hands. He stood still in the middle of the cave panting, and realized the splatting noise had stopped. The last of the sizzling sound died away and he could smell the burning rock throughout the cave. Suddenly aware he was still holding the stick monster; he dropped the two pieces with a shudder and backed away a bit, looking to see if it was really out of commission. The stick monster pieces looked just like two sticks should, motionless and quiet. He sighed and his knees became weak as he sank to the cave floor. He sat that way for a few minutes, feeling certain his legs would be too weak to lift his body. The sound of a groan from Dim a few moments later brought Charlie back to reality. He forced his legs to stand as he stumbled over to the hairy gremlin.

Collapsing next to the goblin he breathlessly asked, "Are you okay?"

Dim groaned out "Do I look okay?"

The goblin's color had turned a pale green and sweat had broken out over his hairy skin. Even in his weakened state he still found a sarcastic edge to his voice as he spoke to Charlie. Amazingly so, this gave the boy a small amount of relief. If Dim could muster up sarcasm then perhaps he would be fine.

"What just happened?" Charlie questioned Dim.

"Well, Knucklehead, I just got shot with Trovac Skrbnik poison," the goblin coughed out. Turning quickly to his side, the weak goblin vomited. Charlie pulled away for a minute at the sight of the vomit and then closed his eyes to keep from vomiting alongside Dim. At home when his sister was ill, their mom always entrusted him to help out, but he drew the line at vomit.

"Whoa dude, that's nasty," Charlie said as he covered his mouth and nose to cover up the stink emanating from the vomit. The odor was similar to that which permeated off the splat when it hit the wall of the cave.

"Geez, sorry. You think I like vomiting up that junk?"

Charlie shamefully removed the hand covering his nose and mouth when he heard the weak reply from Dim. "Sorry. It's just that your upchucking made me want to upchuck as well." He scooted back closer to the ill goblin and tried to ignore as best as he could the stink floating around the cave.

"Enough about my vomit already," Dim wheezed out. He closed his eyes and his breathing became heavy and he began to shake.

"Dim! Dim!" Charlie shouted as his hands came down to steady the short hairy body. He realized within moments it was useless. Dim's body had its own mind now. He sat next to the goblin in near panic and all he could do was wait for his stout body to stop trembling. Then he became still. The heavy breathing was gone and he no longer trembled. Charlie slowly reached out and touched him. "Dim?" Charlie weakly asked. "Dim are you okay?" He felt a great sense of fear at the possibility that the goblin was no longer among the living. What would he do if he was left alone here in this strange land? He knew he'd likely die without Dim's help. He shook the goblin in hopes that he was wrong and Dim was still with him. "Please answer me!"

A weak groan came from the still form and Charlie lowered his head, covering his eyes with relief. Dim still showed signs of life. But for how long?

He sat quietly beside the green Imp for hours, not wanting to leave the safety of the cave. He had checked the wound on the goblin's arm, and it didn't look good at all. It wasn't very bloody, but that's because the edges of the wound were all seared and burnt. Nasty looking liquid was oozing from the damaged arm, and he found a piece of cloth in Dim's knapsack that he gingerly covered the wound with. His best hope of survival was for the goblin to recover, but it did not look promising. Soon, he'd have to make a decision on what to do next, but for now he sat vigil at Dim's side.

The sick goblin stayed still for some time with only an occasional groan. Charlie kept alert, awaiting the groans and feeling relief for those moments. It at least gave Charlie comfort to know he was still with him. He wasn't certain how Dim had wiggled his way into his heart in such a short time, but Charlie felt a fondness for him, goblin or not. He couldn't shrug off the helpless feeling just sitting there watching the hairy kobold fade away.

A slight sound from the mouth of the cave startled Charlie. He turned, mentally preparing himself for the beak of a Raptor Soarer to reemerge or worse yet another stick monster, but instead he found himself looking down an arrow into the face of a very intent-looking female. Instinctively, Charlie moved to cover Dim never taking his eyes off her and the arrow. She followed his movements with her bow, the arrow never leaving Charlie's sight, and he held his breath, afraid she would loose her arrow at any moment. As she turned slightly to follow his motions, he was startled to notice the shape of her ears. They were elegantly shaped and came to a point towards the top of her head. If his eyes were to be believed, he must be looking at an Elf! An Elf armed with a bow and a nocked arrow pointing directly at him! Still, he was a bit mesmerized, having never seen a real Elf before. And this one was beautiful. Her skin was silken brown, and her eyes were a piercing dark chocolate color. He couldn't look away from her gaze. She appeared to be as mesmerized with him as he was with her.

Neither spoke for a long minute. Charlie was the first to break the silence. "Are you planning to kill me?" Charlie asked, glancing from the Elves' eyes to the bow still pointed at him and then back to her eyes.

"Depends on what you are doing here and what you have done to Dim."

"You know Dim?" Charlie looked from the Elf to the goblin in surprise.

"I think you are not the one in the position to be asking questions right now. Once again, what are you doing here and what have you done to Dim? Do not make me ask again." The Elf readjusted her bow to fixate it between Charlie's eyes.

His hands went up in a surrender motion to ward off the Elves' bow. "I know Dim as well. Oh, I wish I could explain this all to make sense of it myself, but it's all so surreal." His hands came forward to cover his eyes for a minute as exhaustion overtook him.

Silence engulfed the cave as he let his head rest in his hands. The Elf just stared at him, summing up the situation. After a few moments she asked, "How do you know Dim?"

The tired boy let his hands drop back down to his sides and let out a deep breath before answering as best he could. "He came to me in my world raving that I must come here to save magic." Charlie paused for a moment as he let his eyes search the Elves' to see if she was taking any of this crazy talk seriously. "He was taking me to someone called Forerunner when we were attacked by some birds...something called a Raptor Soarer, and Dim hid me in this cave, but in the process this stick monster," Charlie let his hand move to point at the broken stick lying on the cave floor a few feet away, "came and shot something at Dim. He said it was Tromac Biscuit poison, whatever that might be. Since then he's gone unconscious and I've just been sitting here with him trying to decide what to do next. Oh, it's all so confusing." Charlie choked back a sob. He refused to cry. The last thing he needed to do in front of this curious beautiful Elf was cry like a baby. He was able to choke out "Can you help him?" before lowering his head once again to hide the emotion that must have been evident in his face.

A few moments later the Elf lowered her bow and moved forward swiftly, bypassing Charlie and kneeling by the goblin's side. She bent low and put her ear to Dim's mouth listening for breathing and then touched his wrist. She removed the piece of cloth covering the wound and frowned at the ugly gaping damage. Within seconds she knew what she needed to do. Pulling out a small vial from a pouch she wore at her waist she gently opened Dim's mouth and let three drops enter.

Charlie watched as she worked and was transfixed by her movements and ease in caring for such a cumbersome oaf like Dim. He slowly scooted next to the Elf and let his hand drop to the unconscious goblin's arm. The normal green color was slowly returning to the goblin as the Elf worked. After the vial, she produced some dark spiny-looking leaves from her pouch and sprinkled the remainder of the liquid over them, crushing the leaves as she did so. She then placed them on the wound, wrapping strands of twine around them to keep them in place. She sat back and they both just stared at the thick hairy Imp.

Minutes passed with neither Charlie nor the Elf speaking. Both were absorbed in watching Dim's breathing. After several minutes the Elf was the first to break the silence.

"He is stable now."

Charlie wasn't sure what that meant. Dim did look better, but he was still unconscious. "So you cured him?"

"No, I do not have what is needed to cure him. I only had a poison equalizer that will buy you time to find the cure."

Charlie's relief disappeared with those words. "How will I ever be able to do that? I don't even know where I am or what I'm doing here without Dim! And look at him. He's not in any condition to help me."

"You need to learn patience. The treatment will work and he will become more cohesive in time. As for the cure, you will need to find an Oleander bush and mix it with Elf blood." The Elf pulled another vial from her pouch and handed it to Charlie. "I can help you with the Elf blood, but you'll have to find the Oleander bush. At one time they were abundant in this world, but now they have become less prevalent. The few that remain are usually heavily guarded by the Trovac Skrbnik." The Elf looked over at the remains of the stick man lying on the cave floor. "But I see you are capable of dealing with them. Yet masses of them will be far more difficult to handle. Where they are fragile and easily broken, in groups you will be lucky to survive unscathed." She paused and looked at Charlie thoughtfully. "In truth, there was an Oleander bush outside this cave, which is what this Trovac was guarding, but it is gone. Something tore it out completely, down to its roots."

"There is no way I'll be able to find an Oleander bush let alone be able to defeat a group of…what did you call them…Trovac Skrbnik? How do you suppose I do this when I don't even know where I am?"

The Elf turned to face Charlie. "You are a mighty impatient boy. But then again it has been awhile since I have been in the presence of a human. I have forgotten how impatient your kind is. If Dim was with you then you must be of some importance to him. It has been even longer since I have seen a goblin in the presence of a human. For Dim to risk his life…these days…in this world…to take great measures to keep you safe means you must be important. Do you not feel the least you owe him is your patience?"

Hearing it that way, Charlie felt shamed and he could feel the blood rushing to his face with embarrassment. "Of course I can be patient. I'm sure you think you know everything about…my race, but believe me you don't. We can be patient when we're supposed to be."

Charlie and the Elf locked eyes. He could read in her eyes that she did not believe his statement, but she still replied, "I do not presume to know your kind, so forgive me if I overstepped my ground and offended you."

"Um, thank you," Charlie politely answered back and they fell silent again for a while. The boy kept his eyes averted from the Elf's and kept them locked on Dim. The Elf on other hand continued to study Charlie and he couldn't help but feel uncomfortable. He felt she was stripping him down and looking into his soul and he wasn't certain he wanted her to be able to see that deep into his emotional state.

The awkwardness of the Elf staring at him prompted him to start speaking again in hopes of drawing her attention from him. "So you never told me your name, or asked me mine for that matter."

"Names did not seem to be important about now, but if you must know I am called Divine Echosby, and I am a proud descendent of Pasha Echosby of the Crystal Elves."

"Crystal Elves," Charlie whispered to himself. He'd never heard of anything quite like that. "Why Crystal?"

Before Divine could answer, Dim's voice echoed weakly through the cave. "I'm lying here dying and you're asking Divine why she is a Crystal Elf. It shows where your priority is, Knucklehead."

"Knucklehead. What an odd name for a human," Divine mused. "The few humans I have come into contact with had such bland names."

Charlie stared at the Elf open-mouthed, trying to determine if Divine was being serious while Dim let out a muted peal of laughter that trailed into a fit of coughing. After determining Divine was serious, he informed the Elf his name was not Knucklehead but it was Charlie and turned and gave a stern look at the goblin for his uncharacteristic sense of humor.

"Well, I see someone is feeling better," he said to the goblin.

Dim slowly brought himself to a sitting position, but a rush of nausea engulfed him and he turned away from the onlookers and vomited. "Somewhat better," he replied, using his hand to wipe the vomit off his face. "I take it I have you to thank for my recovery," Dim addressed the she-Elf.

"It is thanks to holy water and Fletcher leaves. In other words, it is a temporary fix," was Divine's answer. "I gave the boy...Charlie some Elf blood. Now all he needs is to find an Oleander bush and you shall have the permanent cure you need."

"Oleander bush. Are there still some around?" Dim inquired.

Divine stood up, gathered her bow and situated it onto her shoulder. "They are hard to come by with the darkness of Nefarious having destroyed so much of the land, but I believe I saw some around Crimson Meadows. If you leave now you may make it there by nightfall." She moved to the cave mouth. "Be careful, Dim. It will be surrounded by the Trovac Skrbnik and where that would not have much of an effect on you now, the boy will be a target. I am assuming you have gone to great lengths to keep him safe so you would not want him to fall to the fate of the Trovac."

"Knucklehead is tougher then you think. And he knows magic."

"No, I don't," Charlie sputtered.

Dim turned his slimy vomit-slathered face to the indignant boy. "Yes, you do Charlie. It's in you. You just don't know it yet."

"So that is why you have risked your life for a human," Divine murmured. "You believe this one will fare better than those humans that have passed before." Divine turned and summed up Charlie from head to toe. "He is no more than a boy. No older than...Ethereal. Why would you believe he can accomplish what all other humans have failed?"

"He's different, Divine. I could see it a few nights ago when he started a fire from magic without any prompting. Forerunner knew it without even having seen the boy. It's there. And if we can find those remaining humans who have secluded themselves away from Czar, together they may be able to bring back our land as we once knew it. It is a given I've never cared for the humans, but we both must admit that we need them." Dim's speech brought silence and they both observed the young human.

Charlie glanced from Divine to Dim and back again. "Stop already. I hate being stared at. And I don't like being talked about as if I'm not here." He moved his weight from one foot to the other anxious for the eyes to stray away from him. "I have no idea why you think I have magic Dim, and if that is why this Forerunner wants me...well he's going to be very disappointed in you and me."

"If Dim says you have magic then I trust what he says. Some may say goblins are untrustworthy, but Dim is not like normal goblins. He has proven that to me many times over. Trust in him, Charlie. Just like patience, your kind needs to learn trust."

"Geez, Divine...such glowing compliments from you. I couldn't be more honored," Dim sarcastically commented.

Twice Charlie had been insulted by Divine. He was not feeling warm and fuzzy with Elves at the moment. "It's hard to trust someone who kidnaps you from your home and drags you to this...nasty place and doesn't explain himself fully!"

"All will explain itself in time, young one," Divine soothingly replied back. "Trust in Dim and he will bring you to safety." The she-Elf nodded to the stunted goblin. "Take care my friend and do not wait too long to find the Oleander bush for this world would not be the same without you." She exited the cave.

Chapter Four
The Battle at the Iron Gate

"So explain to me again where those Raptor Soarers disappeared to. Why would they give up on us so quickly?"

"Raptors have small brains and short memories," explained Dim. "Once they see their prey they attack, but if they do not succeed within a short time they forget the goal and move to the next prey they see. Let's just say we are lucky they are gone or Divine would never have found us and I'd no longer be here."

They walked through Majestic Caverns. For the most part both were lost in their thoughts, but occasionally Charlie would ask a question. "This is a town? Where are the people? How much longer will it be?"

Dim would answer in short sentences. "Yes, this is Majestic Caverns. Most humans are gone...except for a few. We are almost to Oubliette."

The diminutive kobold was able to keep a pretty good pace even though Charlie didn't feel Dim's color was very good. He also noticed Dim was walking with a bit of a limp and seemed to take longer to lift his arms. When they finally stopped for camp, the goblin's breathing was heavier. But when Charlie asked if he was okay or if there was anything he could do for him, Dim changed the subject. Divine had said the fix was temporary, but Charlie had no clue how long they had before the Trovac poison would take what was left of his hairy green guide from him.

That night when sitting at the fire Charlie once again brought up Dim's health. "Are we any closer to finding the Oleander bush? I can see all this walking is exhausting you. I'm worried we won't be able to find the cure in time."

Dim took a deep breath and let out a sigh as he leaned back against a rock. "Must we have the same convasasion every hour?"

Charlie smiled at Dim's misuse of the word and realized this was the first time in days he felt anything seemed funny. "I'm going to keep asking until I get an answer. Divine thinks humans aren't patient and don't trust easily. What she didn't mention is we're persistent as well."

"Fine," Dim weakly answered. "We aren't looking for Oleander bushes, Charlie. I'm taking you to Forerunner. That was my mission and that is what we are doing."

"You must be joking!" Charlie was stunned by this revelation. "You'll die if we don't find these Oleander bushes. Surely Forerunner can wait!"

"Look around you, Charlie. Does it look like Forerunner can wait? Does it look like any of us can wait? Our world is crumbling around us. My mission is you...not me. So no, we are not going to look for Oleander bushes." Dim let out a heavy breath and closed his eyes at the exertion this day and conversation were having on him.

Charlie jumped to his feet at Dim's statement of martyr-dom. "You're crazy if you think I'm going with you quietly to see Forerunner! I'm not letting you sacrifice yourself for me. Look at yourself! You can hardly keep your eyes open anymore and just hav-ing a conversation with me is exhausting you. You'll never even make it to Forerunners besides. We can just take a quick diversion and find you some Oleander before finishing up this trek."

"Sit down, Knucklehead. Like I told you already we are not stop-ping for Oleander. Either way it's too late for that. We passed the only known area to have Oleander bushes when we passed Crimson Meadows today. We are not going back."

"We passed Oleander bushes and you said nothing? You *are* a crazy goblin! We could have easily picked some and it wouldn't even have diverted us!" Charlie was yelling at the hapless goblin now.

"I'm not letting you get shot up by Trovac Skrbnik, BOY! My mission is getting YOU back safely to Forerunner. Not making me feel better!"

Charlie was steaming angry at Dim's martyr act and refused to talk to him the rest of the evening. The weakened goblin gave Charlie the stones to make the fire. They ate in silence and the young human pulled up his hoodie and lay down next to the fire without another word to Dim. He might think he can control me, but I'll never let him know how little control he really has. Add controlling to the lists of things humans are! He'll show that stubborn goblin!

He waited until Dim's breathing became heavier. He knew the night before that the goblin had not been able to stay awake to stand guard, so he assumed the same would happen tonight. Dim did not disappoint him.

Charlie pulled himself up and tried to steady his nerves to venture into the dark. He hoped he'd remember the path back to the town. It had only been a few hours back if he recollected right. He pulled the fire rocks from his pocket. It sure came in handy that Dim was weak and tired from the poisoning. He never realized that Charlie hadn't given the rocks back. Perhaps he could use them to help guide him through the darkness, but he'd want to be a distance away before trying. He did not want the green imp to awaken and be able to follow his trail. He could just imagine the anger Dim would have when he awoke and found him gone, but the goblin should know better than to think Charlie could ever allow Dim to sacrifice himself. He was not brought up to think one life was more important than another. His parents would be proud. The thought of his parents brought a sudden wave of homesickness that he mentally pushed down to remain hidden for the time being. He'd never be able to continue on if he thought of them or his sister. Charlie picked up a solid stick lying next to Dim that he figured would make a good torch and quietly set out into the darkness.

He worked from memory as he slowly moved into the night

heading in the direction he believed the town was in, and he said a little prayer that he was right. He walked about five minutes before trying the magic rocks and was easily able to ignite his torch. He wasn't sure how much longer Dim had, but from the weakened state he witnessed tonight, he guessed only a few more days. He hoped again he was not wrong and that he was heading back in the right direction to find the Oleander bushes. It never occurred to Charlie that he had no idea what an Oleander bush even looked like. He wasn't thinking with his brain, he was thinking with his heart.

Charlie had been walking for what seemed like forever but in actuality was only about forty-five minutes when the ground became more treacherous and he had to stop for a minute and mentally refocus on the path they had taken when they first passed this way. He could not remember the ground being this rocky and slippery, but honestly he could not remember much of the trek earlier in the day. He had spent most of the time worrying about his stubborn companion. Could he have passed along this treacherous path earlier and not noticed? It was possible, after all his mother had told him many times over that he was forgetful. She used to tease him mercilessly that if his hands were not attached he'd certainly leave them somewhere and never notice for days they were missing. When his mother said those things to him he had felt offended, but today the memory only brought a smile to his face and an ache in his heart where she lived, now that he was here and she was absent.

He turned around in a circle using the torch to try and see as far into the distance on each side in hopes of seeing something familiar. He didn't recognize anything, and he was becoming concerned he was going in the wrong direction. For the first time since leaving Dim, he was thinking perhaps he made a poor decision going off alone in the dark. He should have waited until daylight before heading back. Dim wouldn't have been able to stop him in his weakened condition anyway, or so Charlie figured. His mom was right. Sometimes he acted without thinking things through. He squinted and tried to make out the terrain ahead of him but torch or no torch the darkness was so thick he couldn't see farther than a few feet ahead of himself.

He'd have to make a decision on what he should do. He wasn't sure staying put was a good idea. Who knew if there were Raptor Soarers or Trovac Skrbnik or any other enemies lurking nearby? However, moving forward did not appeal to him either. The ground was rocky and slippery. If he fell here, he could be lost, becoming easy prey if he became immobile. After pondering his choices, Charlie chose the lesser of the two evils and chose to stay put. He couldn't be more than an hour from the town and daylight wasn't too far away. He'd hate to take any more chances with his life. But how was he to stay safe here? The rocky terrain put an end to collecting fire wood. He'd have to make do with his torch and hope the fire would last. It seemed as if the fire wasn't burning the wood as much as dancing on the torch. Maybe it was because it was magic fire. And sleeping was out. He had no idea what might be in the darkness stalking him. Sleeping would just make him easier prey.

Charlie looked around the ground below him and collected as many rocks as he could gather into the pouch of his hoodie. He certainly had not been thinking when he had left Dim. He should have taken a sword or some sort of weapon from the goblin. Now all he was armed with were medium size rocks and the base of his torch. He'd have to make do.

Charlie settled down on the cold slippery rocks and tried not to think about how cold and scared he was and tried to place himself back at home, sitting on the couch with Kassie watching a season of Lost one of their favorite TV shows. He daydreamed of home and family until he slowly faded off into sleep against his best laid plans.

Isabella had been watching this strange human for many miles now. Charlie had stumbled right by her camp in the dark. He'd been only ten feet away from her as he slipped and fumbled his way on the rocks and he hadn't even noticed her. She, however, had noticed him. She did not recognize him in the firelight from his torch, but she was certain she knew the few humans left in Pulchritude Amity seeing as how she was one of them. She and the others had made a pact to stay a great distance apart and keep hidden until The One made his appearance. It was too dangerous for them to stay together, for if they were found then all was lost, whereas if only one was found then at least the others still kept hope alive. The solitude was fine, as far as Isabella was concerned, and she had become accustomed to being alone quite easily. She couldn't remember the last time she had stumbled upon another human, however, and now that she had, it was a human she'd never laid eyes on before.

Isabella's curiosity, and though she'd never admit it to anyone, her loneliness as well, had prompted her to follow this human. Perhaps he was a decoy or even worse a disguise of Nefarious' to pull her into the open. But then again, perhaps he was The One. She wasn't certain she even believed The One existed. Her mother had told her tales as soon as Isabella could walk that they would not have to live in constant danger this way, forever afraid of Nefarious. Tales that The One would bring beauty and kindness back into this world and would bring with him intelligence humans had not seen in decades. An intelligence that would bring a natural aptitude to learn magic as had never been seen before.

At first Isabella listened to her mother's stories as any child would to a parent they love. Then as she grew older she became leery of what her mother said, taking the tales as just that… tales. Life was not kind to humans while Isabella grew up. Nefarious was hunting them down and enslaving them for his use, but when he was not able to truly find what he so desired from the humans he started executing as many as possible. Before humanity realized what was happening, it was too late for them to stop it. Many of Isabella's friends and family had become victims to Nefarious' evil before her mother scooped her up and fled. They had spent most of Isabella's younger years fleeing from one location to another. At the end of her mother's life, they ended up in a cave with three other teenage humans, having come to the conclusion they were all that was left of their race. Her mother tried hiding them, and she cast a spell of protection on each of them. Then she gave each a piece of magic to guard from the hands of Nefarious. Isabella had the book of Potions; Henrietta had the Pen of Knowledge, and Riot the wolf boy had the Book of Truth. Alone they were useless. Together they were all powerful, so Isabella's mother decided dividing them among the three and sending them in different directions throughout the land would give them the best chance to keep the items safe. Nefarious' minions finally found Isabella and her mom. Henrietta and Riot had already separated and were gone. Isabella's mother had pulled her behind her and whispered "I love you. Always know that. Protect the book well. The One will come and save you three. Believe." Then she whispered 'Olonso Pulleis', and Isabella's form disappeared. She became translucent. The minions charged forward and attacked. Her mother fought a strong fight and took out many minions before succumbing to death. Isabella stood frozen and invisible, unable to intervene, watching in horror as her mother died. A great deal of time had passed since that fateful day and she still had not forgiven her mother for allowing her to witness her death. Perhaps she never would.

Now she finds this strange boy wandering alone in the dark. Isabella knew it was unlikely he was The One, but she felt she owed it to her mother's memory to at least find out what this boy was doing here and where he came from. Could there really be another human alive? Did they assume they were the last and were wrong? Isabella doubted that to be the case.

She wasn't sure what the right course of action would be. In these situations she missed her mother so much. She'd know what to do and she'd be able to sense if this was The One or just a trick of Nefarious'. She had been fortunate to have learned a bit of magic from her mother, but she did not know the spell of *Sensing*. It would have been useful about now. Of course, even if she had known the spell, it probably wouldn't work since magic was nearly extinct.

She quietly followed behind the boy and stopped a short distance behind him when he halted and used his torch to look around him. He certainly didn't look dressed as any human she had ever known. He also seemed a bit confused and uncoordinated. This one was different, but Isabella decided she needed longer to observe. It could be a trick and after all this time she could not fall prey to Nefarious and let her mother down.

The boy dug a hole in the ground to settle the torch and pulling something over his head lay down on the rocks. He was settling in which meant Isabella would be settling in as well. She'd stay watch over the night and see if this boy met up with anyone. If not, she'd have to make a decision in the morning whether she'd take a chance and approach him or let him continue on his way. She moved away from the boy and found a boulder to lean up against. She whispered *Olonso Pulleis* and felt the tingling that preceded the invisibility and settled in for a long night of spying. She looked over at the lump on the ground that was the boy and listened closely. A soft snore could be heard. He was asleep.

Something was tickling his nose. Charlie swatted at it without opening his eyes. The tickling continued and he swatted again feeling his hand touch something which startled him awake to find some sort of bug the size of his palm crawling across his fingers. He stifled a scream as he sat straight up out of his daze and shook his hand to shake the bug off him. It fell on the rocks below and scurried away. Charlie sat dazed watching as a disgusting looking bug took refuge between some rocks. It took him a minute to recall where he was and why he was sitting on a bunch of boulders with a sore back.

A light bulb in his brain went off as he recalled the stupid trek in the night to find the Oleander bush and the uncertainty of where he was. Then finally acknowledging he was probably lost and sleeping on the rocks. He glanced around himself to see rocks and boulders practically surrounding his location. He did not recall having come this way yesterday. He was certain now he had taken a wrong turn and was indeed lost. And what to do now, Charlie was uncertain. The day was slightly brighter than the night, but he still could not see too far into the distance with the constant fog that hung over this land. He'd have to head back the direction he had come from in the night to see if he could find where he had gone astray. Dim would be awake by now and knowing the hairy goblin as he already did, he was sure that even in his weakened state he would soon be out looking for him. If Dim found him before he was able to find the Oleander bush, he'd insist that he accompany him to see Forerunner. He was determined not to sacrifice the goblin for himself especially for some hair-brained idea that Charlie possessed some natural talent in magic. Dim was misguided, or so Charlie believed.

He picked up his now burnt out torch and backtracked his steps from the night before, starting down the crooked slope of rocks. It only took him about an hour to reach the bottom and get back to the pebbles he and Dim had traveled over the day before. He turned right rather then left at the bottom of the rocks and headed away from where he and the goblin had made camp the night before, feeling confident that he was heading the right direction towards the town they had passed yesterday… and felt relieved not to be lost anymore.

Charlie's stomach grumbled as he walked and he realized for the first time since leaving Dim how hungry he was. He cursed himself for not having thought to sneak a few servings of that dried food the hairy goblin had force fed him. Even that sounded appealing to him about now. He had anticipated having already found and acquired the Oleander, not getting lost among the rocks heading up into the mountains. He'd have to ignore the continuous grumbling of his stomach and move faster. Besides making it back to the town before Dim found him, the faster he went the quicker he could get back to Dim and eat something. He was certain it wouldn't take the goblin long to figure out he was heading back to the town for the Oleander bush. Charlie had not let the subject go yesterday. The goblin was brighter then he appeared. He'd need to reach the town before Dim.

He moved at a good pace only stopping a few times to look around him. He felt a prickle go up and down his spine a few times certain he was being followed, but there weren't many places for someone to hide and Charlie saw no one. He shook off the feelings and continued to move forward. He was relieved when about an hour later he stumbled across the abandoned town. He let a smile creep across his face that he was able to find his way back without any direction from Dim. He felt pretty proud of himself. Now to find these Oleander bushes. He couldn't recall seeing any plants when he had first traveled through this town yesterday, but he hadn't really been that observant either.

He'd have to consider what he would do if he found the bush and it was surrounded by the Trovac Skrbnik like Divine said they would be. What was his plan to evade them? He was certain he could never defeat a troop of Trovac without being poisoned. He hoped that either Divine was wrong about the Oleander bushes being guarded or that only one or two guards would be there. But first he must find the bushes.

He felt his best chance of finding the Oleander would to be to go off the pebble trail and look behind or around the homes situated throughout the town. He felt an eerie feeling creep over him as he wandered among the deserted buildings. As he crept and peeked around homes in the town looking for Oleander bushes, Charlie could not stop the prickling along his neck that he was being watched. He stopped every so often and glanced around, never finding anyone.

He had been looking for what felt like hours when he stumbled across an unusual occurrence. Behind an old home built from granite was a magnificent garden. It was the first sign of color Charlie had seen in this dreary world. It was bordered by a stacked rock wall and an iron gate. As he glanced around the corner of the home he could see bushes and flowers of assorted colors inside the rock wall. He was mesmerized by the colors and sweet smells emanating from the garden. He felt drawn to it and stumbled from behind the wall of the home out into the open and dazedly moved towards the gate.

Charlie was halfway to the iron gate of the garden when he first noticed movement to his right. It took all his willpower to pull his gaze away from the wonders extruding from the garden and turn towards the movement. He halted when he saw a row of the Trovac Skrbnik poised to fire at him. Charlie realized he'd been stupid to have wandered out into the open so carelessly. He didn't know what had come over him. He had walked right into their trap. He knew there was no getting out of this predicament. Unlike Dim, there was no Divine to save him. The best he could do was fight and hope he'd outlast them and then if at all possible he'd be able to gather some Oleander from the bush to save him and the sick goblin. The problem was he didn't know what Oleander looked like. He had not anticipated a garden full of plants when he had gone searching for Oleander bushes. Foolishly, he thought he'd only find the Oleander and he'd be able to just pick some. He did not think he'd have to identify the plant itself. He cursed Dim for not having just stopped here on their way yesterday. Certainly he'd know what Oleander looked like.

Now he'd have to fight the awful stick monsters and then if lucky enough to survive the fight he'd have to pick every available plant he could find in the gated garden and hope one was Oleander. Charlie slowly reached into the pouch of his hoodie, hoping to grab some of the rocks he had brought with him when the first Trovac fired its deadly missile. He let himself collapse to the ground and the shot went over his head. Before he could pick himself up another shot was fired. Charlie rolled to his left and the splat landed a foot away from him. Picking up two rocks as he rolled he brought himself back up to his knees and aimed and threw. The first rock missed the target by inches, but the second hit a Trovac Skrbnik, crashing him to the ground. Charlie felt elated and pumped his fist into the air. His enthusiasm almost cost him dearly as two more Trovacs fired at him, pinning him down where he kneeled. Charlie's only hope was to jump from his knees to his feet and make a dive into the air to overshoot the splats. He surprised himself and succeeded in doing just that, diving inches over one of the splats and falling face first into the pebbles against the rock wall. The fall stunned him which gave the Trovac stick monsters time to move forward and close in on him. Charlie slowly pulled himself up and saw how fruitless this all had been. He would not be able to save Dim. The hairy goblin had been foolish to believe he was anything special. It was obvious he was only a normal failure of a boy.

Charlie lifted his head up in a sign of pride. He would not die hanging his head. He took a stance and shoved his hands into the pouch of his hoodie. He let them rest on the stones he had taken from Dim. The fire stones! Perhaps they could be useful about now. He was uncertain if they would be of any use in a situation like this, but he was about to die, so he decided it was the best chance he had. He could hear the click of the Trovac Skrbnik as they prepared to shoot at him. Charlie grabbed a stone in each hand and pulled them from his pouch, clapping the stones together once, then twice. A blaze of bright fire ignited from them, and Charlie released the stones directly into the crowd of stick creatures in front of him. Then he lifted his arms up to his eyes and turned towards the rock wall as the fire flared up and engulfed the Trovac.

It only took a few minutes to disintegrate the stick-like guardians into ash. The raging fire licked the back of Charlie's legs and back as he faced the wall, and he felt the seething brand of the burns. He cried out in pain and collapsed to the ground near the wall, trying to brace himself against the rock structure. He'd burnt himself before when taking a pan from the oven at home, but then it was just his fingers. The pain in his fingers had been intense and taken days to fully heal. This pain was worse. The back of his legs had taken the brunt of the fire and the burning made him feel faint. Charlie had succeeded in destroying the Trovac Skrbnik only to possibly succumb to death from the burns. The pain was so severe that he could not sit on the ground without feeling faint and nauseous. He stayed upright holding on to the rock wall and tried to fight through the pain. If only he could make it into the garden. Perhaps there would be something to help with burns, but then again Charlie didn't even know what the Oleander bush looked like, so how would he even know what could heal burns? After several minutes of bracing himself against the wall and fighting the nausea that overwhelmed him from the pain, Charlie made the decision to crawl over to the Iron Gate and enter the garden. He'd eat whatever plant he could find and hope by some miracle it would heal his wounds. The worst case scenario is he would eat something and die. At least he'd be put out of his misery.

It took Charlie several minutes to convince himself to move his legs. But when he did he moved quickly to get the pain of moving over as fast as he could. He entered the gate and stumbled over to the first plant inside, collapsing before it. It was a beautiful bush with purple flowers and the fragrance was intoxicating, but Charlie didn't notice any of that. He was too absorbed in his pain. He reached up and pulled a piece of the flower off the plant. Now that he was here he was not even certain what part of the plant was required to heal Dim. He had no idea if he was pulling off an Oleander flower or some other random plant. He'd just have to hope it was a plant that if it didn't help it would at least put him out of his misery. Charlie went to place the flower into his mouth when something stopped his hand.

"You don't want to do that," the voice of the hand that had grabbed him said. Charlie could barely comprehend what the voice was saying. All he knew was the excruciating pain, and he just wanted it to end.

"Leave me alone," Charlie cried out to the voice. "I can't stand the pain. Let me die and be put out of my misery."

"I'm afraid I can't do that. You are too important I fear. You must not die."

Charlie's grip loosened on the flower he held and it dropped to the ground. The pain finally won and Charlie passed out. The last thing he saw as his eyes closed was the stern face of a beautiful blonde blue eyed girl.

Isabella let go of the boy's hand and let it go limp with his body as the pain overtook the young human and he passed out. She had followed him here still unclear whether he was human or a decoy or disguise of Nefarious', but after the use of magic, Isabella had determined he was for real. Czar Nefarious did not know magic. It was the purpose for which he had enslaved humans long ago. He had hoped to learn what gave humans such power with magic which he and his kind had never succeeded in learning. So this boy with the magic must certainly be the real deal. Whether he was The One was yet to be determined, but first Isabella would need to heal him in order to find out more about him.

He may know magic, Isabella pondered, but he certainly wasn't too bright in how he used it. Throwing fire so close to oneself certainly would result in backlash thus the severe burns he had received. Certainly anyone adept at magic should at least know that much. Isabella wasn't even certain why he was about to eat Larkspur. It would certainly cause severe seizures, paralysis and possibly death.

He was fortunate she had interrupted him before he could do anything so foolish.

Isabella pulled out a blanket from her bag and laid it out onto the ground next to the boy. She gently rolled him over onto his stomach. Then taking her knife from her bag, Isabella cut through the strange clothes the boy wore. Some of the clothing was embedded into the boy's skin and Isabella knew removing all the pieces would be painful, but necessary. She was thankful the boy had passed out.

She worked quickly. Pulling back the clothing from the boy's back and legs she used her water to clean the burns. At times like these she wished more than ever that her mother was here. She was masterful in healing. But then again she was masterful in magic and battle as well. She was one of the few humans in Pulchritude Amity to be so adept in all three areas. Isabella was skilled in battle but she was only adequate in healing and magic. Her mother had taught her as much as possible about the healing arts before her death. As with most humans Isabella tended to be talented more in one area than another and battle was Isabella's talent. She had been fortunate in her youth to have spent time in both, the school of magic and the school of battle. As Isabella tended to the boy's wounds she was thankful, not for the first time, for her mother's persistence in teaching her healing.

The wounds were not as severe as Isabella had first anticipated. The boy was fortunate he had collapsed in the middle of a bountiful feast of medicinal plants. She was certain she'd find what she needed to heal his wounds and do so quickly before any other wandering enemies stumbled across them.

It only took Isabella a few minutes to spot the two plants she needed. One of the plants, Histamine, she would crush the berries into a paste and mix with crystal dust and holy water. Luckily she had crystal dust and holy water. Once she spread the paste over the wounds the healing would be fairly quick. The other plant, Lidicaine, could be eaten, but in the boy's case likely dissolved under his tongue to ease his pain.

Isabella put a few leaves from the Lidicaine under the boy's tongue and held his mouth closed for a few minutes to allow them to dissolve then she went to work on the paste. She then used leaves from a maple tree to slather the paste into the burns and cover them with cloth she ripped off a minotaur's body after slaying him. Isabella was amazed the boy never moved or cried out in pain during the treatment. She'd never used Lidicaine before but now felt certain it truly worked. She'd make sure to gather all she could before they left this area. It certainly would come in handy. After all this was the first time Isabella had even come across such a lush garden since before her mother's death. She was puzzled how it had stayed so vibrant.

Evening would be here soon, so Isabella went about constructing a makeshift shelter to keep the boy protected, so he could continue to rest and heal. She, on the other hand, would be staying awake guarding the boy. She'd cast *Olonso Pulleis* if necessary. She wanted to protect this boy, but she knew it would be foolish to do so at her expense. She still did not know who this boy was, but she knew whoever he was she could not bargain herself for his life. She carried too much of importance to do that. She'd have to hope they would not be found.

Chapter Five
The Fate of Dim

D im woke several hours after dawn. The poison had weakened his limbs and caused a fatigue that would not go away. Luckily, they only had about another day of travel and they'd reach Forerunner. He forced his eyes to stay open as he looked around him. It took a few minutes to register that Charlie was no longer within his eyesight. Dim's eyes opened wider and took a thorough search of the area. Due to the fog he could only see so far into the distance. Charlie was not anywhere in his view.

"Charlie," Dim croaked out weakly. No response. Dim pulled himself up to his feet and wobbled for a few minutes as a rush of dizziness overtook him. "Charlie," the goblin mustered up enough energy to yell. No response again.

Dim became concerned that while he was passed out overnight cannibals or something worse had taken it upon themselves to attack and take Charlie. However, Dim wasn't sure why they'd have passed Dim up if that was the case. He needed to sit for a minute and think. Where standing had caused so much exertion, sitting was easy. Dim just let his legs collapse and a sigh escaped him at the relief of not expending so much energy standing anymore. Now to think.

He let his mind wander back to the night before and the conversations he had with Charlie. The last conversation he remembered having was about the Oleander bush and the city they had passed. Charlie had been outraged they had not stopped to find the Oleander bush at Crimson Meadows. Certainly he was not stupid enough to have gone back there himself. Dim's eyes closed as exhaustion took over his body once again. The tired part of him wanted to forget Charlie and let him get himself killed if that is what he wanted to do. But then the loyal part of him chastised him for those thoughts. Forerunner was counting on him. And after all if Charlie did go back to Crimson Meadows it was a noble act that led him there. He was trying to save Dim's life. Though the goblin figured Charlie would likely lose his in the process.

The debate of what he should do exhausted Dim even more. The loyal side won the battle and Dim mentally prepared himself for the trek back to Crimson Meadows. The goblin hoped he was correct and Charlie had gone back that way. He stood and let the dizziness come and go before heading toward Crimson Meadow, disappearing into the fog.

Charlie awoke in the dark and felt warm and snuggly. He pulled the blanket up to his chin and rolled to his side then winced as soreness passed over his body. How did his back and legs get so sore? His mind felt a bit foggy and he couldn't think straight. He sat up from the cushion of his bed and looked around him. He was greeted with darkness. His room was never this dark. Charlie reached out in front of himself and his hand touched something slick. He ran his fingers down the object. It seemed to surround him. Charlie felt a panic as he started to wonder if he was imprisoned in some sort of casket. He pushed at the slick wall in front of him and it moved. Charlie pushed harder and the slick wall lifted up over his head and he was out in the open in the middle of a dark garden. The memories of where he was and what had happened came crashing back to him.

He reached behind himself to touch his back and the back of his legs and found to his amazement that he was wearing some type of strange clothing. Not only was that surprising, but where he still felt pain at touching the burned areas, the pain was tolerable. There was also some sort of moist cloth placed over his burned skin. Charlie knew he never placed them there, so the question was who had.

Charlie went to pull off the cloth from the burned area on his back when a crisp voice stopped him midway.

"I wouldn't do that if I were you." Flames leaped up suddenly from the end of a torch.

Charlie looked up startled. His eyes met the piercing blue eyes of a young girl. It only took minutes for Charlie to place where he had seen them before. "You," Charlie stammered, "You were the girl I saw before passing out." He stared at her for a moment. "So I suppose these weird clothes are yours?"

"Well, it's good to see you still have your memory intact, and, yes, you are welcome by the way," Isabella answered as she swatted his hands away from playing with the cloth on his back.

Charlie stared at the girl still trying to place where she had come from. Dim had told her that Pulchritude Amity only had a few humans still alive. How was it possible that one of them would be standing over him? Was Dim lying about the amount of humans left in order to play on his sympathy to keep him from going back home?

"You're human," Charlie stated.

"Well, look at you. Not only do you have your memory, but you know what a human looks like. Funny thing, I was thinking the same thing about you...being human that is."

"But I thought most of the humans were gone from here."

"So they are. And those still alive I know personally...minus you. So my question is who are you and where did you come from?"

Charlie stopped himself from answering as he pondered what she was asking. Who was she and could he trust her? He felt uncertain what to say and who to trust in this land. He sure wished Dim was here just then.

As if having sensed Charlie's thoughts a figure stumbled into the garden and stood before them. Isabella twirled around pulling her sword from her sheath and took stance to attack. Attack was not necessary, for as Isabella turned the swaying figure collapsed, first to his knees and croaked, "Charlie..." before falling face first into the dirt at Isabella's feet.

"Dim!" Charlie cried as he quickly moved forward to the goblin's side.

Isabella watched as Charlie slowly, painfully knelt down and cradled Dim's head in his lap. "Dim! Dim, can you hear me!?"

"You know this goblin?"

"Yes, he's a...friend," Charlie hesitated only for a second before calling Dim friend. He looked up at Isabella. "Put that away," Charlie said angrily. "Dim would never hurt you. Look at him. He isn't even capable of hurting anyone right now."

Isabella put the sword away after taking a closer look at Dim to be certain he was not in any condition to harm them. "Now you have me curious how a boy like you knows a goblin." Isabella's suspicion of this boy came back full force at the sight of him cradling the green imps head.

Charlie couldn't decide whether to tell this abrupt girl with piercing eyes about him and the goblin. He didn't know who to trust, but if he didn't trust someone, Dim would die if he already wasn't dead.

"Dim brought me here. He was taking me to meet Forerunner. He said something about how I was supposed to bring magic back to the land. Personally, I think he's crazy."

The expression on Isabella's face changed at what Charlie said. Her eyes squinted as she pondered over his words. "So this goblin, Dim you call him, was bringing you to someone called Forerunner because you were bringing magic back to this land. And where did he get you from?"

"Ummm, that's a good question. He took me from my home. My home is earth. I can't tell you exactly where that is from here. I just know Dim showed up in my dryer and pulled me in with him. Then somehow turned the thing on and after knocking around in it I passed out. The next thing I knew I was waking up in this depressing world."

"That's crazy," Isabella spurted out. "Dryers and knocking around and a place called earth. Are you a story teller?"

"I'm sure this all seems crazy to you, but put yourself in my place. THIS is all crazy to me. Goblins and magic and Trovac...whatevers!" Charlie rocked the goblin's head back and forth in his lap. "And now Dim is dying. I wasn't able to save him. I put my life in danger to save him and I can't even succeed at doing that. How could Dim even think I was important to this world?"

Isabella processed all that Charlie had just told her. Perhaps there was another world somewhere with things called dryers and maybe this is where The One would come from. It sure seemed like this goblin thought this boy was important.

"Here, move over," Isabella commanded Charlie as she handed him the torch. She bent down to the goblin and turned him over. She knew very little about the care of goblins. She wasn't even sure if goblins had the same illnesses that humans had or if their organs were even the same as theirs. But if this boy felt strongly about this hairy gremlin, then it would be in her best interest to do all she could to save him. She needed this boy to trust her and perhaps this was her only way to do that.

First she checked to see if the goblin was even breathing. She put her ear down to the goblin's mouth and felt the slight breath coming from him. "He's still alive," Isabella stated.

Charlie let out a sigh of relief. "Then the poison has not killed him yet. We need to find the Oleander bush then."

Isabella stopped what she was doing. "So you know what is wrong with this goblin?"

"This goblin has a name and it's Dim. And yes I do. He was protecting me from the Trovac Skrbnik when he was shot with the poison," Charlie said as he got to his feet and grimaced at the pain that still emerged from his wounds. "I need to find the Oleander bush so I can help Dim before it is too late." Charlie proceeded to hold the torch in front of him as he surveyed the plants and bushes surrounding them.

"Do you think it is wise to go picking through plants you have no knowledge of? It was only this morning you were about to poison yourself with Larkspur before passing out." Charlie stopped midway to touching a plant with beautiful pink flowers attached to it.

"Are you saying I almost poisoned myself this morning?" He couldn't even remember what he had been doing before passing out. The pain must have been so severe that he wasn't even coherent to the choices he was making.

Isabella took a leaf of Lidicaine and put it under Dim's tongue and held his mouth shut. "It's very dangerous to mess with plants when you have no knowledge of them."

After the Lidicaine dissolved under the goblin's tongue, Isabella carefully laid his head down on the ground and stood. She pulled out a book from her knapsack and held it under the torch, thumbing through it. It only took her a few minutes to come to a page that described Oleander bushes to her. *The Oleander bush has thin long green leaves and pale pink flowers that have 5 petals and a yellow middle.* Next to the description was a hand drawn picture of the plant and flower.

"Hey, what is that?" Charlie asked as he observed Isabella studying something in a book. Charlie moved closer to Isabella to get a better look.

Isabella slammed the book shut and quickly placed it into her knapsack before whispering *Onso Protecto* and waving her hands over the pack. "None of your business," was Isabella's curt answer as she slung the knapsack back over her shoulder and snatched the torch from Charlie's hand. "Look after Dim while I get a better look at the plants in this garden."

Charlie felt offended by the tone in Isabella's voice, but he grudgingly obeyed. If Isabella was able to heal Dim, then the least he could do was listen to her and watch over the sick goblin. He went back to cradling Dim's head on his lap. He sat there a bit uncomfortable and uncertain what to do now. He decided all he could do was talk to Dim and hope that he'd hang on long enough for Isabella to find Oleander.

He watched as she disappeared into the foliage of the garden and tried to think of something to talk to Dim about. "So...um...you know back home I write stories for my sister. They're not that great really, but she sure enjoys them," Charlie said as he put two of his fingers onto Dim's neck and felt to see if he could get a pulse and was relieved when he felt one. "Anyway, I wrote this one story once about a goblin. Well, at least my version of a goblin. He was tall and fat and very green. He had these sharp fangs for teeth and growled when he spoke. He was a nasty dude, mean and scary. He also liked to eat humans when he caught them." He stopped talking for a minute as he felt Dim stir.

"Dim?" Charlie questioned, but didn't receive a response. He let disappointment overtake him. He had hoped the goblin was waking. He wasn't medically educated, but he assumed the longer Dim was unconscious the less likelihood he'd ever wake. He sure hoped Isabella would have some luck finding Oleander soon.

"Well, after meeting you, Dim," Charlie continued, "I realized how wrong that description is. I don't think I'd have ever described a goblin as being noble and loyal or self-sacrificing." Charlie trailed off as he let himself remember Dim's selfless act of hiding him and leaving himself vulnerable to being attacked with poison. "I'm proud to call you, a goblin, my friend." Charlie felt himself fighting a sob.

Just then, Isabella made her reappearance. "I found it," Isabella proclaimed as she raised a stem of green leaves with pale pink flowers over her head.

Charlie choked down the sob and lifted his head to see the flower she was waving about. "And you are certain it's Oleander?"

"As certain as I can be. So, what I do know about Oleander poisoning is you need to mix it with Elf blood, and I'm pretty certain we are not going to find that here."

Charlie brightened up as he recalled that Divine had already given him Elf blood. "Oh, I forgot to mention that I already had that," Charlie proclaimed as he pulled a vial of Elf blood from his pants pocket. He smiled as he held up the vial for Isabella to see.

"Normally, I'd ask where a boy like you found Elves blood, but I'll presume you came by it innocently. If not, I do not want to hear about it. After all, the majority of the Elves you'll find in this land have long been allies of ours, so I sure hope you found this honestly." Isabella reached over and took the vial from Charlie's hands.

Charlie watched as Isabella pulled out a clay bowl from her bag and placed the leaves from the plant into the bowl, letting seven to eight drops of Elf blood fall over them. She smeared the blood around the leaves and then took them into her hands.

"So where was Dim shot?" Isabella asked.

Charlie pointed to Dim's left arm. She bent down and saw the skin of the goblin's arm was eaten away. She took the blood smeared leaves and put them over the wound. Then taking more of the cloth from the minotaur that she had used earlier on Charlie's wounds she placed it over the leaves and tied it in place with some thin vine that was tied to her wrist.

"Well, that is the best I can do for him. Now to wait and see if we were too late." Charlie sure hoped they weren't.

The next day passed quietly. Isabella kept moving from the front of the garden to the back with her sword in hand. Occasionally she'd stop by Dim and feel his pulse and place more Lidicaine between his lips. Otherwise she spoke little and guarded the area. Fortunately for them no other creature made an appearance. Obviously this pretty little garden had not been discovered by anyone else.

Charlie on the other hand sat vigil at Dim's side. He told tales that he once told Kassie and kept a constant eye out for any signs of recovery. But the goblin remained the same. When not telling tales Charlie would sit quietly and go over and over all that had occurred in his life the last few days. It was already becoming difficult to remember his old life and it had only been a short time. The only constant thought was that of Kassie. He missed her vibrant bubbly personality especially in a world that lacked anything vibrant or bubbly.

When evening came the goblin's condition had not changed. Isabella moved away from the borders of the garden and sat down beside Dim and Charlie. "You need to eat," she stated. She pulled a cloth from her pouch and unwrapped some sort of meat. She handed it to Charlie along with some greens she had picked from the garden. It only took him minutes to devour the meal handed to him. After only eating some sort of dried junk that Dim had been feeding him, the meat and greens was a welcome treat.

Isabella sat back against the garden wall and slowly munched on some of the meat herself and watched as Charlie ate his food like a starving child. She couldn't quite place who this boy was, but the longer she had to think about all the events of the last two days the more she was convinced he was either The One, or knew of The One. She would be a disappointment to her mother if she did not take notice and cultivate the relationship between her and the boy. If he was The One then the next step would be to find the other two humans and bring them all together. Together with the Pen of Knowledge and Book of Truths and her Book of Potions, they could begin the destruction of Czar Nefarious and the reemergence of the human race, though in that area they would need some help. Isabella decided they'd worry about bringing back the human race after the destruction of Czar. "One step at a time," she softly whispered.

"What?" Charlie asked.

She looked up at Charlie as she realized she had said those last words out loud. "Oh, nothing. I was just talking to myself."

She sure hoped Dim would make a recovery. She was not friend to the goblins, but she had never truly considered herself an enemy of them either. Dim had obviously been friend to one human, Charlie or else he had made Charlie believe that. Perhaps Isabella could get answers from the goblin that she could not get from Charlie.

"Perhaps you should get some rest," Isabella stated as she brought herself to her feet.

"What about you?"

"Don't worry about me. I'll be fine. I believe you and Dim will fit under my makeshift shelter from yesterday. That way you can keep an eye on him and get some rest."

Charlie wanted to protest, but he could barely keep his eyes open. It was amazing how sitting and talking all day could exhaust one. "Okay. I am tired, but when you need a break just wake me and I'll take over for you."

Isabella nodded at him. "Okay." She knew better than to allow this inexperienced boy to guard anything. She'd just have to take some wake potion to keep her alert all night. As long as she didn't do that too many nights in a row she'd be okay. After several days she'd get side effects, and she didn't need that, but for tonight she'd be fine.

Isabella helped cover Dim and Charlie in her leaf and mud covered shelter. Then once they were settled underneath, she pulled out the small vial of wake potion and drank it. She gagged once at the pungent taste. Within minutes she stretched and felt as if she had just taken an 8 hour nap. Then she quietly whispered *Olonso Pulleis* and waved her hands over herself, crouching down at the garden gate and settling in. With magic continually fading, she didn't know how much longer her spells were even going to keep working.

The first half of the night went quietly. It was a rare clear night and the moon was in full force. Isabella spent some of the time peering through her potion book at the types of plants listed in it, and the rest of the time looking to see if some of the plants were in the garden they were camped in. Isabella knew it might be a long time before she was lucky enough to stumble across such a bountiful garden as this one. She could still remember when this world had an abundance of gardens. Now they were hard to come by.

She checked in on her guests several times to find Dim about the same, though she swore his color was looking better. Charlie slept soundly next to Dim and had his hand lying across the goblin's arm. She couldn't help but watch Charlie for a short while as he slept. He looked way too innocent to be of any help to them.

Midway through the night while Isabella was picking the dirt out of her fingernails with her knife, she heard footsteps in the distance. Putting her knife back into its pouch on her belt, she quietly pulled the sword from its sheath. She'd have to make a decision quickly about whether to wake Charlie or let him sleep and hope the shelter would be overlooked. The sounds of the footsteps became louder and she could tell from the loud thump that whoever was coming closer was of big girth.

Isabella had survived years alone. Now having to take care of this boy could be costly. She'd have to be careful to keep anything from happening to herself or the book. She took her pack and whispered *Onso Protecto*. She must keep the book safe regardless of what happened to her. She knew just enough magic to be able to do that.

The footsteps were closing in. Isabella took a stance in front of the shelter. She had decided keeping the boy out of this would be the best recourse. Seconds later a figure made an appearance through the darkness. It only took her seconds to discover the intruder was a burly cannibal. He was about as round as he was tall and his orange complexion almost glowed in the dark. His fat hung so low it nearly touched the ground. His bare fat feet sunk a few inches into the ground as he walked. He did not walk alone. Behind him he was dragging a goblin. He had the goblin by his foot and tugged him along as he walked. In the darkness Isabella could not tell if the goblin was dead or alive. She saw no movement from the goblin, so she assumed he was dead and perhaps the goblin was to become the cannibals late night snack.

Isabella held her breath as the cannibal stopped at the gate of the garden. *Olonso Pulleis* spell was keeping her safe, but she was uncertain if the cannibal would be smart enough to discover the shelter behind her or worse what was underneath it. She kept still and held her breath as the cannibal let go of the goblin leg and pounded his way through the gate. He moved slowly and carelessly as he toppled plants along his way. She kept still and watched as the cannibal stopped a few feet in front of her. She knew this was her opportunity to take him out before he knew what was happening.

Before she could act she heard more footsteps behind the monster. The burly cannibal turned slowly to see as well. Out of the darkness another orange shimmering cannibal appeared stopping inches from the goblin's body.

"Nooooo," this huge booming voice came from the cannibal in front of her. Isabella was not expecting such a loud voice to come from him and she jumped at the sound of it.

"Mine!" was the response from the other cannibal as he reached down and grabbed the goblin's head and started pulling the goblin towards him.

The cannibal in front of Isabella stomped his foot hard into the ground, "Not Yours, Mine," he yelled back.

Isabella felt the shelter behind her scrape across her legs and she panicked realizing that Charlie had been awakened by the commotion. She turned to pull the shelter back over Dim and Charlie before the cannibals noticed, but she was too late. The cannibal holding the goblin's head made a strange garbled sound of surprise to see Charlie and Dim that he dropped the goblin and it fell to the ground. Isabella knew killing one cannibal would be difficult, but killing two would be near impossible alone. Though their skin looked flabby as it hung around them in actuality, it was tough as nails. And where they rarely carried a weapon other than a club their massive fists could do more damage than most humans could with a weapon. She was in a predicament as to what to do. She had the element of surprise since she knew the cannibals could not see her, but while engaging one cannibal the other would likely attack Charlie and Dim who from what Isabella could see still had not regained consciousness. She could gamble on Charlie to use some magic to help her, but she didn't know enough about him to know what magic he knew. If fire was all he had, that would not help in this case. Cannibals were immune to fire.

As she tried to determine her best recourse, Charlie sat frozen next to Dim staring at the cannibals as they stared back. Before he could do anything the closest cannibal moved forward and came within inches of Isabella and grabbed the boy, "Mine."

Charlie cried out "Isabella!"

She wanted to respond, but knew it would be better for Charlie if she remained unseen. She'd have to take her chances and see what happened with the cannibals. She'd intervene if they harmed either Charlie or Dim. Otherwise, she'd wait until the beasts were distracted and she'd sneak them away. But with Dim still unconscious she was not certain she'd be able to handle rescuing both of them. She'd have to make a choice which in her mind was easy. It would be Charlie, but would he ever forgive her if she left the goblin to the fates of cannibals? She thought not.

Isabella moved quietly and quickly to the garden wall and stood back to watch what would occur and said a quick prayer to her God to keep Charlie safe.

"Isabella!" Charlie called out again.

The other cannibal picked up the goblin by his head again and dragged him along behind him as he stomped into the garden stopping at Dim's unconscious form. The brute looked at the goblin he was holding then back to Dim and back to the goblin he was holding again. He dropped the goblin he was holding and picked up Dim's foot and brought it to his face and sniffed. The cannibal looked back down at the goblin he had dropped again confusion swallowing up his face. Then his gaze went back to Dim's foot.

"Put him down!" Charlie screamed at the cannibal. This pulled the cannibals attention from Dim and drew it towards Charlie. "Isabella!" he cried out again. This was the last sound the boy made as the cannibal holding Dim's foot slapped Charlie hard and knocked him unconscious.

"MINE," he said as he dropped Dim's foot and grabbed Charlie from the other cannibals grip!

Chapter Six

A Menu for Escape

C harlie forced his eyes open and grimaced at the pain that small movement caused. He groaned and lifted his hand to his face. He couldn't believe how strong that, that...thing was. He was certain it broke his nose and he could tell his face was swollen. His eyes only opened halfway and the swelling kept them from opening any further. He did his best to look around him but the thing wasn't anywhere in sight. But lying on his left side was a goblin and on his right was another goblin. With his hindered vision he couldn't tell which one was Dim. Neither goblin was moving.

It took Charlie a few minutes to realize he was no longer on the soft ground of the garden but was lying in some sort of cave. The memory of calling for Isabella and her not coming to help returned and he felt anger well up inside him. He should have known better than to trust her. Now both Dim and himself where in worse trouble than before. That is if the goblin was even still alive.

Charlie sat up slowly and felt the ache from the burns and struggled with the dizziness from the injuries to his face. He sure was feeling beat up these days. He turned towards the goblin on his left and tried desperately to see through his swollen eyes if he was Dim. With the injuries hindering his vision, Charlie had to lower himself to within a few inches of the goblin's face before he could focus on it. Once lowered to within inches of the goblin it only took Charlie a few seconds to determine this goblin was not Dim. He was much fatter in the face and his ears were huge. Dim's face was only mildly chunky and he had small ears.

Charlie turned to the goblin on his right. Lowering himself to within inches of this goblin's face he hoped this goblin was Dim. He stopped inches from the goblin but before he could determine if he was Dim, a deep voice made him jump.

"Get any closer and we will be kissing and I ain't kissing a human."

"Dim!? You're alive!"

"I would hope so," Dim said as he slowly lifted himself to a sitting position groaning as he moved. "I sure feel like fish scum. I would think if I were dead I wouldn't ache so much."

Charlie couldn't hold in his delight at the goblin's recovery as he lurched forward and wrapped his arms around Dim.

"Hey, Knucklehead let's not get all touchy feely." Dim pushed Charlie away from himself showing his uncomfortableness at being hugged. The goblin looked around his surroundings as Charlie tried to hide his embarrassment at being pushed away. "Where are we? And what happened to your face. You've always been ugly, but now you're hideous."

Charlie's embarrassment vanished at Dim's typical abrupt self and he let out a laugh. "I'm not certain where we are. Some fat slobbery... thing brought us here I would think. And as for my face...my handsome face by the way...the slobbery thing hit me."

"Well, I don't see this slobbery thing around us now, so I would think we'd be wise to get out of here before it comes back."

At that precise moment the ground shook and a commotion was heard outside the cave. Charlie stumbled over to peer out the cave entrance only to see one of the things beating on the other with some sort of club yelling, "Mine" over and over.

"Uhhh, we need to leave now," Charlie said.

Dim tried to bring himself to his feet but dizziness overtook him. "I'm not sure I can." Charlie turned towards the weak goblin and away from the cave's mouth.

"We need to! I'll help you."

Charlie stumbled back to Dim in order to help support him. As he walked he discovered that the dizziness from his facial wounds caused him to weave a path back to the goblin. He stopped several feet from Dim and crouched down as he vomited.

"Hey, Knucklehead, I don't think you're in any shape to be helping anyone."

The commotion outside continued as one slobbery beast beat on the other beast repeating "Mine, mine, mine," over and over again.

"It's useless," Charlie said has he stayed crouched on the cave floor. "Neither of us is in any shape to be going anywhere."

A rustling sound was heard near the cave's mouth and Charlie slowly lifted his face up assuming he'd find the enemy coming for them. His surprise engulfed his face as he saw Isabella make an entrance.

"We need to leave now," she said as she looked from Charlie up to Dim without showing any surprise at Dim's consciousness. "It's our best chance to sneak out of here while the cannibals are battling."

"Oh, yeah," came Charlie's disgusted response. "Where were you when we needed you? You think showing yourself now is doing you any favors?"

"We do not have time now to be discussing this." Isabella no longer was talking to Charlie but was concentrating her statements to Dim and Dim alone. "Talk sense into him Dim. We need to get out of here while the opportunity has arisen."

Dim wasn't sure who this brash girl was and was even more stunned to be staring at another human. He knew there were only three other humans left in this land, so how was it he was staring at one? Were they multiplying now? He was certain of only one thing though and that was they needed to run while the opportunity was there even if that meant Charlie went with this girl and he stayed. The important thing was getting Charlie out alive.

"Neither of us is in the shape to walk out of here," was Dim's response. "But I know you are right and we need to run while we can. Charlie," the hairy goblin turned his attention towards the young human boy. "You need to go with this human. I will find my own way out of here and we'll meet up later to head to Forerunners."

"I'm not leaving you Dim. You can't imagine what I've had to do to keep you alive. I'm not leaving you now."

Dim stumbled his way to Charlie and gripped the boy's shoulders to steady himself. "You'll be doing me a favor Knucklehead. I will be better off finding my own way out of here. Besides, I shouldn't leave Boris here to the fates of the cannibals," Dim stated as he turned and glanced down at the other goblin who had been left forgotten on the cave floor. "Trust me, Charlie."

The two of them stared at each other in silence reading from each other eyes what the other was saying. Charlie could see how serious Dim was about this. The words from Divine came back to him "Just like patience, your kind needs to learn to trust more."

"We need to leave *now*," Isabella said again as the commotion outside rose to a fever pitch and the chant of "Mine, mine, mine" changed to "Eat, eat, eat."

"Okay, Dim. I'll trust you. I'll go with Isabella, but I expect you to keep your word. You better get yourself out of here." Then for good measure he added, "Forerunner will never forgive you if you don't bring me to him safe and sound and I need you alive in order to do that." Charlie knew the mention of Forerunner would weigh on Dim and spur him to escape.

Either from the relief of finally getting through to Charlie or the dizziness from the effects of the last of the poison in his system, Dim let go of Charlie and allowed himself to collapse to the cave floor. Charlie stumbled without the aid of the goblin as his dizziness returned and the blurriness of his surroundings caused him to turn and retch again.

Within seconds of vomiting Isabella was at Charlie's side and pulling him to his feet to aid him in walking. "I'll take care of him Dim. Look to the east where minotaurs are few and the trees still bear fruit even though most are rotten and foul. Beyond that you'll find the waterfalls. Go under them and you'll find an opening if you search it. That is where you'll find us."

Dim nodded as best he could as Isabella and Charlie exited the cave.

They stopped about a mile from where they had begun. They were fortunate they had exited the cave when they had. One of the cannibals had beaten the other to death and was busy skinning his remains and never glanced back as Isabella and Charlie exited. Charlie had wanted to stop shortly after leaving the cave due to his poor vision and dizziness hindering his movements, but Isabella had let him lean on her the whole way only stopping occasionally while Charlie vomited. Finally they stopped about a mile later when the burden of carrying his weight had worn her down.

"This is as good a spot to camp as any," Isabella stated as she deposited Charlie's weak form to the ground leaning him up against a boulder. She surveyed her surroundings to see how hidden she could make them for the evening. She was fortunate she had slept the night before while waiting for the cannibals to vacate the cave. She had hoped Charlie and Dim were still alive and was delighted when a fight between the cannibals occurred and she was able to sneak in to find both were not only alive, but conscious. Even though Charlie's wounds were painful to him and hideous for her to look at they were actually minor compared to what the fist of a cannibal could do. A bonus was the medicine had worked on Dim and he was now conscious. She was disappointed he was not here with them, since she was anxious to ask him what Forerunner wanted with Charlie. But if he was as competent as most goblin's, he'd find a way out of that cave and meet up with them at the location she had described to him. She just hoped his dizziness would not hold him back too long. Even though the cannibal had satisfied his hunger for the evening, a cannibal's appetite was huge and likely by morning he'd be looking for something or someone else to devour.

Isabella became busy putting together some sort of shelter with what she could find in her surroundings as Charlie leaned back onto the boulder behind him and closed what little was still open of his swollen eyes.

"I'll help with your wounds once I've been able to get us shelter for the evening," Isabella said.

"You left us," Charlie choked out.

Isabella stopped gathering and turned to Charlie. "Yes, I left you," she answered back. "Sometimes you have to make hard decisions for the best of others. Leaving you to the cannibals was a gamble, but I needed to take that gamble."

Isabella could tell by the confused look on Charlie's face he did not understand. To him she had deserted him. To her she had done what was necessary in order to find a safer way to save Charlie and Dim. Sure it was a gamble. She may have found them dead or eaten, but it was very unlikely one small human could defeat two hungry cannibals. She was not willing to sacrifice herself that way at least not until she knew more about Charlie. She had to keep reminding herself her role in magic was important. So even if Charlie were The One, he'd need her to guide him in the recovery of magic as well as Henrietta and Riot. He'd never be able to do that alone.

Isabella slowly lowered herself to the ground across from Charlie. "I know you're angry. I know you don't understand. But one small human would never be able to defeat two cannibals. I did what I needed to keep us both alive."

Charlie stared suspiciously at Isabella. After a few minutes of a stare down Charlie repeated, "You left us." Turning his gaze away from her he pulled up his hoodie and pulled his sleeves over his hands and lay down next to the boulder.

Isabella took her cue and stood up letting her hand glide down Charlie's arm as she stood. "I'm sorry, Charlie."

Chapter Seven
The Elves of Crystal Valley

E scaping the cave unnoticed would not have been so difficult if it hadn't been for the side effects of the poison still seeping out of his body. And then there was the issue of dragging Boris with him. The frumpy goblin was barely breathing, but Dim felt if there was any chance he might recover, Boris should get that chance. Most would claim goblins didn't have feelings and were robotic warriors and though that was true more often than not, it certainly didn't apply to Dim. Where goblins rarely had mushy feelings like humans they still felt anger and loyalty and concern. And surprisingly goblins also did what they could for their own kind. Where the rumors of the viciousness of goblins was true, that usually only pertained to those of other kinds. Dim liked to believe he was one of those vicious goblins, but unfortunately he never acquired those same traits. It was likely that was the reason Forerunner chose Dim to bring back Charlie. Any other goblin would have likely beaten the bratty human to death by now. Dim found it a curse to not share in the vicious trait. He particularly felt it now as he dragged Boris a few feet at a time, only stopping to steady himself. It would be so much easier to leave Boris to the fate of the cannibals. Any other goblin would have.

He had decided that going through the cave would be his best recourse. He did not have the speed to go out the front of cave without being caught and besides he needed the support of the cave wall to lean against as he went. He just hoped there was another opening further back in the cave. The alternative would be to get as deep into the cave as possible and hope he could hide there for a while until the dizziness subsided and then make an escape through the front of the cave.

The going was slow. Having to stop every few minutes to steady himself against the cave wall annoyed Dim. It was taking too long to make any progress. He could only hope the cannibal wouldn't make an appearance any time soon. He did notice that the cave walls and ceilings were narrowing as he went, so he was counting on that to keep the cannibal away. If the walls and ceiling kept the steady progression of narrowing, he was certain the cannibal would never fit through them, thus he'd be safe, at least for a short while.

It took Dim double the time it would normally have taken him to make his way deeper into the cave. It didn't take him long to realize there wouldn't be an opening on the other side. Even if there were an opening he'd never fit anyway. The cave was becoming a bit narrow even for him.

He stopped his forward progress and let go of Boris exhausted from having dragged a three hundred pound goblin for so long. Dim let himself sink to the ground next to Boris and rest. After a while he pulled his dried food from his pouch and munched on it. It felt great to rest and eat again. Now he just needed to wait out the poison. He didn't have much knowledge on how long poison took to exit a body; he just hoped it wouldn't take long.

The coolness of the spray coming from the waterfall chilled Charlie to the bone. They had already made their way across the lake, and now standing soaked with the mist of the waterfall blowing on him made Charlie certain he would catch pneumonia. Standing with his arms crossed and hands rubbing up and down over his arms, Charlie waited as Isabella stood observing the rocks behind the waterfall.

"What are we doing here?" Charlie asked.

"This is the safest place in Pulchritude Amity for you to recover," Isabella replied.

Charlie wasn't certain whether to trust her or not, but in his condition he didn't have much choice. He sure hoped Dim wouldn't take

long to join them. He watched as Isabella let her hands move effort-
lessly over the rocks until she came to a smaller one that was loose.
She pulled on it and the rocks vibrated and slowly moved to the left
leaving a narrow opening through the rock wall.

"After you," Isabella said as her hands pointed towards the opening.

Charlie moved forward cautiously and glanced through the opening, but with his hindered vision he couldn't see what was behind the
rocks. Divine's words came to him again "Just like patience, your kind
needs to learn to trust more." Charlie closed his eyes and squeezed
through.

Once on the other side Charlie opened his eyes as best he could.
He let his gaze move around him with his mouth gaping open. The
wonders he saw amazed him. After the drabness of this world he had
seen so far he stood shocked at the beauty surrounding him. The walls
of the mountains were made of crystal. They glistened and sparkled
in all directions. Below them was a valley still lush in greenery and
blooming plants. At the foot of the valley was a kingdom built of clear
bright crystals.

"How is this possible?" Charlie asked when the shock wore off. "I
thought without magic this world was slowly dying yet I walk into a
mystical place of beauty."

Isabella had just finished closing the space in the rocks they had
traveled through when she turned to see Charlie still surveying his
surroundings. She moved next to him and glanced around as well.

"Yes, it is beautiful, but Crystal Valley is seeing the wear of magic
leaving our land also." She touched Charlie on the arm and pointed
towards his right. "All those crystals were vibrant with colors, pink,
blue, purple, but they have lost all color and now stand clear. This
land below," Isabella continued as she pointed now to the valley, "used
to be scattered in blossoms of various flowers and plants, but now
they have lost their blossoms. Sure the greenery is still there, but that
too shall eventually fade."

"Crystal Valley?" Charlie repeated. "That seems a fitting name." He continued to absorb the beauty around them. Then it occurred to him; Divine was a Crystal Elf. This was Crystal Valley. "Is this where the Elves live?"

Isabella didn't answer immediately. Rather she took Charlie's arm and guided him down steps made of crystal leading to the valley. "Be careful. These steps can be treacherous even to one with perfect eyesight."

As they descended down the steep steps Isabella kept ahold of Charlie's hand, leading the way down and guiding with her words. "Watch your step here" and "Slowly, this step has a groove on the right." When they made it to the bottom Isabella finally answered Charlie's earlier question. "Yes, this is where the Elves live."

As if on cue, an Elf stepped out from the bushes in front of them holding a sword encased in crystal and inscribed. Behind him was what appeared to be another Elf on horseback. "Who are you to think you are allowed in this Valley?" the Elf holding the sword said sternly.

Isabella took a stance in front of Charlie to shield him as she replied, "I'm Isabella the descendent of Gunnar and Akila Aindrea. Divine told me once that I could come here to find refuge if needed."

The Elf's eyes never left Isabella's as she spoke. They stood that way in silence for a few moments. Without even glancing at Charlie, the Elf asked "You said you had permission to seek refuge. So who is the human boy and where does he fit into all this?"

Isabella never let her eyes stray from his either and responded back, "He is of great importance. Far more importance then an Elf guard is privy to know."

The horse stomped his hooves back and forth at that statement in disproval of Isabella's tone, but the rider said nothing knowing his place was only one of support. Charlie's attention turned from the sword-wielding Elf to the horse at the motion and was stunned to see that what he had thought to be an Elf on horseback was actually the head and torso of an Elf merged with the body of a horse...an Elven centaur!! The Elf with the sword allowed more time to lapse as he intimidatingly stared at Isabella. After a moment more had passed he commanded, "Savageskin, go fetch Divine." The Elven centaur wheeled and galloped away.

Ethereal had been observing the newcomers from a distance, and as they descended the wide valley stairs she could not quite make out who they were. She only knew if they planned to invade the valley, they'd be hard pressed to find a better armed valley. As the couple descended the stairs and came closer she became aware the girl in the lead was definitely human. She had not seen a human in a very long time, but she had not forgotten how they looked or presented themselves. This girl presented herself just like the humans Ethereal remembered with confidence and cockiness. She had long sweeping blonde hair and was adorned with a sword and spear that Ethereal knew would never get her past Aelfhere, their most proficient guard.

The second newcomer appeared to be human as well. Ethereal was certain he was male, but she only presumed he was human. She couldn't be certain since he did not share the girl's confidence and cockiness. His face was swollen and of various colors of black, blue and yellow. His eyes peeked through slits and Ethereal could not fathom how this creature could possibly be able to see. He walked unsteadily and seemed to rely highly on the girl's guidance in order to descend the stairs. He exuded very little that would have drawn attention, but for whatever reason, Ethereal could not take her eyes off him.

Her mother had told her that humans were extinct in this land, so Ethereal could not understand how she could be looking at one if not two humans. She could only remember having met one group of humans before and it was a long time ago. Her mother and the others did not speak highly of them. They felt humans were selfish, impatient and emotional creatures and if it wasn't for their natural talents in magic, this world never would have needed them. Now that they were extinct the land had lost its lushness and beauty. It was now being controlled by a demon ruler, Czar Nefarious, who was harsh and unjust. His evil had brought disorder and death to the humans and death to the land. He enslaved all creatures he could find to do his deeds. Some of her kind had been captured and never heard from again. No creature had been left untouched. So the Elves had chosen a life of solitude. So far Nefarious had not discovered the hidden valley. But eventually, he would. Yet before that happened their land may lose all the elements they needed to survive. The Crystals had already turned clear leaving them less energy and soon the resources they needed to survive would also disappear.

So lately a few of the Elves had taken it upon themselves to leave the valley to hunt and gather whatever plants they could use for medicine or sustenance. Her mother Divine had volunteered to be one of those searchers. Her mother had just returned a day ago with several leaves from plants that aid in the healing of crepicy, a fatal illness that attacked the nerves. They had a case a few months ago and no longer had the ingredients for healing the disease and the Elf had died. So Divine was thrilled to have found the leaves needed in use of the cure. But every time her mother left, Ethereal feared she'd never return. She had already lost her father in the Battle of Minotaur. She could not lose her mother as well.

She watched with interest as Aelfhere stopped the strangers and eventually sent Savageskin towards her home. She would have loved to be there to hear what was being said. At one time her mother could hear other people's thoughts and Ethereal had inherited that trait, but unfortunately, with the loss of magic they had lost that ability. There was something about the male stranger that gave Ethereal a desire to hear what he was thinking.

The stomping of Savageskin's hooves and the opening of the door below drew her attention from the strangers. Her mother had answered the door and Ethereal heard her calm voice. "What can I do for you Savageskin?"

"There are two humans that have entered the valley and the human girl claims you gave her approval to come. Aelfhere has sent for you."

So they were both humans. Ethereal glanced back to the strangers still being held by Aelfhere. The boy certainly did not look like any human she had encountered, but then again she had not encountered many.

Her mother closed the door and accompanied Savageskin to the entrance of the valley. Ethereal stayed on the balcony and watched the meeting of her mother and the strangers with interest. Then as her mother left the entrance of the valley in the presence of both humans, she thought perhaps she'd find out more about this boy after all.

Ethereal moved quietly to the first floor. She was curious about the humans, but knew if her mother caught her spying she'd be sent away. She came upon the room to which her mother had taken the humans. She hesitantly moved to the edge of the room and stood near the door and listened.

"How did this happen?" Divine asked.

"He took a fist from a cannibal," Isabella answered.

"Cannibal? That is what that thing was?" asked Charlie.

"Those were cannibals. At one time they were human like us, but they have done much evil among other humans and then started cannibalizing. Eventually, they evolved into something no longer human," said Isabella.

"You mean like a wendigo," said Charlie.

Isabella just looked quizzically at him for a few seconds. "I don't know what that means. They are cannibals."

Divine interrupted the conversation asking "How did this boy end up in your company? The last I saw he was traveling with a goblin."

"You know Charlie?" a shocked question from Isabella.

"I have made his acquaintance. The last I saw he was with a goblin that had been seriously poisoned by a Trovac Skrbnik," said Divine.

"The two of you are talking as if I'm not even in the room. Divine is the Elf that helped neutralize the poison in Dim and gave me the Elf blood," Charlie stated.

"And where is Dim now?" Divine directed the question to Charlie.

Before he could answer Isabella said "He is in a cannibal cave west of here. He was too weak to travel with us. He should hopefully be here in a few days."

"Goblins are not allowed in Crystal Valley. He will not be allowed past the guards," Divine said. "What are you expecting from me and from sanction here with the Crystal Elves?"

"Charlie needs healing. His wounds are slowing his travel. We would not be asking to stay for an extended time. We'd only stay as long as it takes for him to heal."

"I can help with the healing, but I cannot promise sanction here to recover. That would have to pass through the council," Divine said as she started to move about the room preparing the dressings that would be needed to be placed on Charlie's facial wounds. "It would be best to give him something to ease the pain, but I am afraid we do not have any more Lidicaine here to use. We have not been able to locate any lately."

"I have some," said Isabella as she pulled some Lidicaine from her pouch and placed it in Charlie's mouth. "Take this, Charlie. It should help with the pain." He did as she asked. He normally didn't like being told what to do, but he was tired of the constant ache in his face.

Divine went to work on the dressings and placed them on his swollen features leaving only the orifices visible. "Take some of this," Divine said as she held out a spoon full of purple liquid.

Charlie scrunched up his face at the sight of the strange looking liquid. "What is it?" he asked.

Divine sighed. Ethereal knew her mother did not like being questioned. "It is a sleeping aid. In order to speed up the healing, you should sleep," Divine reluctantly answered.

He opened his mouth to protest, but the stern look in Divine's eyes told him that would not be a good idea. He opened his mouth and closed the slits of his eyes as she deposited the purple liquid onto his tongue. Charlie closed them and gagged at the foul taste of the liquid but forced it down.

Divine turned to Isabella "I will need you to accompany me to the meeting of the council. They will want to hear from you. I fear they will not be pleased with harboring two humans in our Valley. We do not want Nefarious to find this place. I know to you that must be a selfish view, but we must think of our kind and preserving them for our future."

Isabella actually did understand her view. It was the same one she had about the remaining humans in this land. "I would be honored to speak to the council, but I'm hesitant to leave Charlie alone."

"He will be safe here. No one will disturb him. Besides the sleep aid will keep him under a deep sleep for some time."

Isabella looked hesitantly from Charlie to Divine. He was already floating away into sleep, so Isabella felt her best recourse would be to accompany the female Elf. She was hoping the council would allow them a few days to recover here at Crystal Valley. She just needed long enough for Charlie to heal and for Dim to make an appearance. Then she'd need to convince the goblin to forego Forerunner in order for them to find Henrietta and Riot. If Charlie was The One, she needed to form a reunion of the humans before Nefarious discovered Charlie was in Pulchritude Amity.

"Okay, I'll go with you to see the council."

Ethereal scrambled around a corner as Divine and Isabella left the room to head up the winding crystal stairs leading to the conference room. She knew that the council would take a while to gather and then they would spend time debating the best course of action for them in this situation. Ethereal realized this was her chance to get an up close view of this human boy they were calling Charlie.

Once Divine and Isabella disappeared up the stairs, Ethereal snuck into the room. At first she stood a distance away and watched as the human's chest moved to the rhythm of his breathing. She still would not be able to see his face close up with the dressings covering it. But she was mesmerized by this human. Something about him drew her to him and she felt a chill go down her spine. She stood for about ten minutes just watching him breathe. He made little *pmff* noises as he exhaled and Ethereal found it endearing. Eventually Ethereal convinced herself to move closer.

She moved silently to the side of the bed and looked down at what was visible of his face. His eyelashes were extremely long for a boy. They curled at the ends. She tried to imagine what his eyes were like under those lids. She pictured blue to go with the golden hue of his hair. His lips were full and a vibrant red that accentuated the pale shade of his skin. She wanted to reach out and touch his lips and feel the moistness, but she held back.

Ethereal allowed her gaze to move from the boy's face to his arms and hands and felt another shiver go up her spine. His arms were young and strong and his hands though bruised and dirty had a masculine shape to them. Ethereal could not hold back and she let her hand reach out and touch them. As her fingertips brushed across the small hairs on his hands she felt a tingling in the tips of her fingers that quickly worked its way up to her hands and arms and into what she imagined to be her heart. A fire was burning there and she was certain whoever this boy was, he was of great importance not only to Pulchritude Amity, but also to her. She closed her eyes as the fire that burned in her heart worked its way through her entire body. She let her fingers grasp the boy's hand and the burning increased and then it happened. For the first time in a long time she heard the thoughts. But this time the thoughts came with visions. She had never had a vision before.

The vision was of a petite blonde haired girl. She was beautiful and had the same shape to her mouth as the boy sleeping in the bed in front of her. She stood outside in some green grass with trees scattered behind her. She wore some sort of flowing blouse painted with flowers and tight pants of blue. Ethereal had never seen such clothing. Next to the girl stood a boy whose face took Ethereal's breath away. His eyes were as blue as the sea. His hair was a golden blonde. From the shape of his nose and mouth, Ethereal was certain this was the boy who was lying in the bed before her. He, like the girl, wore some sort of shirt with a hood over it that had some strange markings across the front of it. His pants were made of a material she did not recognize. He stood with a round object in his hands that he tossed up and down while talking to the girl.

"So, I thought we could toss the ball around while waiting for mom and dad," the boy said.

The girl who seemed to have a permanent smile plastered on her face answered back, "Sure, Charlie."

Ethereal watched as they threw the round object back and forth and talked and laughed telling jokes and stories. She sensed she'd love this young girl. The girl was bright and happy and just seeing her made Ethereal feel happy as well. But she couldn't take her eyes off the boy for the most part. He mesmerized her and drew her to him. She knew these two were exceptional and important.

She could have spent hours watching the two chat while tossing the object around. Just as she was relaxing in the bliss of seeing a vision and hearing a thought she heard the sound of voices and footsteps coming down the stairs.

"Divine said the boy was in the room to the right."

"We will check to see if he is conscious and if he needs his dressings changed," said a second voice.

Ethereal let go of the boy's hand and the vision disappeared from her mind. She'd have to think quickly as to explain why she was in this boy's room.

The Elf twins walked into the room and halted at the sight of Ethereal. "What are you doing here?" said the twin named Jerushah.

"I…ah…I was walking by and thought I heard someone crying out from this room, so I thought it would be best to check out the sound," Ethereal hesitantly answered. She sure hoped they wouldn't see through her lie.

The other twin named Aafke glanced from Ethereal to the boy on the bed. "The boy made a sound?" Aafke asked as she moved swiftly to the bedside and took a hold of the boy's hand. "Are you in pain?" she asked the boy. She did not receive a response. Ethereal felt a slight pang of guilt over the lie about the boy crying out.

"Hmm, if he was in pain, he certainly seems okay now. He seems in a deep sleep again," said Aafke.

Jerushah never took his eyes off Ethereal. She could feel his glare and suspicion from across the room. She felt uneasy, but having learned from her mother how to mask her feelings, she stood tall and proud with her head held high as though she didn't even notice Jerushah's gaze and hid her uncomfortableness well.

"That is strange. Perhaps he unconsciously cried out in his dreams and is now fine. I am not a healer, so cannot explain his reactions," Ethereal explained. "Who is he anyway?"

Jerushah answered before Aafke could. "That is none of your business. Please leave now. He is in good hands."

Ethereal knew better than to argue with Jerushah. He was strict and by the rules where Aafke would have been more apt to have answered her kinder. Ethereal bowed her head to Jerushah out of respect for her elders and left the room.

She thought a lot about the boy and the girl in this human's thoughts as she took the stairs back up to the balcony. She had not entered anyone's thoughts in a very long time and she had never seen a vision before. How could this boy bring that out in her? And was it the boy or had she just recovered that ability again? She'd have to test it out on someone else. All she knew for certain was that she needed to be near this boy. She'd have to make sure of that. She felt certain he was a piece of her somehow. She was sure they fit together. She had been told once that her mother and father had been destined for each other and had known it immediately. There was a magic that swelled between them and a tingle that didn't go away even when the other was not present. Ethereal had not understood those feelings, but she now did as a tingle went up her arms as she walked. She had found her destiny.

Chapter Eight
A Plea for Sanction

Isabella was a bold girl. She found little that scared her. It was certainly a trait that had helped her survive these harrowing years. However, walking into a room of twelve Elf elders and four Elf centaurs left her at a loss for words. She had fought and defended herself against many creatures, but all the time she had been alone she had only encountered one Elf, Divine. She was a bit in awe of her. She was wise and helpful, but she never came off menacing. This group of Elves stood behind podiums in a massive room and took turns talking. Their dark skin and dark hair created a menacing and intimidating appearance. They stood erect with heads held high. Among them were a few Elves with grey hair that had the same long, smooth and straight look. Their eyes were dark as coal and appeared to look straight through one.

Isabella tried to comprehend why this group of Elves intimidated her. She had fought minotaurs and ogres without hesitation. But then again she was fighting and that was where her comfort lay. She was not comfortable speaking and certainly not among some of the most intelligent beings in Pulchritude Amity. Intelligence was not her best trait. She hoped Divine would take the burden of the speaking.

Divine walked into the room exuding confidence just like the elders. She certainly did not have any problems speaking among this group. Isabella couldn't help but admire her.

"Good day," the she-Elf greeted. The Elves turned and gave their attention to Divine and Isabella and all talking ceased. "I called you all here to discuss our current situation." Divine put out her hands to Isabella who stepped forward placing her hands into Divine's. "We have a guest here today seeking sanction with us along with her companion…a human boy. He would be here today, but he was in need of healing. He is under the care of Jerushah and Aafke until I return. It needs to be decided among the elders whether sanction can be granted for the humans."

With that Divine became silent. Starting to their left the first Elf questioned, "Where did these humans come from? We all know there are only three humans left in this land. Are these two of the three?"

"We are only assuming there are three humans left in this land. Though we have told our people humans are extinct, we in this room know better than that. We know the importance of the three remaining. I would think we would want to aid in their quest if at all possible," answered Divine.

"How do we know this is not a trap? We have been fortunate to remain hidden from Czar Nefarious' eyes. We would not want to bring that evil here," the second Elf on the left intoned.

"We cannot be certain this is not a trap. We have to trust our instincts on that, thus I brought the girl here for you all to see." Isabella felt uncomfortable as all eyes moved to her.

"How long do they seek sanction?" the third Elf to the left asked.

"As long as they need to heal and prepare plans for what they seek," Divine answered.

"We see the girl and she radiates goodness, but we cannot say the same for the boy without seeing him," the fourth Elf to the left stated. Isabella wondered how she radiated goodness. It was never something she truly considered herself before. She wondered what the Elves were seeing.

"As I said the boy was not able to come with us today, but I promise we will bring him to you when his health is better."

"I believe we would be hard pressed to allow sanction until we have laid eyes on this boy," said the fifth Elf from the left.

Before Divine could reply, Isabella spoke up. "He's The One." A hush engulfed the room at Isabella's statement. She hadn't been certain if they knew about The One, but after the hush she suspected they had. All in the room stood in silence for a minute as their eyes searched hers including those of Divine. Isabella wasn't certain if telling them he was The One was the right thing to do since she wasn't positive herself, but her gut told her he was.

"The One?" the sixth Elf from the left asked. "How do you know this?"

"He is strong in magic and only The One would have that right now. Sure I have a small amount myself, but it is dwindling without a magic writer. When you touch him you can feel the magic coursing through his body," Isabella stated. The Elves hushed again as they comprehended what Isabella was saying.

"We will need to see this boy ourselves to determine if you are correct," stated the seventh Elf to the left.

"When will he be healed enough to stand before us?" asked the eighth Elf to the left.

"I would think within a day. He is under a sleep aid presently, so he would not be able to stand before you today."

"Then we will meet here tomorrow with the boy at dusk," said the eighth Elf from the left.

"We will want the girl to come with him," said the ninth Elf from the left.

"This is to be kept between the circle of trust until a decision has been made," said the tenth Elf to the left.

"We will provide sanction for the night, but no longer than one night until we meet again," said the eleventh Elf to the left.

"Good night," said the twelfth Elf to the left to dismiss the meeting. It was not lost on Isabella that each Elf had a say before the meeting was over. She assumed that was protocol or coincidence. However, the Elf centaurs never spoke. Perhaps they were merely guards. Isabella and Divine exited the room.

Charlie awoke feeling rested and peaceful. He hadn't felt this way for quite some time. Whatever Divine had given him had done wonders. He lifted his hands to his face and removed the dressings and surprisingly he could see through his eyes and the swelling was gone. After days of stumbling around because of his facial injuries, Charlie was relieved to feel normal again. He sat up and glanced around the room looking for Isabella or Divine, but he found himself alone. Strange, he was certain while he was out that he had felt a presence that was comforting. A tingle went up his spine just remembering the feeling. He had also remembered having a dream of his sister whom he missed terribly. Perhaps that was the comforting presence he had felt.

Charlie stood and walked to the door, peering out the entrance. Seeing no one he decided he'd explore and see if he might be able to find Isabella or Divine. He was eager to see if Dim had made an appearance while he was sleeping. There was a long hallway to the left and a hallway that turned left on his right. Then there was crystal stairs in front of him. It only took him a few minutes to decide he'd go upwards. Taking the stairs two at a time he found a lobby with an opening to the right that went out to a balcony. Charlie walked onto the balcony and looked over the edge to see the valley below him. It was dark now, but he could see fire burning in various areas of the valley indicating where life might be.

He was so absorbed with the view that he did not hear the steps behind him. A hand reached out and touched his arm and he jumped in surprise. The surprise continued when he turned and stood face to face with a young beautiful dark haired Elf. She reminded him of Divine, but a younger version. She stood erect and proud her eyes never leaving his. Charlie felt a tingle go up his spine.

"I'm sorry," he said. "I know I didn't ask to look around, but I awoke alone, so I thought it would be okay to go looking for Isabella or Divine."

"Of course, you may go wherever you please. As long as you have sanction here with us, you have access to all that we have access to," the Elf with the dark eyes said.

She let go of Charlie's arm and looked out over the ledge of the balcony, letting her hands rub against the crystal that made up the ledge. Charlie was mesmerized by the movement of her hands and watched quietly as she stood staring off into the valley. This Elf transfixed him and took his breath away. He felt peaceful just being in her presence.

After a few minutes of watching her hands soothing the crystal, Charlie pulled his gaze away and turned to face the outside world. "I'm Charlie, by the way."

"Ethereal, proud warrior daughter to Bibhatsu and Divine Echosby of the Crystal Elves."

So this was Divine's daughter. Charlie could see the resemblance, dark, proud and mysterious. Unlike how he felt around Divine who made him a bit uncomfortable, Ethereal on the other hand made him feel at ease just standing near her, silent. He had to fight the urge to reach out with his hand and touch Ethereal's hands that were still caressing the crystal ledge. He couldn't understand how having only met this Elf, he felt so drawn to her.

"You are human," Ethereal stated rather than asked.

"Yes, I'm human."

Ethereal turned her body to face him. "I was told your kind was extinct. But as I stand here staring at you, a human, I realize that is not truth, but a falsehood. I have never been so close to a human before. I find your kind seems to carry emotions in their faces. That can be a weakness here in Pulchritude Amity. Perhaps that has not helped your kind to survive."

Charlie turned to face Ethereal and allowed their closeness to heat his body. They were so close that he could feel her breath caress his face as she spoke. "Emotion can be a strong trait as well. It depends on how you view it. Without emotions would we be a breathing creature?"

"I am not questioning there being a place for emotions, but displayed across our faces for all to see is not where emotions belong. Do you know my emotions from viewing my face?"

Charlie allowed himself to search her face from the smooth skin of her cheeks to the dark pools of her eyes and the straight lines of her mouth and found he could not. Yet he longed to know what was beneath all that beauty. What thoughts this beauty possessed. "No, you hide your emotions well."

Ethereal moved a few inches closer causing Charlie to catch his breath. She was so close he could almost feel their mouths touch. "Ah, but you I can read. You feel desire. You wish to touch me. Perhaps to feel my lips to see how soft they are," She whispered. Ethereal took a step back from him. "Emotions. They are displayed like a hand written letter across your face."

Charlie squirmed slightly at the accurate description of his emotions. "That is only a guess. You don't know that's what I was feeling."

"So you do not desire me? I have misread you?"

He didn't want to lie to Ethereal. He felt the best decision was to change the topic and leave it be. He turned back to stare out at the valley. "Crystal Valley is a beautiful place."

Ethereal turned as well to view the valley again. "At one time it was beautiful. Now it is losing its beauty. Perhaps you could bring that back to us."

"Me? Why would you think I could bring beauty back to your valley? I'm just a boy...I mean man." He felt the need to clarify the difference between a boy and a man. This wise Elf could not possibly find a boy of any interest, but perhaps a man she would.

"You have magic coursing through you. That magic could bring beauty and kindness back to our land. Crystal Valley is not immune to the disappearance of beauty. It is just slower in showing it. Sort of like how we are with emotions. Slow in showing them," Ethereal stated.

"If I have magic in me, then why do I not feel it? Why don't I just snap my fingers and fix all the issues in Pulchritude Amity?"

Ethereal stayed facing the valley, but turned her head towards Charlie. "It does not work that way. I am a warrior. It is in my blood. My father was a warrior. His father was a warrior. Thus I am a warrior. It is in my blood. But that does not mean I can just fight without the training. It has taken years for me to be able to wield a sword like my father. The same would be for you."

"But my father is a physics professor and my mother is a nurse. Neither of them knows magic. So how could magic be in my blood?"

"Perhaps you do not know them as well as you believe." Ethereal looked back out over the valley. "Or perhaps you are unique. But one thing I am certain of is that you are strong in magic. Stronger then I have felt in a long time."

Charlie stood silently looking out over the valley. Daylight was slowly creeping in over the mountains. The fog Charlie had become used to during his travels in Pulchritude Amity did not swallow up the valley, but the sun didn't burn strong here either. A cloudy hazy day extended over the valley. He was so transfixed on the crystals and uniqueness of the place that he didn't realize until now that the valley was covered in haze and some of the trees in the distance were losing their leaves as they spoke. Ethereal was accurate in her description of the valley. It may still hold some of its beauty, but soon that would disappear as well. It was just slower to occur than the rest of the land.

Perhaps Ethereal was telling the truth. Maybe there was magic in him and he just had not realized it. After all it sure seemed Isabella and Dim also believed it. Maybe they all knew something he did not. Dim. He had meant to find out if Dim had made an appearance to Crystal Valley.

"Has a goblin shown up looking for me?" Charlie asked.

"A goblin? Not that I am aware of, but then again I am not supposed to be aware of you. However, it is our policy here at Crystal

Valley to not allow goblins into our city. Is this goblin that which you are seeking sanction from?"

"No, no. He's…a friend."

"Strange. I did not know goblins and humans were friends. You would want to ask Isabella if a goblin has come for you. She did not want to stay in our home. She felt more comfortable outside. You will find her camping in the woods behind us," Ethereal said.

Charlie did not want to leave the she-Elf. He was afraid he'd never see her again. However, he knew he needed to find Isabella. "Thank you, Ethereal." He hesitantly turned and headed back down the stairs to find Isabella.

He found her under some trees. She was sitting cross legged and reading a large, leather bound book. As he came into her view she closed the book and quickly placed it into her knapsack. Charlie had seen that book twice now. Isabella sure seemed secretive of the contents in that book. Now his natural curiosity was revving up.

He squatted down across from Isabella. "What ya reading?"

"A book," Isabella said with a smirk. "So I see you are better," and she reached out and gently touched his face in awe of how the swelling had disappeared and the bruising had changed to a mild yellow color. "I'm going to need to find out from Divine what she used to heal your wounds so quickly."

It did not go unnoticed by Charlie how Isabella had skirted over his question about the book. His curiosity was definitely peaked now. He'd find out some way or another what was in that book. "So, Dim has not showed up yet?"

Isabella let her hand drop from Charlie's face and dropped her eyes from his. "No I'm afraid not."

"You think something has happened to him, don't you?"

"It is possible," Isabella stood and put her knapsack on and kicked dirt over the fire in front of her. When she stood she had hoped Charlie would stand as well. She realized his expression showed one of concern. She was being insensitive to his feelings about Dim again. "That doesn't mean anything has happened. Goblins are slow. It's possible he just has not found this place." When Charlie didn't say anything she tacked on "I'm sure he'll be here soon."

Charlie stood slowly. "If he doesn't show soon I'm going to go looking for him."

"That would be foolish. You don't even know your way around and there are terrible creatures in this land looking for a human like you. And my guess is you don't even know how to use a weapon. Am I right?"

"According to you I don't need a weapon. I know magic."

Isabella shook her head at his statement. "It doesn't work that way. If you are The One you would be strong in magic, but we need The One as a magic writer. The old magic has faded. We need new magic to be written and taught. That is what you would be doing. That alone will make you a key target for Nefarious. It would be my job to keep you and the magic safe."

Charlie had never really put a lot of thought into where magic came from. It certainly had never occurred to him that someone wrote it. He had no idea how to do that. He wanted to protest again that he did not know magic, but then Ethereal's statement just a short while ago came back to him. For whatever reason where Dim and Isabella had failed, Ethereal had succeeded. He trusted her and couldn't understand why since he really did not know her. She believed he was strong in magic. Perhaps she was right and he just had not discovered that for himself. Maybe Isabella would be able to help him with that. But he felt disloyal to Dim. The goblin wanted him to go to Forerunner, but Charlie was sensing that was not his calling now. He felt Isabella and her path was his calling.

"I won't go with you without Dim. When or if we find him, we can do whatever it is you believe I'm here to do, but not until then."

"We may not have a choice. We may be forced to leave here whether we want to or not. We were granted sanction for one night. The council would not extend that without you being present. We go back at dusk to face the council again."

Charlie had no idea who made up this council Isabella was talking about. All he knew was he wasn't ready to leave this place. Truthfully, he didn't want to leave Ethereal. He wanted more time to explore what was between them or at least what Charlie believed was between them. He couldn't read the female Elf. He just hoped she felt something for him.

"Did you want to leave soon?" Charlie asked.

"I thought it would be best for us to stay a few days to make sure you were one hundred percent and to give me time to make a plan."

"A plan? What plan?"

"To find the other humans of course," she said as she walked away towards Divine's home.

Chapter Nine
A Council of Elders

Charlie felt extremely nervous as he walked into a room of Elves and Elf centaurs. Divine alone made him nervous. Twelve Elves and four Elf centaurs made him ill at ease. The only Elf he had met that did not make him nervous was Ethereal. He looked around the room hoping he would find her here at the council, but was disappointed. He knew it was unlikely she'd be there since the council was made up of wise older Elves, yet he couldn't help but wish she were there. He had looked around all day for her, but never came across her again. He hoped the council would see fit to allow them sanction for a few days more. He didn't want to leave without speaking with Ethereal at least one more time. Besides, he would never be able to continue with Isabella without Dim. He hoped a few more days would give enough time for the goblin to find them.

Divine stood on his left and Isabella on his right. Across from them at twelve podiums were twelve Elves. On the left side of the twelve Elves stood two Elf centaurs. On the right side of the twelve Elves stood two more Elf centaurs. When Divine, himself and Isabella walked into the room all talking ceased. Divine was the first to speak.

"I have come tonight with Isabella and the boy, Charlie. As you can see his wounds have healed enough for him to walk in here himself," she said. Charlie would have expected her to seem proud that he had recovered so well, since she was the cause of his recovery, but she stood and talked as if it was of no special significance that she had single handedly healed him. If she were human, she'd be talking herself up and giving herself all the credit. He was impressed she did not do that.

All the Elves turned their attention to Charlie and nodded as Divine spoke.

"We see he looks well and capable," said the first Elf to the left.

"Do you two still seek sanction with us now that he is well and capable?" asked the second Elf to the left.

Isabella answered this time. "Yes, we would like to stay a few more days. We would want to be as certain as possible that Charlie is totally healed. Otherwise, he would slow us down and that would put both of us in danger."

"Both of you staying for even another day longer will put the Crystal Elves in danger as well," said the third Elf to the left.

"This is true, but in the long run you would be saving your kind by saving this boy and isn't that more important?" said Isabella.

"That would only be true if this boy is The One and we have not determined that of yet," said the fourth Elf to the left.

The Elves became quiet and all eyes went to Charlie. He felt uncomfortable being the center of attention. He did not like being stared at. He moved his weight from one foot to the other as he felt the urge to run.

"Please step closer," the fifth Elf from the left commanded.

Charlie could feel his knees shaking and hoped he could move forward and not collapse and make a fool of himself. He glanced towards Isabella. She nodded to him in reassurance. Charlie moved forward until he was standing within a few feet of the Elves. Then the Elves moved around the podiums one at a time and stood before Charlie. Each Elf bowed their head and reached out with one hand touching him either on the hand or arm or shoulder. None of them said a word as they touched him and stood that way for a few minutes before they moved on. Charlie felt awkward allowing so many strangers to touch him. It took all he had not to bolt from the room.

After the last Elf touched him the sixth Elf from the left said, "You may move back now."

Charlie stepped back until he was even with Divine and Isabella. He looked searchingly at Isabella hoping he'd find out through her eyes what that was all about. All he got from her was a shrug of the shoulders.

"You may stay for as long as you need to get well," said the seventh Elf from the left.

Charlie assumed that meant he had passed whatever test they had just put him through. He was thrilled they could stay longer. That would give him plenty of time to find Ethereal.

"Does that mean you believe he is The One?" Isabella asked boldly.

The Elves looked from one to another before answering. "He is more than just The One," said the eighth Elf from the left.

Charlie had just become a little bit comfortable with being called The One. He wasn't prepared for being told he was more than that.

"More than just The One?" Isabella asked.

"He is sacred here in Pulchritude Amity. You can feel it in his blood and spirit," said the ninth Elf to the left.

"We would be foolish not to harbor and heal this boy," said the tenth Elf to the left.

"We will do our part to bring this world back to where it once was. This boy can do that for us," said the eleventh Elf to the left.

"Good night," said the twelfth Elf to the left.

Divine ushered the two humans from the room. Charlie wasn't ready to go. He wanted answers. If he was more than just The One what more was he? Didn't anyone think he at least deserved answers? He knew he wasn't going to get them from those Elves or from Isabella. Even Dim didn't provide him with enough information. Only one presence in Pulchritude Amity had provided him with any direct answers. He knew that was who he needed to find.

Ethereal sat in the midst of the forest on an old tree that had fallen years ago. It was one of her favorite places to go and think. The forest was on the edge of their valley and wasn't very deep. It was surrounded by walls of crystal, much like the entire valley. It kept their home hidden and had for centuries. Now Ethereal had heard the Elves were talking about the likelihood of Czar Nefarious finding them. One of the Elf centaur scouts had seen the minotaurs not too far away. He was certain they were looking for the humans, and was convinced it would not be long before they discovered Crystal Valley. Ethereal knew enough about minotaurs to know they could not swim, so she wasn't sure how the scout figured they would make it across the lake to the waterfall. It was the only entrance to Crystal Valley. The lake had kept many creatures from finding their home since so few of the beings in Pulchritude Amity could swim. It was one reason Crystal Valley had remained hidden for so long.

She sat on the log and watched the leaves fall off the trees. Once upon a time she would have sat here and reveled in the beauty surrounding her. Now she felt deflated watching as the leaves turned brown and the fruit that some of the trees still bore was rotten and inedible. Her favorite spot was no longer a place of beauty. She felt helpless to stop the decay. She was disappointed that the Elves had remained distant from helping save this land. Didn't they realize eventually Czar Nefarious would enslave all those around them and they would be next? Her father would never have allowed the council to sit back and just watch. He was a mighty warrior in his time and had fought in the Battle of Minotaur. He had died for the cause. Ethereal was so proud of her father for sacrificing his life to better the lives of all those around him. She had inherited his fight and warrior trait. She wanted to do something to help stop Czar Nefarious. But without the approval of the council the Elves in Crystal Valley would never fight. She hoped with the arrival of the humans perhaps the council would change their views. Now that The One was here in person, she felt certain they would. Her mother did not agree. She said nothing but death would change the council's decision to stay out of the fight. The council still remembered how many of the Crystal Elves had died in the Battle of Minotaur. They were not ready to go through that again.

Ethereal felt the urge to go against the council and she saw her opportunity with the arrival of Charlie and Isabella. If she could help to stop Czar Nefarious, she would feel better than sitting here in Crystal Valley and doing nothing. If that meant she had to sacrifice her life, then she'd be more than willing to do so. There was never a more honorable death for a warrior than dying for their cause.

She was not too absorbed in her thoughts to miss hearing the rustle of leaves behind her. Someone had followed her. She quietly stood and pulled her bow from her back and nocked an arrow. The sound was behind her and to the left. Whoever was there was not light on their feet. Anyone could have heard them from miles away. She was certain there wasn't an Elf in Crystal Valley that would make that much noise when walking.

The rustling became louder. Without turning Ethereal shouted, "Halt whoever walks with crashing sounds behind me or else I will send an arrow through your heart."

The rustling behind her stopped. She turned and her eyes met the piercing blue eyes of the human, Charlie.

"Would you really shoot an arrow through my heart without even knowing who I was?" Charlie asked.

"In a heartbeat," Ethereal answered back as she lowered the bow and arrow. "It's never wise to sneak up on anyone let alone an Elf. You may find yourself with several arrows through your heart if you do that again."

Ethereal could see the shock cross Charlie's face as he absorbed what she had just said. He was so easy to read. She did not know how that would be a good trait for The One to have, but then again he was human and there wasn't much he could do to fix that. Perhaps she'd be able to teach him to hide his emotions better, but she doubted it.

"Why are you following me?" she asked.

"I...ah...I...just wanted to see you," Charlie stumbled over his words.

Ethereal had wanted to see Charlie as well, but she was not about to let him know that. She hadn't worked through the feelings she was having every time she was around him. All she knew for certain was she did not want to be away from him for long. She had also wanted to see if she could hear thoughts again with him being close by. She had tested it out on another Elf after having heard and seen Charlie's thoughts, but it had not worked. She wasn't sure if she could only see and hear Charlie's thoughts or if he was a portal to hearing and seeing those of others as well. She was eager to try it out again.

"I hear the council has allowed you sanction for a few more days," said Ethereal. "I also know the community is unhappy to hear there are two humans among us."

"They are? Why would they be unhappy about two humans being in Crystal Valley? Do humans and Elves have a bad past?" Charlie asked.

"We have been lied to by our own council. The majority of us had been told humans were extinct here in Pulchritude Amity. I believe most of the Elves here feel betrayed."

"But that isn't our fault. Isabella and I did not tell them humans were extinct. I can't see why anyone would tell them that. What would they gain from telling their people we no longer exist?" asked Charlie.

"It is the council's way of keeping peace in Crystal Valley and keeping everyone here under their control. No doubt if some of the Elves knew there were still humans in the land, they would have gone to find them. We are wise enough to know that the only way to reverse what has already been done by Czar Nefarious is to have humans bring back the magic."

"Speaking of magic," Charlie started, "the council said that I'm not only The One but that I'm more than that. They said I'm sacred here in Pulchritude Amity. I don't understand. What do they mean by all that?"

Ethereal did not know what the council was speaking of, but she could feel when standing in Charlie's presence that he was more than just The One. What that meant, she could not be certain. She also knew something the council probably did not. The girl in Charlie's dream, the one that looked similar to him, was also of great importance to the land. She could not describe how she was important yet, but she could see and feel it from the dream that she would make a difference here at some time. Perhaps Charlie didn't even know this. He didn't seem to know very much about his importance to this land, so he likely did not know about the girl's importance either.

"I wish I could answer what you ask, but I do not know that myself. All I know is that you radiate a magic none has seen in this land ever. It can be felt merely by touching you. You should be able to write strong magic that has never been written before," she answered as best she could.

"Write magic? Is this what The One is to do?" He asked.

"Yes, that and so much more." Ethereal stepped closer to Charlie and put her hands on each of his arms and the tingling she already had felt just being in his presence overtook her whole body. Immediately his thoughts engulfed her.

I wish she would stay this close forever. I've never felt this way about anyone before. It sort of scares me. However she makes it hard to think straight. Wow, she's so surreally beautiful. So beautiful that I want to reach out and touch her to be certain she's real.

Ethereal let her hands drop off Charlie's arms. She was flattered and thrilled and a bit concerned about his feelings towards her. She stopped listening to his thoughts since she somehow felt she was invading something private that she should not be hearing. Now she knew Charlie was certainly some sort of portal for her to hear thoughts again. Next she'd have to test if she were near him and someone else if she would be able to hear their thoughts. Ethereal was certain that the magic Charlie carried was what brought back this ability. Perhaps when he wrote magic again, Ethereal would get this talent back without having to be near him.

"What are yours and Isabella's plans once sanction is over here at Crystal Valley?" Ethereal changed the subject. She remained close to Charlie not only because she knew he wanted her close, but because she wanted that as well.

"I'm not sure. I know we are waiting for Dim to meet up with us. I'm actually getting a bit worried about him. He should have been here by now. Isabella felt certain he'd be able to escape the cannibals, but I'm not so sure myself."

"Goblins are resourceful. I am sure if Isabella felt he would escape then he likely will. Be patient."

Charlie didn't say anything and just looked into her eyes. Ethereal stared back. Looking into his eyes was like floating in a sea. Blue and tranquil and she could easily get lost in them. She had never seen blue eyes before. The Crystal Elves eyes were usually dark as coal. There were a few who had a dark brown tint to them, but the majority of Elves here had black eyes. She found blue a soothing color, which gave a sense of trust and innocence to them. She had always found the darkness in the eyes of the Crystal Elves lent them to feel hidden in motive and somewhat aloof. She had never thought that to be a bad trait. It aided them in battle often. Now after seeing the blue of Charlie's eyes she could see how it would be easy to follow his lead. His eyes hypnotized her and she assumed it did the same to others.

Ethereal was stunned when Charlie reached out and let the back of his hand caress her cheek. It was a bold move and one Ethereal should have discouraged, but she did not. She stood completely still and let his hand touch her skin and send tingles throughout her body. She suppressed the urge to hear his thoughts as he touched her. She did not want to ruin the moment invading his personal thoughts. She had her own thoughts to contend with. She knew at that moment she would not be able to allow this boy to leave her valley without her. She would follow wherever he led. Ethereal knew it was her destiny. Her mother would not see it the same way, but Ethereal was no longer a child and she refused to allow her mother to dictate her life. She was certain this was what her father would have wanted for her. She was after all her father's daughter.

Charlie's hand hesitantly dropped from Ethereal's cheek and she longed for it to return. He stepped away from her and left a little distance between their bodies and she felt as if Charlie had taken a bit of her with him.

"I want to go with you and Isabella when you leave here. I believe I can help keep you safe. I am a warrior, like my father before me. I would like to aid in your cause."

Ethereal could see the conflict cross over Charlie's face at her statement and she felt hurt. Did he not want her to go along with them? Why would he feel that way? She was certain he felt the same way about her she felt about him, so why would he not want her along? She had to suppress the urge to touch him again to see what his thoughts were.

"I'd have to ask Isabella and see what she feels about that," Charlie stated stiffly.

Ethereal kept the emotion from her face as she answered him. "Please let me know as soon as you have talked with her." She turned abruptly and headed out of the forest into the valley.

Isabella watched the interaction between Charlie and the young Elf from a distance in the forest. She had been out looking for medicinal herbs. She hadn't liked being so close to the valley the night before, especially since she preferred keeping her distance from others after her mother's death. She was used to being on the alert, left to her own skills, and did not want to chance being too close to the valley in case trouble erupted. She had not expected to encounter anyone else in the forest. So she was surprised when she heard voices and one of those voices was Charlie's. She had done the best she could to stay far enough away not to be noticed, but close enough to hear some of what was said. She had only heard bits of the conversation and none of which made sense. However she could read more from the body language between the Elf and Charlie then she ever could have up close. The chemistry between the two was undeniable and it caused a doubt to form in Isabella. Did Charlie know this Elf from before? Had he told her the truth about whom he was or where he came from? Or was the chemistry a newly discovered one? Either way Isabella wasn't certain she liked it. This Elf could put a wrench in her plans for Charlie. He was needed to write magic and Isabella knew they did not need any distractions, which this Elf was. She needed to find out more about her.

She found the Elf on the balcony of Divine's home. She stood staring into the valley. "It took you a long time to find me," Ethereal stated.

"How did you know I was looking for you?"

"I knew you were in the forest long before you knew I was in the forest. You forget this is my home. I am aware of the sounds that come from it. The sound of a human girl scrounging around the forest floor is not one of them."

Ethereal continued looking over the valley. Isabella couldn't help but feel a bit intimidated by this Elf. She never felt comfortable around Elves anyway, they kept too much hidden. Isabella liked it better when she could read others thoughts from the looks on their faces. She couldn't do that with Elves.

She moved next to the Elf and let her elbows rest on the crystal balcony but rather than looking out over the valley she kept her eyes on Ethereal. "I'm Isabella, but somehow I assume you already know that."

Ethereal continued looking forward not even giving Isabella a glance. "I am Ethereal, descendant of Bibhatsu and Divine Echosby of the Crystal Elves."

Isabella didn't know many Elves, but she knew of Bibhatsu Echosby. He and a group of Crystal Elves had ridden alongside the humans in the Battle of Minotaur. He was legendary among the humans. When the keeper of the Book of Truths was surrounded by minotaurs, Bibhatsu Echosby had jumped in front of the human and sacrificed his life so that the keeper could escape. He was a hero among humans. The end result was the slaughter of the Crystal Elves and humans fighting in that battle, but the Book of Truths had been kept safe.

"I'm honored to meet you," Isabella said humbly. Her view of Ethereal changed slightly after hearing she was the descendant of a great warrior. Yet she still couldn't help but feel curious as to why Ethereal had been alone with Charlie, and so intimately at that.

"I am assuming you want to ask why I was with Charlie," Ethereal stated.

Isabella felt unnerved that Ethereal could read her so easily. "Well…yes, I am curious why you were out in the forest alone with him."

"We did not intend to meet if that is what you are asking. It just happened." Ethereal turned to face Isabella and let her hand glide across Isabella's arm as she did.

"When I saw you two, you seemed…well," Isabella felt herself blush, "intimate."

"You were seeing us from a distance. Eyes can play tricks on you from a distance," Ethereal lied.

Isabella tried to recall what she had seen again. She thought Charlie had caressed Ethereal, but perhaps he had just been remov-ing something from her face. Maybe Ethereal was right and from a distance what she thought she saw wasn't what had really happened.

"Then if it wasn't intimate, what were you doing together?" Isabella asked.

"I was telling Charlie I felt you would be remiss in not inviting me to join you two when you left Crystal Valley. I have my father's blood and I feel it is my calling to help you in your quest whatever that may be."

Isabella was not expecting that answer. What she had viewed between Ethereal and Charlie seemed like an intimate meeting, but Ethereal was stating it was to plead her way into joining them. She wasn't certain how she felt about taking along an Elf. She already had her hands full with Charlie and a goblin. That is if Dim ever put in an appearance. She was beginning to think leaving him behind had been a mistake. She had been certain he was resourceful and would have a better chance of escape without a dizzy unhealthy boy keeping him back.

"I...don't know if that would be a good idea," Isabella answered Ethereal. "I believe I'm capable of protecting Charlie myself. I don't know that bringing an Elf, and pardon me if I say so, but an Elf that has likely never left Crystal Valley, along with us would be of any benefit. I think you'd more than likely just be in the way."

In one swift movement Ethereal stepped back and pulled her sword from her sheath. Isabella instinctively stepped back as well and pulled out her sword in defense. Ethereal moved forward quickly and twirled her body in a circle to bring her sword against Isabella's cheek before Isabella was even able to move. She was shocked at the speed with which the Elven warrior moved. Perhaps she would be of use in protecting Charlie after all. Two warriors were better than one, right?

Ethereal lowered her sword and put it back in its scabbard on her hip. "I believe I would be of great use on your journey." Ethereal moved back to the balcony wall to allow her elbows to rest on them. Isabella cautiously put her sword away. "Perhaps you are right."

The next day Charlie found Isabella camped out in the forest. He had never met anyone so comfortable with nature. Charlie felt awkward with nature. He was more comfortable sitting in front of his computer back home. "I've been looking for you," Charlie stated.

She was sitting by the fire cleaning a knife she had just used to kill some sort of critter she was now roasting. Charlie couldn't stand the thought of her killing an animal. He tried to block that vision out of his thoughts.

"I wanted to talk to you about Ethereal," Charlie said.

"I've already spoken to Ethereal. You don't need to ask for her to join us. I agree that she'd be useful to us," Isabella said.

Charlie was flabbergasted at Isabella's response. He had come here to tell her that the young she-Elf wanted to come along, but he didn't think it was a good idea. He hadn't expected Ethereal to go to Isabella. He had not wanted her to join them. He did not know what lay ahead, but the one thing he knew for certain was there would be life-threatening danger, and he did not want Ethereal put in harm's way, certainly not at his expense.

"I wasn't going to ask you to let her join us. I was going to ask you to not allow her to join us."

Isabella scrunched up her face in confusion. The young Elf had made it appear as though Charlie had wanted Ethereal to join them. She hadn't mentioned that Charlie was against it. "I don't understand. I thought you two were meeting in the forest to discuss Ethereal joining us being she is a descendent of Bibhatsu, one of the greatest Crystal Elf warriors in their history."

Isabella knew they had met in the forest? That surprised him for a minute as he recalled the intimate caress Ethereal and he had shared. He hoped Isabella hadn't noticed that part of the meeting.

"What is this about Bibhatsu?" Charlie asked.

Isabella told Charlie the story of Bibhatsu and the Battle of Minotaur. He was moved at the sacrifice Ethereal's father had made. "The Book of Truths? What is the Book of Truths?" Charlie asked.

"You'll find out more about that later. What I'm trying to convey to you is Ethereal is her father's daughter. His warrior blood runs through her veins just like my mother's warrior blood runs through mine. We could use her protection."

Charlie did not know what to say to that. Perhaps she was correct. Isabella and Ethereal could probably protect him. But who would protect them. He wanted to ask Isabella precisely that, but he could sense her mind was already made up about Ethereal.

"Why are you against Ethereal joining us?" Isabella suspiciously asked.

Charlie thought carefully for a moment before answering. "I'm not. I was mistaken."

Chapter Ten

Dim's Arrival

D im stumbled to the lake and knelt down to gather some water in his huge palms to drink. It had taken him longer than he had expected to rid himself of the dizziness. Boris had become slightly conscious enough so that he could stumble his way out of the cave with Dim once the cannibal had left in search of something to eat. He had managed to keep Boris alive in the narrow part of the cave for a few days waiting the flesh-eater out. He was relieved that the cannibal was not bright enough to realize his captives had escaped, but the lumbering hulk also did not find Dim and Boris hidden deep in the cave. The goblins had run out of water and dried food by then. Once out of the cave Boris went his way not even interested in Dim and what he was doing. Dim went in search of the waterfalls to the east that Isabella had described to him. He was relieved at first to see the lake. He had eaten very little since leaving the cannibal's cave. There was very little sustenance in the land between the two locales. Most of the edible plants had died and there was so very little wild life left to kill for dinner. Dim was feeling a bit weak by the time he finally stumbled across the body of water. After drinking from it he became aware of the waterfall at the other end. Isabella had not mentioned there wasn't a way over to the waterfall other than to swim to it and, unfortunately, Dim could not swim. He sat back onto the hard ground next to the lake and rested, pondering how he would make it behind the waterfall. There was a jumbled rock outcropping along the walls on both sides. He might be able to climb along the wall over the ledge and behind the waterfall. He was pretty stout with big feet which could be difficult climbing a rock wall, but it appeared to be his only choice. He just hoped he would not lose his footing and fall into the water below. He would surely drown. It was not his preferred way to die. He would rather be eaten by a cannibal or beaten and sliced to death by a minotaur than to die cowardly flapping around the water until his death. But he knew he had no choice.

He leaned over the lake's edge again and lapped up more water. He needed to gather more strength before venturing up the rock wall. As he sat back away from the water his eyes wandered back to some tall weeds that were still green. He'd looked them over earlier and had come to the conclusion they were edible, so he grabbed a fist full and ate them. He supposed if he was wrong he'd be dead within a few hours, but he needed something of substance to build his strength before attempting the climb.

Dim sat next to the lake for hours sipping water and munching on weeds, waiting until the hunger dissipated. When he felt as strong as he believed possible after going days without food and water, Dim walked along the lake's edge until he came to the rock wall. There was roughly twelve feet from where the wall met the edge of the lake to where it connected to a rocky ledge behind the waterfall. He hoped he'd have enough strength to make it over to the ledge. He'd have to climb up the wall about eight feet then maneuver to his left the twelve feet to reach the rim. He examined the wall to find any handholds he'd be able to put his feet in, and for the most part he found gashes and crevices for the eight feet up, but going to the left would be tricky. Perhaps a bigger creature with longer legs would be able to make the steps to each handhold easily, but goblins were shorter, heftier creatures and Dim's legs were particularly shorter than most goblins. It would be a stretch for him to be able to place his feet into the crevices to get to the ledge.

Dim felt sweat forming over his face and his palms as he contemplated the path he would take. Bending down to the ground he wiped the sweat from his palms before grasping the first notch in the rock face. He quickly made his way up, openly feeling brave, knowing at this point that if he fell he'd fall onto solid ground. Once up about eight feet, he paused a moment, mustering his will, and then made his first step to the left. He felt his legs quiver weakly, but he stretched as far as his short legs would go and just made it to the next gash. He felt shaky as he clung to the wall. He'd have to remove his right foot from the crack and slide his left foot over to make room for his right foot in the same notch. He held on for a few minutes trying to steady his shaking and preparing him to let go. In one quick movement he removed his right foot from the notch in the rock and using the strength in his hands he pushed his body to the left and let his left foot slide as he moved his right foot into the same gash in the rock that held his left foot. He let out a breath as he had climbed about a third of the way over in just one long movement. Now he had to grasp with his left hand the crevice over to his left. His arms were longer than his legs which were disproportionate to his body, but most goblins were out of proportion in the same way. In this case his longer arms came in handy. He stretched easily to the left and grasped the notch above his head with his left hand. The next notch to his left for his feet wasn't as long as the first and he was able to stretch easier to get his foot there and bring his right leg over with it. He was three fourths of the way over. He glanced down to his left and the ledge was close. He felt certain he could do this. Dim easily moved his hands to the next crevice to his left. Taking a deep breath he took the long stretch to get his foot into the next notch on the rock wall. He strained his body as far as he could and barely made a foothold into the notch. All that was left was for him to bring his right leg over. He removed the right leg from the notch and in doing so felt his left slip on the wetness on the rocks from the spray coming off the waterfall and he let out a groan as he was left hanging from only his arms with his legs dangling weakly below him. He wiggled and grasped as much as he could with his feet but he could not get them back into the notch on his left, and he felt his hands slipping as sweat moistened his palms. His only chance of not plummeting into the water was to swing his body and jump the four feet to the ledge next to him. It wasn't the ideal way to make it to the ledge, but the alternative was to fall and drown.

He put all the strength he had left into swinging his body first to his left, then to his right. He allowed himself a few swings to build momentum before making the jump. The jump was precise and he hit the ledge, but he hadn't factored how slippery the rock would be from the waterfall and he felt his feet slip under him, causing him to slide backwards towards the water below. Panic engulfed him and he flung his arms in all directions grasping for anything to save him. His right hand brushed something long and he took a death grip on whatever it was, pulling his body forward until his feet were once again solidly on the ledge. He reached forward with his left hand and moved onto the ledge a bit further. In this way he walked hand over hand deeper into the ledge until he felt secure enough to let go. The rock wall near the edge of the ledge was jagged and Dim had fortunately grabbed onto the long projecting rocks to save himself. He moved a few feet on the rim behind the waterfall to get as far away from the water below as possible and let his head rest on the rock wall before him. He closed his eyes and let the shaking in his body cease.

When he had more control of his body he looked around and saw a smooth rock wall to his left. He moved in front of it and searched for some sort of opening. His strong hairy hands found a loose rock in the wall and he pulled on it. A small opening silently appeared. Dim studied the narrow gap with a scowl on his sweaty face. How did Isabella think a fat goblin like him could ever fit through that opening? O well, Knuckleheads will be Knuckleheads. He sucked in his breath the best he could and shoved his way through feeling the pain in his body as he scraped by the rocks of the opening. He was relieved once he was through the thin passage, and wiped the dripping sweat from his forehead, only to look up into a bristling mixture of arrows and swords in the hands of some Elves and Elf centaurs.

"Where do you think you're going, goblin?"

Ethereal watched as a short fat goblin squeezed his way through the opening at the top of the crystal steps. She also watched as the guards stood ready for his entrance. It was time. She knew she'd be leaving within the hour. She had not told her mother she was leaving. She felt it was best to wait until the time came. Divine would fight her on it if Ethereal had told her when they were alone, but if she stated it in front of the other Crystal Elves her mother would not make a commotion. Ethereal felt she was betraying her mother, but it could not be helped. Someday her mother would understand. Just like her mother eventually understood Bibhatsu's decision to leave and fight with the humans. This was Ethereal's calling. Her mother surely would understand that. She was not meant to sit idle here at Crystal Valley while the rest of Pulchritude Amity died off. She had this gift of a great warrior from her father and she needed to make use of it. Besides, she was certain Charlie was her destiny. She could never leave him now.

She moved quietly down the crystal steps of her home and into the forest taking in all that was around her. She reveled in the shine that was still clear on the crystals and the greenness that was still evident in various areas of the valley. She would miss Crystal Valley. It was her home, but she hoped someday to return and perhaps it would be back to the lush valley it had once been. If she did her job right, then magic would return and Czar Nefarious would be defeated.

Ethereal found Isabella and Charlie where she had expected them to be. Both were sitting huddled around a fire. Charlie looked more Elf than human by the light of the fire now that Divine had given him some of Bibhatsu's old clothing. He wore armor over his chest and on his shins. He looked uncomfortable in them as he fidgeted on his rock. Yet these clothes were more practical than the old ragged robe he was wearing when he showed up here. Ethereal stood back for a moment as a mixture of emotions swept through her at the sight of her father's clothes on the human who she felt was her destiny.

Isabella looked up from the fire when she noticed Ethereal coming into view. "It is time," Ethereal stated.

Charlie looked confused as he looked from Ethereal to Isabella, but Isabella understood immediately. She took the remainder of the meat from her kill and stored it in her pouch, then kicked dirt over the fire. "It's time to go Charlie," Isabella said.

Charlie stood slowly and he glanced from the young she-Elf to the young human warrior. "But Dim hasn't even showed up yet."

Isabella looked into Ethereal's eyes to try and read them. "I believe Ethereal is saying that Dim has shown himself?"

Ethereal just nodded in agreement. Isabella pulled her knapsack over her shoulders, attached her pouch to her belt, and took ahold of Charlie's arm, guiding him out of the forest.

"Dim's here? He's alive?" Charlie asked, following Isabella's lead.

"For the moment he is alive," Ethereal firmly stated.

When they emerged from the forest into the valley Charlie noticed a commotion. In all his time in Crystal Valley he had seen very few Elves, but now they were emerging from all directions. All the Elves were heading towards the crystal steps that he and Isabella had descended the day they had arrived. He felt both Ethereal and Isabella's hands on either side of his arms as they hurried him towards the steps. Ethereal pushed and shoved her way through the crowd that had formed at the bottom. Charlie bumped against one Elf after another as Ethereal guided him from the front and Isabella held his arm and shoved him from behind. He couldn't help but say "excuse me," and "pardon me," as they shoved through the Elves in the crowd. It only took them a few minutes to make it to the top of the crystal steps where Ethereal halted and he collided into her from behind blurting out an "excuse me," to Ethereal.

"You can let him be, Savageskin," Ethereal stated in her most authoritative voice.

Savageskin barely gave notice to Ethereal's request. "We do not allow goblins into Crystal Valley. Any that penetrate our walls are sentenced to death. We cannot allow this goblin to go free or our hidden city will no longer be hidden."

"This goblin is not a threat to your city," Isabella stated unconvincingly. She wasn't even certain of that herself, but she knew for Charlie's sake she must defend Dim.

Charlie stretched to look over the heads of the few Elves around him and caught a glimpse of a short hairy green goblin. "Dim," Charlie shouted. "Dim, you're alive!"

"Of course I'm alive Knucklehead," Dim shouted back. Then he looked around at the Elves surrounding him. "I'm not sure how much longer I'll be alive though. You could have told me that they don't allow goblins in here, Isabella," Dim accused.

Isabella shrugged. "I didn't know that myself," she answered back.

"You know these humans?" Aelfhere asked Dim.

"Yes, I travel with the one known as Charlie," Dim answered back.

The Captain of the Guard looked from Dim to Charlie than back to Dim. "This does not change anything. We must execute this goblin regardless of who you travel with. Goblins cannot be trusted."

Then Ethereal heard a voice she was very familiar with. "Let him go Aelfhere. He is of no concern of yours. This goblin can be trusted."

Ethereal turned and saw her mother move through the crowd on the steps as she made her way to the top. Aelfhere also turned at hearing Divine's voice. Her mother was neither one of the council nor a leader of any sort in Crystal Valley, but she held a lot of respect. Bibhatsu had left her mother that much from his honorable death. But Aelfhere still hesitated to let Dim go. "He is a goblin and he has penetrated our hidden valley. We cannot let him live."

Divine and Dim made eye contact for a moment before she spoke.

"This goblin will not betray us. He travels with the boy. He is responsible for The One being brought to our land. He should be left alone."

Hearing her speak of The One, the crowd of Elves quieted and all eyes turned to Charlie. He fidgeted as he realized he was now the center of attention, and he cut quite a figure wearing Bibhatsu's Elvish armor.

"You would not have to allow him into the valley. We will be leaving now," stated Isabella. Aelfhere turned his gaze to her. Ethereal could actually see the conflict on the Captain of the Guard's face. It was not often emotion was so readable on an Elves features, but occasionally it did occur. The conflicted guard Captain looked again at Dim. "Fine, you may live," said the Captain of the Guard. "But you must leave Crystal Valley." Then turning to Divine he pointed a finger at her chest and stated, "And if he comes back here with more of his kind or worse, Czar Nefarious himself, that will fall on you."

Ethereal pulled on Charlie's arm and dragged him up the last step next to Dim, who was already squeezing back out the passage. Isabella followed Charlie. "Thank you Divine for your help in giving us sanction," Isabella said as she stopped next to The One at the top of the stairs.

"You are welcome, Isabella."

"And thank you for allowing Ethereal to help us on our journey," Isabella continued as she started following Dim through the opening.

Divine turned her gaze from Isabella to Ethereal, then let her eyes drop to Ethereal's hand holding Charlie's arm. The young she-Elf waited for some sort of shock or disapproval to cross her mother's face, but there was none. She had, after all, learned long ago to control what emotions were displayed on her face. Divine's eyes moved from her daughter's hand back to her coal black eyes and they stared at each other. Ethereal squeezed Charlie's arm and concentrated on her mother's thoughts and she wasn't disappointed.

Stay safe, my love. I know you feel this is your destiny and who am I to stand between you and destiny. Know I love you and you have made my life complete all these years. It is now your turn to explore and learn what it means to be with one that completes you. I've had it twice with your father and with you. I wish that for you. Know this is always your home and I'm always here, my love.

Ethereal let a smile reach her face and was graced with one in return from her mother. Charlie had begun squeezing through the opening behind Isabella, and as she squeezed through the opening of the entrance she stared into the pools of darkness that were her mother's eyes and felt a sense of sadness that one part of her life had ended in order for a new one to begin.

Chapter Eleven

Riot

They were met with the spray of water from the waterfall. Isabella stretched out her arms with her head facing the sky and allowed the spray to fall over her body. She felt freedom once again. Not that she was ungrateful for the sanction the Crystal Elves had given them, but she felt confined when in the presence of so many. She enjoyed the solitude of the outdoors and being surrounded by nature. Ethereal however had already taken Charlie by the arm and jumped into the lake. They were already swimming their way across. Isabella put her arms down and turned to Dim.

"You go next," she said. Dim just stood and stared into the water below. After a few moments she asked, "What's the hold up? Don't tell me a big burly goblin like you is afraid of the water," she said in her best baby voice.

"No...um...I just prefer to go a different way," Dim stuttered.

It never occurred to Isabella that Dim wouldn't cross the water. He had obviously made his way across the first time or how else had he gotten into Crystal Valley. "We don't have time to waste on finding another way. Let's go!" Before Dim knew what was happening Isabella had grabbed him and shoved him into the water below. The goblin hit the water with a plop and splash. His wet hairy green head bobbed to the surface, then his arms started thrashing and he started to sink. Isabella watched with mild alarm as it suddenly occurred to her the reason most creatures in Pulchritude Amity had never found Crystal Valley was because most creatures here did not know how to swim. From the thrashing Dim was doing in the water, she realized the goblin was one of those. Isabella put her hands together and dove into the lake a few feet to Dim's left and came up next to the sputtering goblin. Putting her arms under Dim's arms and across his chest she shouted "Calm down or you'll drown both of us!" He stopped the thrashing and went limp as Isabella leaned backwards and with her free arm started stroking them towards shore. He was heavy and she had to stop a few times and tread water to get her breath but eventually they made it to the shallow part of the water's edge. "You can stand up now," Isabella stated, a bit annoyed at having to drag a goblin across the lake. Charlie better appreciate her for saving his stupid goblin once again. Dim was becoming more of a hindrance then a help.

She dragged herself out of the water and plopped next to Charlie who was sitting at the edge watching them. Ethereal stood a few feet away erect and alert. Isabella watched her for a moment as the young Elvish warrior looked around surveying the area. Ethereal was going to be useful even if she was a bit annoying. She didn't like being overshadowed, and the young she-Elf's presence was enough to overshadow anyone, let alone Isabella. The young human woman would just have to focus on the usefulness of the young Elven woman's skills. And then she had to deal with a useless boy and a pain in the butt goblin. The journey to find the other humans could be a long one.

"Why didn't you tell anyone you couldn't swim?" Isabella accused Dim.

"It never came up! Swimming is not something goblins do very often, okay," Dim snapped back, muttering under his breath.

"What I don't understand is how you got into Crystal Valley if you don't know how to swim," she retorted.

The bedraggled goblin looked away from her as he tried to shake off the weight of the water that clung to his hairy body. "None of your business," he snapped again.

Isabella was about to retort back when she saw the pained look on Charlie's face at their terse conversation and she thought better of herself. "Fine, we need to be moving along anyway," she snapped back.

"Moving along where?" Dim snarled.

"To find the remaining humans of course," she retorted. Ethereal still stood erect and alert and Isabella wanted to smack her a few times to see if she would loosen up some. She bent down and snatched Charlie by the arm and yanked him to his feet.

Dim scrambled forward and grabbed Charlie's other arm. "He's not going with you. He is going with me to meet with Forerunner."

Isabella pulled on Charlie's arm trying to loosen Dim's grip. "No he is not. He is The One and The One has no use for a goblin leader. He is coming with me to take his place as the magic writer."

"Over my dead body," Dim growled baring his sharp teeth as he did.

"Stop it already," Charlie shouted as he yanked his arms free from both Isabella and Dim. "You're talking about me like I'm your possession and I'm no one's possession."

Ethereal spoke up just then. "You are right Charlie. You are no one's possession. You know your own mind. Where do you think we should go?"

Isabella gave Ethereal a dirty look for interfering in the conversation. Dim stood looking at Charlie waiting for his response.

"I...I...I don't know. I can't think with all the shouting and shoving and pulling going on," he said as he let his hands go to his head.

Within seconds Ethereal was at Charlie's side. She brought her hands up to his and gently pulled them from his head and held them, letting her gaze meet his. "It is okay, Charlie. Take a few deep breaths. And just think about it for a few minutes." He stared into the bewitching young Elf's eyes and his heartbeat calmed down as his breathing slowed. Isabella watched with interest at the connection between the two and came back to the conclusion there was something intimate between them. She was certain Ethereal had played her. She obviously had some sort of control over the boy.

After a few minutes Charlie answered while still staring into Ethereal's eyes. "We go and find the humans."

Dim groaned. "That was not the plan Charlie."

Charlie let his eyes leave the Elf's and turned to the squat goblin. "I'm sorry, Dim. I know you are supposed to take me to see Forerunner, but I feel finding the other humans is what I'm supposed to be doing right now. After I've found them, I'll go with you to Forerunner."

"That's assuming I'll stay with you now that you have your own agenda, Knucklehead!"

"I think you will. I think you'll see this through no matter what the hiccups are," Charlie said.

Dim stood silent not acknowledging whether Charlie was right or wrong. Isabella broke the silence.

"Well, the boy has spoken. So we head east. I don't know for sure where the other humans are, but I have suspicions of where they might be. At least the vicinity they are in. I'll lead. Ethereal you take up the rear." Isabella started forward not waiting for a response.

Charlie wasn't used to walking for such long periods of time. They had been traveling since early in the morning and now the world was becoming dark. He had wanted to stop hours ago but Isabella had been snapping at him all day, so he thought it would be best to keep quiet and keep moving. He sure hoped he had made the right decision to trust Isabella and find the other humans. Quite frankly with the way she was acting, he was starting to doubt it. He had looked back at Ethereal several times throughout the day, but had not really had the chance to talk to her, yet he felt the reassurance in her eyes. He could tell she supported his choice. Dim, on the other hand, grunted and grumbled the whole day. Charlie had tried to talk with him a few times, but the grumpy goblin refused to answer. At least Charlie was correct and Dim had continued with them.

He let out a sigh of relief when Isabella declared they were stopping for the night to set up camp. The young human warrior sent a dirty look his way making Charlie feel ashamed of his physical weakness, but he was not used to so much physical activity in one day. Normally about now he'd be sitting on his couch with his sister watching television. His mind went back to those days and his sister and he felt a longing to see his loved ones again. Never in his wildest dreams would he have imagined he'd be sitting here at a fire with a goblin, an Elf and a human warrior.

Ethereal sat down next to him brushing her hand across his arm as she sat. A shiver went down his spine. He never tired of being near the young Elf. But it was getting harder and harder to keep from reaching out to touch her. Somehow he thought Isabella and Dim would frown on that. He wasn't even sure if Ethereal would approve.

Isabella sat down and started skinning a critter that looked a lot like a mix between a cat and a ferret. She had come across it during the trek earlier that day and used her spear to kill it. It was shocking to Charlie that she could throw the spear with such accuracy. He turned away from the scene, preferring not to watch her skin the animal. He felt a little squeamish, since back home humans kept cats and ferrets as pets. He couldn't imagine killing and skinning them. He wasn't sure how anyone could believe he was The One. He was not made to kill and skin an animal or live in the wild. He was a computer kid. He enjoyed a good book. He liked writing and reading and sitting on his couch and watching television with his family. He was as far from a hunter and killer as they came.

Ethereal stood and grabbed Charlie's hand and as she did so she pulled him up with her. "You need to learn to use a weapon."

It was eerie how Ethereal seemed to be on the same thought process as him. He had just been thinking about his lack of physical ability and here she wanted to teach him to use a weapon. "I'm not sure I'm the right person to wield a weapon. I doubt I could ever kill anyone."

Dim piped up from his seat on the ground. "Well you didn't have a problem taking out that Trovac Skrbnik."

Charlie looked over at the unhappy goblin. "You mean the stick? I wasn't talking about a piece of a tree; I was talking about a living breathing being."

"It was a living being, even if it didn't breathe," the goblin grumbled.

"You would be surprised what you would do when you or a loved one is threatened," Ethereal stated.

The she-Elf looked him over and picked up his hands, turning them palm side up and letting her fingers soothe over them. She let her hands roll up his arms to his shoulders and squeezed his biceps as she went, stopping when they reached his broad neck. Charlie stood completely still as he allowed his body to enjoy the sensation of her touch.

"I think a simple sword would be the best fit for you," Ethereal said after having finished her inspection. She still let her hands rest on either side of his neck.

"Are you teaching him to use a weapon or giving him a massage?" grumbled Dim.

The young Elven warrior let her hands fall from his neck having forgotten they had an audience. He felt the disappointment of losing his physical connection with Ethereal.

"I have the perfect weapon for someone your size," the she-Elf said. She pulled a long sword from a sheath that was strapped to her back. Charlie stared at the glistening beauty in the sword. There were three Crystals embedded in the hilt. All three crystals were clear, but he imagined that at one time they were of different colors as Ethereal said the crystals in Crystal Valley had been. He reached out and let his finger graze across the handle.

"Go ahead," Ethereal said as she shoved the sword towards him.

He hesitated for a minute as he looked in his Elvish teacher's eyes for positive assurance to hold the sword. He saw the encouragement he needed and he let his hand reach out and grasp the hilt. It felt cold and heavy in his hands, but once he lifted it he saw a blue glow rise from the blade.

"The sword glows the color of one's soul. Blue is the color of trust and peace. It also means loyalty and integrity. I am not surprised your sword would glow blue," Ethereal whispered. Their eyes met and he could see a smile form within them. "When my father used this sword it would glow a deep brown which means serious, down-to-earth and relates to security and protection."

"This is your father's sword?" Charlie asked in awe at holding the sword of a great warrior.

"Yes, it was the one he used in the Battle of Minotaur. It was recovered by Savageskin when the Crystal Elves went back to claim the bodies of those who were slain."

Charlie twirled the sword around watching the blue glow swirl through the air. It was a masterful sword. He knew this without ever having touched a sword before. "It's beautiful. I never thought of a weapon as beautiful before. But I can't use this. I'm not a warrior like your father. This should be yours." He handed the sword back to Ethereal.

The Elf put her hands up to halt him. "You cannot give that back to me. It is bad luck to return a gift. This is my gift to you. You may not be a warrior in the physical sense, but you are a warrior at heart. You will discover that one day."

He looked down at the sword and tried to determine what Ethereal meant by being a warrior at heart. He liked the sound of it, but if she meant one day he'd be fighting a battle where he must kill, he could not envision that. But perhaps she meant something more. Warrior at heart could mean a warrior in ways other than physical. He could see himself that way.

"Thank you for the gift," he said as he swirled the sword around again watching the blue glow.

"It's not a usafuul gift if you plan to toss it around looking like a crazy being," growled Dim. "Stop the twirling already. You're making me dizzy just watching it, Knucklehead."

Charlie grinned at Dim's mispronunciation of the word useful. He felt even closer to this goblin who affectionately called him Knucklehead. Whether the goblin would ever admit it, Knucklehead had become his term of affection for the young human. It was the first sign of forgiveness he had seen from the grumpy goblin since the young human lad had chosen to follow Isabella's path rather than Dim's.

Ethereal reached forward and placed her hands on his as they grasped the sword handle and stopped his twirling. "Let me show you first how to hold a sword and then how to use one." They spent some time practicing the art of swordsmanship while Isabella cooked the dinner and Dim grumbled on and off over Charlie's lack of technique. They stopped when he showed signs of fatigue and the meat was cooked through for dinner. Charlie tried to think of something else other than the cute cat/ferret he was eating in order to finish his meal. He was hungry and it was tasty. He just kept envisioning his pet cat and felt a pang of guilt for each bite he ate. He silently sent a sorry message to Frodo his cat back home.

It didn't take him long to fall asleep next to the fire that night. He had wanted to lie down next to Ethereal, but Isabella had insisted the Elven warrior take the first watch and so the young human warrior lay down next to him. He couldn't help but wonder if it was intentional to keep them apart. He sensed Isabella did not like his relationship with the young she-Elf. Dim on the other hand distanced himself from them all sleeping sitting up against a tree overlooking the fire.

The second day of travel was rougher than the first. Isabella had them climbing over rocky hills. She watched as Charlie struggled to climb over the rocks. He looked more like one of them wearing Bibhatsu's clothes, but he still wore the funny looking shoes he came here in. They did not look solid enough to withstand all this climbing. She wasn't sure how he'd fare if they had to run. She hoped he could handle it. She knew they were entering Wolf Country. They could have gone around, but somehow she suspected Riot would be found in this area. When he was a child he had raised a wolf from a pup and found himself more attached to the wolf than to humans. Factoring that in she assumed he would find Wolf Country the area to take refuge. It was only an instinct, but she relied heavily on her instincts and they were rarely wrong.

She knew they would have to be careful while traveling in Wolf Country. The wolves were neither under Czar's or human control. They were their own kind and were unpredictable. With so much of nature dying, the wolves may be looking very intensely for prey to devour. She'd need to stay close to Charlie now since he would be their weak link. She knew Ethereal would take up any attack from the rear, and she had the front covered, but she wasn't certain where Dim fit in. He hadn't done much other than grumble and complain since they had left Crystal Valley. She didn't trust him and if it were up to her she'd have rather sliced his head off and be done with him, but Charlie still seemed attached to the dumb goblin, though his attachment to Ethereal seemed to be deeper than that which he had with Dim now. Isabella didn't know if that was a good thing or not. The Elven warrior had helped him come to the conclusion that finding the other humans was the right one, so she was thankful for that, but she didn't like the looks they exchanged or the occasional touch that they thought went unnoticed. Isabella noticed them all.

Dim moved ahead of Charlie and behind Isabella. "You do realize we are in dangerous grounds now?" he asked sarcastically.

"I know exactly where we are, Dim," Isabella stiffly answered him.

"Is there a reason we are going across Wolf Country when we could have taken a path down below around this area?" Dim asked suspiciously.

"We are not going across Wolf Country. Our destination *is* Wolf Country," she answered curtly.

"You're a crazy person if you believe one of the humans could ever have stayed alive in Wolf Country! No one lives here but the wolves," he ranted.

"I know you believe I have no idea what I'm doing, but I have lived years alone in the land and I've been just about everywhere there is to go. Trust me when I say there is a human living among the wolves."

"All I know is if you put Charlie in danger, I will grab him up and we'll disappear. I don't care what happens to a crazy human and a love sick Elf. My job is keeping Charlie safe. I won't allow you to let him walk into a wolf den," Dim growled at her.

Isabella stopped walking and turned to confront him. "Do you think your threat frightens me? You are nothing but a short fat goblin who thinks because you were lucky enough to find The One that it gives you some right to rule his life. I could have killed you long ago. You only remain with us because of Charlie, so be grateful or get lost," she stated through clenched teeth.

The goblin let his hand drop to his broadsword. She reached for her spear, ready for whatever Dim wanted to throw her way. Charlie had caught up to them breathing heavily from climbing over the rocks below. "Are we stopping," he asked looking from one to the other. Ethereal appeared within seconds behind Charlie and glanced from Isabella to Dim. She grabbed Charlie's arm and pulled him a few feet away from the two, sensing the danger in their body language and battle ready stances.

Dim lowered his hand from his broadsword at the sound of Charlie's voice and Isabella eased hers away as well. "We'll take a few minutes to break while I determine where we are heading next," she answered. She never let her eyes stray from Dim's until the hairy goblin moved a few feet away from her and she felt the threat dissipate.

Dim positioned himself close to Charlie and glanced around as the young human sat down. Ethereal could sense the fear in Dim's stance thus she stood on the other side of Charlie surveying the area. The fog kept them from being able to see too far into the distance, but danger could be felt in the air.

Charlie seemed oblivious to his surroundings. He was just relieved to be able to sit and rest. The day was mostly over and he was exhausted from the trek over the rocky hills. "Are we camping here?"

"No," shouted both Ethereal and Dim simultaneously. Charlie glanced from one to the other feeling the anxiousness oozing from them both. He turned to see what Isabella felt about camping here. "We're going to continue on tonight?" he asked her specifically.

Isabella looked from Ethereal to Dim and then to Charlie. "We might go a little further, as I'm not sure this is the safest place to camp."

The young human warrior had wanted to go a little further anyway. They were only on the outskirts of Wolf Country and somehow she assumed Riot would be hidden farther in near the wolves' dens. Dim would not be happy her plan was to find the lairs of the wolves, but somehow she felt Riot would be among them. She however did not want to be walking into the wolves den in the dark of the night. Perhaps they could go another few miles and camp near the four oak trees. That would give them a place to climb if they were to encounter any wolves during the night. If she could get Charlie and Dim up into the tree then she'd have them sleep there, but she didn't think the fat goblin could climb a tree and Charlie may not be physically able to climb one himself. Somehow she was certain Ethereal would have no problem getting into a tree. She'd have to figure that out when they got to the location. She just hoped they wouldn't meet any wolves on the way.

After a short break they moved on in their journey. Isabella could feel Dim breathing down her back as he had taken to walking right behind her turning occasionally to make sure Charlie stayed close to him. Ethereal was never far behind Charlie herself. He was well protected.

In this order they trudged along until they made it to the four oak trees. "We will camp here," Isabella stated. Charlie let out another sigh of relief and he collapsed to the ground in exhaustion. "Not there," Isabella stated. "There," and she pointed up into the trees.

Charlie looked where she pointed and then stared incredulously at her. "In the trees?"

"Yes, in the trees," Isabella said.

"Even if I could climb up there I'd never be able to sleep up there. I'd fall," Charlie said nervously.

"That is what this rope is for," Isabella said matter-of-factly. "You can tie yourself up there."

"I don't understand. Last night we camped on the ground near a fire. Why tonight must we sleep in a tree?" Charlie asked.

"What Isabella isn't telling you Charlie is that she has taken you deep into Wolf Country. I told you not to trust her. She has put us all in danger," said Dim.

"Wolf Country? What is Wolf Country?" Charlie asked a bit panicky.

Ethereal moved next to Charlie and put her hand on his arm. "I have heard the tales of Wolf Country," she said. "Only wolves reside here. The tale is that the wolves and humans used to live here side by side. Then one day a human hunter betrayed Aierowf by trapping one of the wolf leader's sons and killing him, skinning him for his pelt. The gold he received for the wolf pelt was not worth what happened, for Aierowf, enraged beyond reason slayed the hunter and exiled the humans from Wolf Country. The wolves went from friends with the humans to solitary animals. They have ruled Wolf Country alone for years. Humans and all other creatures have since avoided this land in fear of what the wolves would do to them."

"So you want us to sleep in the trees to stay safe from the wolves?" Charlie asked.

"Yes, Ethereal is right. We are in Wolf Country. I can't be certain we will be safe from the wolves. But the tale Ethereal told is just that... a tale. There is no evidence that any of that is true. My mother told me to be leery of stories. They have been passed down for generations and by the time they get to us they have been altered and it's hard to tell what is true and what is false," Isabella said. "But we will take precautions regardless thus sleeping in the trees."

Charlie looked up at the tree and tried to see what he would use as a handle if he were to climb it. "Okay. If we must sleep in trees I'd rather do so with Ethereal. I'm sure she'd not mind helping me climb up?" He said as he longingly looked at the she-Elf to see if she was okay with that.

"I will do whatever you want to keep you safe," Ethereal said in a whisper.

Isabella almost gagged at the affection between the two. Did Charlie think she was foolish enough to believe he wanted Ethereal with him to protect him? She knew better than that. But if that is what it took to get him up in a tree, then so be it. "Fine," she snapped. She turned her attention to Dim. "So goblin, do you think you can climb a tree?" she sarcastically asked.

Dim didn't give her the courtesy of an answer and began climbing. It only took him a matter of minutes to reach a safe crevice in the tree. Isabella felt a bit surprised at the physical ability the fat goblin had. She underestimated him.

Charlie climbed the tree slowly while Ethereal stayed directly behind him using words of encouragement and whispering words Isabella could not hear. She waited until they had made it to a safe place in the tree before she began climbing. Dim was in the tree to the right of Charlie and Isabella took the tree to the left of him. She made it up the tree in no time. Isabella had considered using *Olonso Pulleis* to keep them hidden for the night, but her magic was slowly fading. Soon it would be gone. She needed to find the two other humans soon or the magic would be gone forever. She had relied on magic these past years to stay alive, but some of it had already disappeared. She was just down to *Olonso Pulleis* and *Onso Protecto* and those had faded. Besides, wolves had wicked eyes and could likely see through *Olonso Pulleis* anyway.

She glanced over at Dim in his tree but the darkness kept her from being able to see what he was doing. She could barely see Ethereal and Charlie, but she assumed they were cuddled up together in the tree and personally she didn't want to see that anyway. She tied herself into the tree with the rope and settled in for the night.

Ethereal was glad to be alone with Charlie without the other's eyes bearing into her. She could sense the disapproval from both of them over her relationship with Charlie. Whatever they believed she truly wanted to just protect him. Of course the attraction was there and she wanted to act on it, but her priority was Charlie's safety.

She could tell Charlie was exhausted from their day of travel. Climbing a tree was the last thing he wanted to do after trekking over dangerous rocky ground all day, but he was a trooper and managed to climb up the tree with little encouragement. What Dim and Isabella didn't understand was Charlie reacted better to encouragement than being told what he needed to do. Isabella and Dim were too busy with their own agenda that they had forgotten Charlie had a purpose here and that is where the focus needed to be. Ethereal just hoped she would be the soothing encouragement he needed to succeed at his purpose here in Pulchritude Amity.

"Here, let me tie us in," Ethereal offered. Charlie handed her the rope and waited as Ethereal made use of it. She tied them up tight together in the arm of the tree. The rope brought their bodies close together and Ethereal could feel the heat from his body. She felt the comfort of being close to him and knew he felt the comfort as well as he hesitantly wrapped his arms around her. After a long day Ethereal couldn't imagine a nicer way to end it. She was glad for the darkness surrounding them. She didn't need to keep her emotions hidden now since Charlie would not be able to see her face well enough to know what she was thinking. Sometimes it was exhausting to hide her emotions all the time. She let her body drape itself against Charlie's and felt the warmth it provided. Leaning her head onto his chest she laid that way listening as his heartbeat sped up. She was sure her heartbeat was in sync with his.

"Are you comfortable?" Charlie asked with a shaky voice.

"Very," she answered.

They stayed silent that way for some time wrapped in each other's arms. Ethereal had assumed he was sleeping by now when he surprised her and asked, "Ethereal, are you awake?"

"Hmmm," she answered back feeling too comfortable to say much else.

"Do you think we are safe up here?"

"Hmmm, as safe as we can be. I have never come across a wolf before, but from what my father used to tell me they cannot climb trees. Isabella was correct to have us sleep up here," she said. She lifted her head while keeping it resting on his chest to see if she could see his eyes and what he was thinking. He lowered his to look at her eyes as well and their lips brushed against each other. Ethereal felt a new heat pass through her body and from Charlie's look he felt the same. She waited to see if he would lean down to complete the act. As desperately as she wanted to kiss him, she knew it was for the best she kept their relationship platonic. The others would never approve of a human and Elf mixing nor would her kind approve. She lowered her head back to his chest and let it rest there listening to his heartbeat and feeling him breathe until she felt certain his breath was deep enough to be asleep. She laid there for hours trying to allow sleep to invade her thoughts. She no longer wanted to think of her closeness with Charlie. For a warrior woman she felt weakness with her emotions over this human boy. At this moment she wished she was anywhere other than in this tree with this human and temptation.

Isabella woke with a start. The day was just beginning so she could see a short ways around her but the haze of the early morning kept her from seeing too far. She listened to her surroundings trying to determine what had awakened her. She could clearly hear the sounds of something or someone moving quickly through the haze on the ground, but could not see any signs of movement. She glanced to the tree next to her and could make out Ethereal well enough to see she had been awakened by the same noise. It appeared as though Charlie still slept. Isabella could not see through the haze to Dim.

Within minutes the cause of the noise made its appearance below. Roving into sight out of the morning haze appeared four gigantic wolves. Isabella had only seen one wolf in her lifetime and that was the one Riot raised from a pup, but she did not remember Riot's wolf being this big. They looked bigger than the wild horses she had seen in the west. And they looked rabid as they stood under the trees growling and foaming from their mouths. She did not know what she had expected when she found the wolves, but she was certain it wasn't what she saw below. Perhaps she was wrong and Riot was not here among the wolves. Even he could not have lived with such crazy looking wild animals.

Isabella did not have a bow as she had not mastered that weapon. She was more of an up close combat warrior, and even though she was good with a spear, she only had one of those. She couldn't recall the goblin having a bow and arrow either, but then again she was pretty sure goblins never used bows. Ethereal however, did have a bow. She twisted around and tried to get the Elven warrior's attention, but she need not have bothered since Ethereal had her bow already positioned to fire. Just then Charlie woke and she could hear him say, "No," as he grabbed at her bow and the arrow misfired high over the wolves' heads, landing somewhere well behind them.

Before Ethereal could push him off her and nock another arrow, they heard a voice shout up to them. "Who dares invade the Wolves' territory?" Isabella froze as she recognized the voice. She waved her arms towards Ethereal shouting, "Don't shoot…don't shoot." But it was too late and Ethereal let another arrow fly. Luckily, Charlie had grabbed at the Elven warrior's arm again and this shot landed behind the biggest wolf and stuck into the ground at the feet of a young human male. Riot.

Chapter Twelve

A Den of Wolves

I t had been a long time since Riot had seen another human. Today
he looked up into the trees and saw not only two humans, but what
appeared to be an Elf and of all things a goblin. He only recognized
one of the humans. He remembered Isabella from the day her mother
had handed him the Book of Truths and told him to keep it safe. She
had cast a spell over him to help protect him but honestly, he hadn't
needed her protection. He relied on only one person and that was
himself. He learned long ago you could not rely on human kind to
do anything of consequence. He had kept the Book of Truths safe all
these years not because Isabella's mother had told him to, but because
he liked the idea of being declared a hero for having succeeded in doing so. He had lost faith in that day ever happening since he had not
seen or heard from another human since. He had assumed Isabella and
Henrietta had not managed to stay alive and had resolved to spend
his life with the wolves. He had won the lupines trust when he and
Elyclaw had rescued a pack of wolves from a fire that had started in
the forest to the north. He had lived here in Wolf Country now for
years and had not crossed the path of any creature other than a wolf
in all that time. Now he was facing four creatures other than wolves.

Riot couldn't say whether he was happy to see Isabella and her
group or not. He had been content here with the wolves and no longer
cared if he saw another human. It took him longer than it should to
decide if he should call off the growling wolves from around the trees.
He could easily walk away and pretend he never saw them and go on
with the life he had become accustomed to, but eventually curiosity
won out and he decided he should find out why they were here.

"*Moshoe*," Riot commanded and the wolves stopped growling and trotted away leaving Riot and Elyclaw standing alone under the tree. "So Isabella, I didn't think you were still alive," he shouted up to her.

"It looks like you are delighted to see me, as usual," Isabella sarcastically shouted back.

"How did you find me?" Riot asked.

"Rude as always," she muttered under her breath, then louder "It wasn't hard to conclude you would want to be where Elyclaw would be accepted. In Pulchritude Amity that only left Wolf Country. Is it safe for us to come down now?"

"As safe as I can make it," he shouted up to her.

Isabella made her way down from the tree and gestured for the others to do the same. As the group one by one made an appearance, Riot realized how much of a mish mash the little party was…two humans, an Elf and a goblin, all traveling together. He couldn't imagine how that had happened. Leave it to Isabella to befriend a goblin. "So, who travels with you?" Riot asked. Elyclaw loped up to each one and gave a show of sniffing them several times looking back at Riot each time as if to say this one is okay.

"This is Dim," and Isabella gestured at the goblin, who was flinching at a slightly growling Elyclaw, who was attempting to stare him down, "and Ethereal of the Crystal Valley Elves and this one is Charlie. He is The One," She said in a quieter voice.

Riot looked Charlie up and down and couldn't help but be surprised there was a human other than Henrietta and Isabella still alive in the land. "The One?" he drawled, addressing Isabella. "Don't tell me you believed all that stuff about "The One." Even I didn't fall for that."

"I know it's hard to believe, Riot, but he is The One. I've brought him with me because it's time for us to join together again. We need to allow Charlie the opportunity to write magic for us. It's been a long time since magic has been written and taught in this land. You still have the Book of Truths?"

Riot toyed with the idea of lying to her and saying no. He didn't know if he wanted to be bothered with all this nonsense about The One and the magic writer. He had never been a firm believer of magic to start with. He came from a humble home. His father had worked hard to provide what they needed since his mother had died when he was young. It was only him and his father and the many pets that Riot had raised from babies. His father had been disappointed that his son showed no interest in hunting. It was how they made their livelihood, but Riot was more interested in saving the animals rather than killing them. However he didn't blink an eye to kill a minotaur or for that matter a goblin. They were unfeeling rotten creatures in his mind and he was not happy to see Isabella bring a goblin into his territory. But then again he might find a use for Charlie and Isabella eventually, so he decided to tell the truth. "Yes, I still have it," he stated haughtily.

"Good," Isabella said with relief. "I thought we could stay here for a few days before heading out to find Henrietta."

Riot had forgotten how bossy Isabella could be. She was in for a big surprise if she thought he was going to go traipsing across Pulchritude Amity looking for Henrietta. If he remembered correctly Henrietta was a meek shy girl who likely was no longer alive anyway. He couldn't imagine how she could have kept herself in one piece all these years. "You're more than welcome to stay here and rest, but you'll be leaving here alone. I will not be going with you."

Riot could see the surprise cross Isabella's face at his statement. Ha, that'll teach her to waltz in here and tell me what to do. He was not about to take orders from anyone let alone a girl.

"Well, okay…it would be easier if you came with us, but I guess we'll just take The Book of Truths and you can stay here if that is what you desire," Isabella said.

"No, you don't understand me. I'm not going with you which means the Book of Truths is not going with you either," Riot declared.

"You don't have a right to keep that book, Riot! It's not yours. It was in the care of my mother for the Human race and it belongs to the Human race," Isabella stated loudly, moving toward him, only to halt after a step and then back up as a snarling Elyclaw appeared directly in her path, hackles raised and teeth bared.

"The last I knew we," Riot pointed to Isabella and himself, "are the Human race now. I'm not giving you the book."

They stood staring each other down neither willing to give in. Ethereal moved smoothly from Charlie's side to Elyclaw and stood before him, cooing to him in a language other than Elvish. Elyclaw's hackles subsided and he stopped baring his teeth. He perked up his ears and stared at the she-Elf, who then advanced and started rubbing his face with her hands, keeping her eyes focused on the wolf's amber eyes. Riot pulled his attention away from Isabella and watched as Ethereal cooed and petted the young wolf. Elyclaw lowered himself to the ground and lay there, breathing loudly with his eyes closed and his tongue lolling out. "Hey! What do you think you're doing?" Riot was astonished. He had never known Elyclaw to take to anyone so quickly before. The young wolf was a loner and didn't warm well to others, yet it was obvious this Elf had a touch with animals.

"Have you ever even met a wolf before?" Riot demanded, stalking up to Ethereal. The she-Elf stopped her cooing and spoke to Riot.

"No, I have not but he is like any other creature in this world. He is just looking for love and affection. It is not hard to figure him out," she answered coolly.

"Not every creature in this world is looking for love and affection. Don't fool yourself and believe that," Riot said. "Come on Elyclaw," he called over his shoulder as he headed off between the trees. "Join me or leave. It doesn't matter to me. You are welcome to stay." The wolf heaved to his feet and loped off after Riot. The two moved through the trees, Riot not glancing back, but it was no surprise to him that the group followed.

Dim didn't know what sort of plan Isabella had, but it obviously was not working the way she wanted. Riot and Isabella were the typical humans in the land. They were full of themselves and difficult to deal with. They reminded him of why he hated humans. Charlie was the exception, but the longer Charlie was around these two humans the more likely they would rub off on him. Dim realized he had been coming at this from the wrong direction. What he needed to do was win Charlie to his side. He didn't need to fight with Isabella. She would alienate Charlie on her own. From what he had observed the last few days Ethereal was the way to Charlie's affection, so Dim just needed to win over Ethereal and Charlie would follow. Then perhaps he could steal him away from Isabella and her plan to unite the humans. And while he was at it, he could swipe The Book of Truths and The Book of Potions from the stupid humans and take them as well. Forerunner would be delighted if he brought those items to him. Perhaps it would keep him from being too angry with Dim for taking so long to deliver the boy.

The chunky goblin decided he would spend the evening getting to know Ethereal better. He had no affections for Elves, they were too holy for his liking, but if that was what he needed to do to get Charlie on his side then that was what he'd do. He'd keep his ears open to where The Book of Truth may be and when the opportunity arose he'd snatch it. He knew The Book of Potions was in Isabella's knapsack. He'd noticed her reading it before. She rarely left the knapsack alone, so stealing the book from her would be more difficult.

Dim wasn't surprised when the wolf human led them to an underground den just like many others surrounding it. Riot seemed like he would be content living like an animal. Dim didn't find it a far stretch from how the goblins lived, so he felt comfortable entering the den. However, Ethereal and Charlie seemed a bit hesitant to crawl into the lair. Isabella on the other hand was a scrapper. She made do with whatever came her way and entered the den with no hesitation, not even noticing how Ethereal and Charlie did not embrace her freeness. This was Dim's opportunity to bond with Ethereal and Charlie.

"Can you believe those st…uh, foolish humans expect us to crawl into that den like an animal?" Dim asked putting as much shock as he could muster into his voice.

"Do…ah…do you think there'll be other wolves in there?" Charlie asked. Dim could see the fear displayed across his face at the thought of joining other wolves in the den.

"Possible. Hey, you two stay close to me. I'll go first and if there is anything to worry about you'll be able to crawl back out and I'll take the brunt of it," Dim offered.

The fear left Charlie's face as he smiled at the goblin. "Thanks Dim. That would be great." It worked on the boy, but he wasn't certain about Ethereal. After all, she was a vicious warrior and Dim was sure her last concern was the wolves inside the den. He assumed she was just battling with the distress of staying in a wolf's lair. It must be a huge change to what she was used to in her precious Crystal Valley. Dim shook that thought from his mind. Those thoughts were not going to gain him favor with Ethereal.

He crawled into the den and wasn't surprised when all he encountered were Riot, Isabella and Elyclaw. He figured Riot lived among the wolves but not necessarily in the same den with them. He motioned to Charlie and Ethereal to follow him into the den and then scrunched down, even though it was actually fairly roomy in the lair. The wild human had obviously made his den deeper and longer than most in order to fit him and his wolf pet comfortably.

They found a place in the den to sit and the squat goblin positioned himself on the opposite side of Charlie and Ethereal but close enough to talk with them, leaving Isabella to her deep conversation with Riot. She obviously thought she would have some luck in changing the wolf man's mind. Where she was graced with physical prowess she lacked in social skills. She'd never convince him to do anything with her demands. But at least it kept her occupied enough to leave Charlie and Ethereal alone.

Dim pulled out his water pouch and sipped from it. "Where did you learn to handle a wolf?" He casually asked Ethereal.

"I have taken care of enough beasts around Crystal Valley during my time. That was before they started dying off. You just need to show them you do not fear them and then give them love and affection. Elyclaw is not any different from those beasts." At hearing his name Elyclaw walked over to Ethereal. He sniffed the ground around her and made a big show of pacing around in a tight circle before lying down at her feet with a suspiciously happy-sounding grunt. She put her hand out and started to rub the huge wolf's back. Dim noticed Riot had stopped in the middle of his sentence to stare at Ethereal as she pet Elyclaw like he were a pet dog rather than a wild wolf.

"Well, you've won him over just like you have Charlie and, well, me," the green goblin added for good measure.

"And how have I won you over?" As she stroked the wolf's fur, Ethereal never let her eyes leave his face. He could tell she was searching it to read him. He would make sure she saw what he wanted her to see there.

"You've taken good care of Charlie and that's all I need to be won over!" he answered.

"Then we share that in common, our concern for Charlie," she stated. Dim couldn't tell if she was being serious or not, but he was hoping he was making headway with Ethereal. Elves were just too hard to read. When the time came and he wanted Charlie to leave with him, he'd know better where the Elf's loyalties lie.

The young she-Elf knew when she was being played, and Dim was doing just that. She had hoped he would not be like most goblins, untrustworthy and vicious, but she was beginning to think he was no different. She would have to tread carefully with him. She also knew she needed to stay close to Charlie. She didn't know what the fat goblin's plan was, but she was certain it involved the newcomer to their land. She squirmed a little in the cramped quarters. She was not used to sleeping in a wolves den, but then again she didn't normally sleep in trees either. She missed having Charlie's arms wrapped around her but she knew Isabella would throw a fit rather than let them sleep that close to each other when it wasn't necessary. She slept close to Elyclaw near the entrance to the den. She felt if anyone wanted to snatch Charlie, they would have to first go through her. It was the best she could do to protect Charlie here in the wolf's lair. She had become exhausted listening to Isabella give reason after reason why Riot should reconsider and come with them, all to no avail. Did she not realize her abrasive attitude was not working on Riot? The rebellious human was not the type to give in to someone's demands.

Ethereal stayed awake for most of the night listening to the breathing of those around her. She missed being in Charlie's arms. She let her hand rest on Elyclaw's fur and felt the warmth of his body, hoping to get the comfort and warmth from him she couldn't get from Charlie. Eventually she drifted off with her hand resting on the furry wolf.

The Elf warrior awoke sometime later when she felt her hand drop off Elyclaw's body. She opened her eyes to see the shape of the large wolf slinking out of the cave. Ethereal looked around her in the dark and found Riot and Isabella sleeping close to her and Dim and Charlie sleeping further inside the den. Elyclaw was the only one missing. Ethereal quietly crawled out of the den and looked around her. It was so dark she could barely see in front of her. But to her left she saw the eyes of a wolf glowing. She turned and whispered, "Elyclaw?" and the eyes in front of her disappeared as a howl went up from the darkness. She realized that to some that would be an eerie sound, but to Ethereal it was magical. Elyclaw was communicating. Perhaps she did not understand exactly what he was saying, but still it was his way of expressing himself. The she-Elf smiled and listened as other wolves howled as well. In a world were beauty was dying, Ethereal found the wolves' howls hauntingly beautiful.

"They're incredible animals," a voice said from behind her.

She turned to find a darker shape in the blackness standing there. "It's beautiful...magical," she answered.

Riot stared hard in the dark and could just make out the young Elven warrior's shape in front of him. Ethereal stared back. She could sense how content he was in his surroundings. She had not seen that air of contentment earlier. Isabella sure brought out the worst in him. She felt anyone that could love an animal that much had a lot of good in them.

"There is something...unusual about you," Riot said. "The way you interact with Elyclaw is amazing."

"He is a creature of Pulchritude Amity just like you and I. He deserves the same respect that we do."

"Isabella said you are a warrior like your father Bibhatsu. I'm bewildered how a warrior who is trained to kill can feel that all creatures deserve respect," Riot said.

"Just because I am willing to fight for what I feel is right and to protect those I love, does not mean I enjoy it. It is a means to an end for me," Ethereal explained.

"And you feel Charlie is worthy of your respect and protection?" Riot asked.

"Yes, he is worthy of all our respect and protection. I do not know who is right about whether Charlie is The One, you or Isabella. All I know is he has a purpose here that has yet to be discovered. I touch him and I can feel it. But do not let Isabella tell you what to do," she said as she placed her hand over his heart. "We all have our paths to take. You need to explore in here what that path is for you." Ethereal let her hand linger on his chest a few seconds before removing it. A look of confusion crossed Riot's face when she touched him. Ethereal could tell he felt something pass between them, something which she felt inside. She could sense it cross his face. Once again he was another human that could not hide his emotions. Perhaps what she passed to him could help him on choosing whether he should stay or go with them. Riot closed his eyes for a second then turned abruptly towards where Elyclaw had been and whistled. The wolf pet howled in return and appeared within moments. Ethereal watched as they walked off into the dark, the young human's arm around the young wolf's shoulders.

Ethereal had softened his heart where Isabella had hardened it, but what Riot couldn't decipher was why he had a vision of a young beautiful blonde blue eyed girl when Ethereal had touched him. The girl had been running barefoot in lush green grass. She was laughing and smiling as she ran. He couldn't see why she was running, but he felt deep down she was running towards him. It confused him. This girl had haunted his dreams for several years, and now he was confused as to why Ethereal's touch had brought this out in him. He had been certain he did not want to go with Isabella, but now he had doubt. Ethereal had said to look deep within and he'd know what to do. He thought he already knew, but now he couldn't be sure.

Elyclaw lay next to Riot, his large shaggy head on his lap as he sat near the den watching the dark turn to day. The wolves were returning from a night of hunting and he loved watching as their massive bodies trotted in unison. He never tired of being here with the wolves. There was no backstabbing. There was no hatred. There was just a pack of wolves working together to hunt and parent. Riot could stay here forever and pretend no one else existed. But somehow he thought that might be the easy way out.

"What do you think, boy," Riot asked Elyclaw as he rubbed his hands along the shaggy coat of fur. "Are you ready for an adventure?" His answer was a huff and a slight growl, and Riot smiled.

The daylight brought Charlie, Ethereal, Isabella and Dim from the den. Isabella looked stern and disappointment was still etched on her face. She would not be easy to deal with if he chose to go with them. He had become accustomed to living life his way. He didn't know that he could go back to listening to a bossy girl telling him what to do.

He watched the swordplay as Ethereal started sparring with Charlie. The boy didn't impress him. His swordsmanship was weak, but perhaps Ethereal's skill just outshined Charlie's. The goblin sat back watching them and occasionally yelling out directions to Charlie on what to do. Riot couldn't place Dim's part in all this.

He couldn't get the barefooted blonde girl out of his mind. She reminded Riot a little bit of Charlie; she had some similarities to him. He didn't know if he believed in magic, or at least he didn't know if he believed the loss of magic had caused this world to fall apart. He just thought it was the natural progression for the world to change as it had. He wasn't even sure if he cared if the human race died off. The humans he had come into contact with had not instilled any wonderful feelings in him. In fact most had done nothing more than foster feelings of hatred and rage. Isabella brought those feelings back in him. But then there was the barefooted blonde girl. He wanted to meet her. She had haunted his thoughts for far too long. Now she was back in his head teasing him. He needed to know why she lived there in his head and who she was.

Riot watched the others all day. He never moved from his spot. Elyclaw had long disappeared into the den to sleep, but Riot stayed put thinking and watching.

Charlie woke and stretched, feeling the soreness in his bones. Perhaps it was sleeping on the hard ground in the den or perhaps it was the work out Ethereal had been giving him the last two days. She said he was getting better with the sword, but to Charlie holding the weapon still felt awkward and strange. Dim had been overly pleasant lately, encouraging him along with his training. He even called him Charlie a few times rather than Knucklehead. He wasn't sure what to make of him. The grumpy goblin had certainly made a complete turnaround in his views of Charlie going with Isabella.

And then there was Isabella...she confused him. She was so abrupt and cold sometimes. He didn't know what to say to her most of the time and after she had so casually left Dim to the fate of the cannibals, he didn't fully trust her either. Riot on the other hand he didn't like. Riot was distant. He seemed to find comfort with no one other than Elyclaw and to his disapproval, Ethereal. He didn't like how he looked at her. He couldn't read the she-Elf's feelings towards Riot, but when Ethereal and Riot were alone they seemed content together. Charlie didn't like the jealous feelings he got when he saw them talking alone. He wasn't used to feeling dislike for someone so quickly, but that was how he felt about Riot. He was just relieved that when they left Wolf Country, the wolf boy would not be going with them.

Charlie looked around and realized he was the last one to wake up that morning. He could hear Isabella talking to Ethereal, and she was saying something about it being time to move on. He was just starting to feel comfortable here! He wasn't sure he was ready to start traveling again. Actually, he hadn't even seen the purpose of having stopped here. Isabella said it was important that they gather all the humans together, and she made it sound urgent that they do so quickly. If Riot would not go with them, Charlie couldn't imagine how leaving to find the last human would do them any good. Maybe he had made the wrong choice following Isabella rather than going with Dim to meet Forerunner.

He crawled out of the den, wanting to join Isabella and Ethereal's conversation, but Dim intercepted him as he emerged.

"Hey, Knucklehead. I hear we are getting ready to move on. You feel okay with that?"

Charlie wasn't sure he was okay with that, but somehow he didn't think his opinion would really matter. "If that is what everyone has decided we do then I guess that is what we will do," Charlie answered.

Dim lowered his voice so that only Charlie could hear him. "If you are having second thoughts about this whole plan of the bossy one, we could sneak out of here at any time. All you have to do is let me know."

Being alone with Dim again was appealing, but he knew he'd never leave Ethereal now. She had left her home and her family to protect him. He could not repay her by leaving her alone with Isabella. "No…I haven't changed my mind," Charlie hesitantly said.

Dim punched Charlie in his arm in a jovial way. "Whatever you say! If you change your mind you know I'm here for you," said the goblin a little too perky.

Charlie saw a flicker of something odd pass across the short goblin's face. He just could not place what it was.

He felt a slap across his back. "Hey there, I see the sleeping dead is awake," Riot said sarcastically.

Charlie didn't laugh at Riot's attempt at a joke. He took his hand and made a dusting motion at his back to wave away Riot's hand. "I've been a little tired with all the training and all," he explained.

Riot laughed which irritated Charlie even more. "You mean what you've been doing lately is considered training?"

Charlie had never had an urge to hit someone before, but Riot was pushing his limits. Somehow he didn't think it would go over well with Ethereal if he resorted to violence. "At least I'm doing something to improve myself! You're….you're just moping around her waiting for us to leave!" Charlie said louder than he had intended. "Don't worry, we'll be out of your hair soon enough!" He stormed away passing the two female warriors who had stopped talking and turned to watch the commotion. He didn't stop walking until he had gone a fair distance away and he realized he didn't know where he was going. There wasn't anywhere to go in this god forsaken fog filled land!

Charlie plopped himself down on the ground right where he stood and struggled to keep from crying. He missed Kassie and the peace of his home. He was tired of being pulled in different directions by Isabella and Dim. He was tired of everyone putting so many expectations on him. He knew he would only be a disappointment to everyone. Isn't that what he did most of the time anyway?

He sat that way with his head in his hands for a while before he realized he was not alone. Glancing up Charlie looked into the eyes of Ethereal. "How long have you been standing there?"

"Not long. I was worried when you went off alone. This is not the safest place. Riot has done all he can to keep us safe from the wolves, but alone, they may decide to attack. We should go back," Ethereal stated.

"I don't want to go back. I want all this," Charlie waved his hand around in front of him, "to go away. I want to go back home and sleep in my own bed. I want to go back home and talk with my parents and my sister. I'm tired of everyone here putting the weight of the world on my shoulders. There are too many expectations everyone has of me."

Ethereal lowered herself next to Charlie and placed her hand on his hand and squeezed it. "It is good for others to have high expectations of you. It would be a sad world if no one expected anything from you. That would mean that you are not worthy or well thought of. Relish in the fact you have a purpose and many of those surrounding you have faith in you to perform that purpose."

Charlie smiled haphazardly at Ethereal. Even though it just sounded like words, he realized that was something Kassie would have said to him. Somehow he could see bits of Kassie in the young she-Elf and that gave him comfort. "I suppose you're right," Charlie grumbled.

Ethereal stood and put out her hand to Charlie. He grabbed it and let her help lift him to his feet. They walked back to the den hand and hand in silence.

Chapter Thirteen
Riot's Decision

As Isabella and the group were packing up their belongings before heading on their way, the wolf pack surrounded them at Riot and Elyclaw's den. Each wolf carried in their mouth an animal they had scored off a recent hunt. One by one they laid their offering at Charlie's feet. He wasn't sure about the mix of emotions he felt, fear and horror chief among them. He was also grossed out by the bloody bounty they placed at his feet. He couldn't help but wonder why he was the lucky one to be given this bloody mass of dead animals. Ethereal who was standing next to Charlie was the first one to speak after the last wolf deposited his offering.

"That is quite a gesture. They are giving you fealty and you should be honored," Ethereal stated. "Even the wolves feel your importance."

An hour ago Charlie would have been annoyed with someone pointing out his importance again, but after Ethereal's conversation about expectations he realized that annoyance had left him. He did feel honored if this offering from the wolves was some sort of peace sign. He looked down at the pile of death before him and tried not to gag at the blood flowing from some of the more recent kills. He just wished the wolves had honored him with chocolate bars and pizza. Charlie longed for chocolate and pizza. He smiled just at the thought of them. The smile brought a response from Riot.

"At least from your smile I see you are pleased with the bounty the wolves have brought you. You must be of some importance for them to give you what they need to survive here themselves, food," Riot stated.

Charlie didn't know what to say, so he just bowed slightly at the wolves. He felt a bit foolish bowing at an animal. But the golden eyes of the wolf at the front of the pack seemed to say "you're welcome". Charlie shook his head. It couldn't be possible for a wolf to feel that. He had to be imagining things. Elyclaw loped up to Charlie and imperiously head butted him gently in the back towards the pile of beasts, as if to say, go ahead, these are for you! Charlie fought back a gag.

Isabella pushed her way passed Ethereal and Charlie and started gathering the bloody carcasses. "Well if you are going to stand there stupidly bowing at a wolf than I suppose I'll be the one to gather the offerings for skinning and cleaning. They will come in handy during our journey," she stated.

Riot looked on with disgust as Isabella started skinning the creatures before her, oblivious to the wolves that had provided them the food for their journey. "Nothing like cutting straight to business now is there," Riot said sharply.

"You don't think he's going to skin these, do you?" Isabella answered Riot, jerking a thumb in Charlie's direction.

The wolf boy looked at Charlie and studied the faintly sick look on his face as he stared at Isabella's work. "No, but at least he has the manners to appreciate the gesture," he said as he turned and went into the den. Charlie felt surprised by the compliment from Riot. But the kind thoughts towards the wolf boy disappeared as Ethereal left his side and went into the den with Riot. Leaving Wolf Country and the annoying wolf boy couldn't happen soon enough for Charlie's liking.

Riot wrapped the skinned meat in banana leaves and placed portions of them into each of their packs. Charlie didn't have a pack, so Riot put one of his old ones together and placed some of the meat in it. The boy of magic didn't want to be thankful for anything from Riot, but the manners his mother had brought him up with took over and he forced out a "thank you" for the pack. The wolf boy could see how much that hurt Charlie to say and he let out one loud laugh, which brought a scowl to his visitor's face. Riot could sense the kid had taken a disliking to him. Personally he didn't care one way or another if any of them liked him. He wasn't about being liked. He had his own priorities and that was all that mattered to Riot.

After filling all the packs with meat, Riot started putting a pack together for himself as well as one that he could tie onto Elyclaw. He wasn't about to leave his wolf after all these years, but he feared taking him away from the other wolves and the safety of Wolf Country could be dangerous. Others in Pulchritude Amity feared wolves and Riot couldn't help but worry that harm would come to Elyclaw once they left the protection of their home. However, Elyclaw had never been away from Riot for even a short time. He couldn't imagine leaving him to his own devices here in Wolf Country, so Riot packed him a pack and tied it onto Elyclaw's back.

Charlie stood next to him watching and after a few minutes he spoke up. "What are you packing for?"

"We are leaving today, right…Knucklehead?" Riot teasingly added the goblin's nickname for Charlie.

"We? I thought you weren't coming with us!"

Riot looked towards Ethereal and their eyes met for an extended moment. "I've changed my mind," Riot said. He turned back to his pack and gathered some rope he had in a corner of the den and packed it. "You have a problem with that?"

The disappointment that crossed Charlie's face didn't go unnoticed. He looked towards Ethereal and then lowered his eyes from hers. "No, of course not," he said flatly. "And don't call me Knucklehead. My name is Charlie and nothing else." The young human pushed his way through the den and out to the fog awaiting them.

"Geez, he's a bit crabby," Riot said to no one in particular.

"I have to admit I'm as surprised as he is that you changed your mind," Isabella said smugly. "I guess you finally saw my side of things."

Riot had to hold his tongue. He wanted to say it was in spite of

Isabella that he was joining them. In fact it was Ethereal that had changed his mind. Not because she had pleaded with him or asked him to travel with them. Ethereal would never have lowered herself to that level. It was something Riot couldn't place his finger on. The Elven warrior gave him hope in humanity once again. She seemed to have faith in Charlie where Riot did not and perhaps he wanted to go along to see how it played out. And perhaps it was because whenever he stood near Ethereal he envisioned the beautiful blonde blue eyed girl that haunted his dreams. He couldn't help but think the she-Elf might lead him to her. It was a long shot, but it was one he wanted to chance.

"Yeah, sure," Riot curtly answered Isabella. The two female warriors crawled out of the den, closely followed by the squat goblin, leaving Riot and Elyclaw alone. He looked around the lair putting his hand on the wolf's fur and absently rubbing him. "Sure going to miss this place," Riot said. "It's been comforting to stay here and not have to worry about anything. I have a feeling it will be a long time before we have that again." Elyclaw butted his large shaggy head into Riot's stomach, panting as he pushed against his friend. Riot smiled slightly and absently rubbed the wolf's head and ears. They then turned and left the comfort of their home with Riot never looking back.

Chapter Fourteen

How to Curse a Forest

Isabella sat around the fire with Riot. Charlie was once again practicing swordsmanship with Ethereal as Dim sat nearby coaching. The group had traveled many miles today, but Isabella wasn't sure where they were going. Where she had a specific location to look for Riot, the female warrior didn't have a clue where to find Henrietta. Riot was correct about Henrietta being meek and weak and perhaps he was right that she had not survived. If Isabella recalled correctly, Henrietta was small, barely reaching four feet tall, and quite thin. She was quick and smart, and Isabella assumed her mother had given her the Pen of Knowledge to keep hidden, banking on her cleverness to keep it safe and herself alive. Isabella had to trust her mother was right and Henrietta had been clever enough to stay alive, but where she had managed to do that was a mystery to her.

"You have no idea where you are going, do you?" Riot accused.

She would normally have snapped at Riot, but this time he was right. She knew they couldn't just keep moving aimlessly around. Where she could keep herself hidden well, she could not keep four others hidden along with her. Eventually they'd stumble across Nefarious' minions. They were nearing his territory. Isabella felt certain Henrietta could not be hidden away so close to Nefarious, so then where was she?

"Actually, I don't. I didn't know Henrietta very well. What I do know of her is she was small and meek. She was smart. Putting those qualities together does not give clues to where she'd hide herself though," Isabella said.

"Sure it does," Charlie spoke up. He was taking a breather nearby from his sword training and had overheard Isabella's statement. "If you were small I would think you'd find a small place to hide yourself."

A small place. Isabella thought about that for a while. She could see Henrietta living in the trees with the miniature dragons, but would they take her in and allow her to stay there? And why would they harbor a small human? What would they gain from doing that? Then there were the Gnomes. She had never seen a Gnome before, but she knew they existed...or so her mother had told her. Her mother had told her the Gnomes had built an underground city somewhere in the Northwest of Pulchritude Amity. It was possible Henrietta could be hiding there. And being she was small, she'd likely be able to blend in with the gnomes, but once again why would gnomes help out a human? She'd heard gnomes avoided humans whenever possible and remained underground for the most part. Then there was the possibility that Henrietta was like Isabella and had been moving around from place to place which in that case finding her would be very difficult indeed. Isabella considered this possibility the least likely. She could not imagine Henrietta having survived years alone wandering this dangerous countryside.

She had to make some sort of decision where to lead the group. They couldn't just wander aimlessly and hope to stumble upon Henrietta. If she had stayed alive this whole time she would not just be standing in an open field somewhere. Riot had gotten up from the fire and had moved to a tree leaning against it with his arms crossed, watching as Charlie returned to sparring with Ethereal. He stood with a smirk across his lips. Isabella could tell Riot felt the same as she did about Ethereal training Charlie in combat. It was a crazy notion to think he could ever amount to anything close to resembling a fighter. He was as far from a fighter as any human could be minus Henrietta. But Isabella didn't interfere with Ethereal's attempts to teach Charlie the skill of using a sword. At least she was keeping him busy and out of her hair as well as keeping Dim busy. Isabella avoided the goblin as much as possible. Every now and then she'd find the hairy gremlin looking at her with a creepy expression and she had to remind herself to let him live for Charlie's sake.

She pulled out her book from her knapsack and glanced around to make sure no one was watching. They were all still so absorbed with Charlie that she knew she'd have a few minutes alone. She opened the book and turning to the back cover pulled out a map. She unfolded it and looked it over. The map was an ancient artifact and held many hidden places in Pulchritude Amity. It once belonged to the old magic writer. When he fled he had left it with his belongings and her mother had been the one to find it. When magic was strong many secrets were displayed on the map, but now with magic having faded the map had faded with it, yet Isabella still used it to help guide her to some of the areas no one else knew about. She saw the miniature dragon's hidden hollows in the trees of the Cursed Forest not too far from where they were camped. She also saw what she believed to be the hidden homes of the Gnomes outlined quite a distance to the Northwest. She decided it would be easiest to head to the Cursed Forest though she wasn't certain it would be a safe place to venture without magic to protect them. She had discovered the night before that her protection spell had stopped working. They would have to be smart about how they entered that area. They couldn't afford to be cursed.

An eerie shrilling cry caused Isabella to stand up, hand on her sword hilt, looking around for the author of that sound. She realized it was Ethereal, and she saw her waving her sword over her head and gesturing towards Charlie, whose mouth and eyes were wide open as he stared at the Elven warrior.

"That is the battle cry of my people," explained Ethereal to the young human magic writer. "It helps focus the mind and prepare the body for battle. It is pulled from one's soul and helps strike fear into your enemies. Now you try."

Charlie shook his head at the Elf. "What, just scream out loud? Do I say words or something?"

Ethereal smiled. "No, this is more emotion than words."

Isabella watched the scene with faint amusement. There was just no way she could see Charlie as a warrior.

He shrugged and took a deep breath. "Okay…" He screwed his eyes shut and opened his mouth wide. The resulting mix of gurgling squeal and squeaky sounds were nothing like Ethereal's battle cry, or any other beings for that matter. Isabella scrunched up her face and covered her ears, staring at the young magic writer with scorn.

Charlie's battle cry trailed off and he opened his eyes to silence. He saw everyone staring at him, Isabella with her hands over her ears. Riot started laughing, and Charlie looked over to see him pointing towards him.

"Did you see his face? And what kinda noise was that?" the wolf boy queried derisively, laughing.

Isabella couldn't help letting out a humorless bark of a laugh. "It sounded more like someone was killing a piglet with a boot," she snickered. She shook her head and sat back down with her map. Out of the corner of her eye, she saw Ethereal rub Charlie's arm soothingly. "That was not bad for a first attempt. We will work on the cry and strengthen it later," she crooned.

Isabella folded up the map and stored it in the pocket at the back of the Book of Potions and put the book away in her knapsack. Charlie and Ethereal joined her at the fire. The boy was out of breath and flushed from the sparring, but the Elf looked as fresh as if she had not even moved a muscle. Even Isabella couldn't understand how Ethereal could not look beat after an evening of physical training.

"How's your pupil doing?" Isabella asked.

"He is coming along," Ethereal said with a smile.

"She's being kind," Charlie said.

"Have you decided on where we are heading next?" Ethereal asked.

She tried to determine if by the Elf's comment she could tell Isabella didn't know where Henrietta was located, but she couldn't read anything from Ethereal's flat expression. "We are headed to the Cursed Forest," Isabella said.

Ethereal just nodded. Charlie's expression however showed one of concern. "The Cursed Forest? That doesn't sound good," he said.

Riot and Dim had joined them by the fire as they tore pieces of the meat from the offerings they had received from the wolves. "The Cursed Forest?" Riot said. "You can't think that's wise."

Dim spat out a chunk of his meat when he heard Riot mention The Cursed Forest. "There is no way I'm going into a cursed forest. And what makes you think a human…a young girl at that…would hide in the Cursed Forest. She'd be crazy to even venture in there alone."

"Then that is exactly why she would go into the forest. She would know no one else would risk their life going in looking for her," Ethereal stated.

"Exactly," said Isabella.

They left for The Cursed Forest the next morning and reached the outskirts by the morning of the following day. Dim only had to take one look into the forest to know entering would be a bad idea. He couldn't imagine why Isabella was determined to take them through there. He still firmly believed there was no way a young small girl would have survived in this forest. From the outskirts the trees hugged each other leaving little room for one to move between them. The trees were so tall that from Dim's small stature he couldn't even make out the top of them. The leaves that grew on these trees were as black as night and Dim figured the lack of magic in Pulchritude Amity was somehow not the cause of the blackness of the leaves. The ground under their feet was sticky and black. When Dim entered into the forest this stickiness made a slapping sound as he walked, and he could feel the debris from the ground attach itself to his hairy feet. As the party entered the forest, what little daylight there was faded to a dusky grey. Dim assumed daylight never really entered the forest. It was likely in a permanent state of nighttime. And worse of all was the stench of death and decay.

They had only taken a few steps in when Dim spoke up. "We should not be entering this forest. I can feel the death surrounding us."

"Don't be a wimp," Isabella snapped at the goblin.

Dim turned and growled at Isabella. Out of the corner of his eye, he saw Charlie gave him a dirty look and he stopped. How he hated this human girl. But to keep peace with Charlie, he stopped talking and went along with the group.

"I don't like the looks of it either, Dim, but I'm working on trusting, so we need to have faith in Isabella and trust her," Charlie whispered. The hairy goblin couldn't help but think what a Knucklehead. Dim trusted only himself. His young human friend would be wise to learn that lesson. Never trust anyone to do anything other than mislead you and leave you. The goblin race had lived centuries with that type of thinking. And the humans? Where were they? They were dead for the most part. "Trusting," Dim spit out in a grumble. "A stupid human idea."

"What?" Charlie said.

"Oh, nothing," Dim spat.

He stopped walking and Riot, who had been looking at the ground, collided with him. "Hey, what are you stopping for," Riot said as he rubbed the spot on his forehead that had taken the brunt of the collision.

"I just think if we are going to go any further into this forest we should protect ourselves from the curse," Dim stated. He watched as all four of his companions stood staring at him. "Just do as I do," Dim continued.

The goblin twirled around towards his left four times on one leg then he hopped onto his other leg and twirled around towards his right four times. Then he bowed down twice and on the second bow he picked up a stick off the ground and broke it over his leg and spit. When he was done his four companions were still staring at him with mouths wide open. Elyclaw growled at the goblin, his hackles raised.

"What in the world was that?" Isabella exclaimed.

"It wards off curses," Dim calmly answered back. "You all need to do it. Trust me; you'll be sorry otherwise when the curse catches you."

Isabella let out a laugh that sounded almost like a cackle. It was the first time Dim had seen her smile let alone laugh. The green goblin resented the laugh being it was at his expense. "That is the most ridiculous thing I've ever heard of or for that matter seen," she choked through the laughter.

"STOP IT!" Charlie turned towards Isabella and yelled. "Who are you to tell Dim what is or isn't ridiculous? Honestly look around you. We are walking in some forest that is supposed to be cursed. I've seen birds the size of dinosaurs. I've been spit at by evil walking sticks. I've almost been eaten by an oversized human turned cannibal, I've walked through a Crystal City, I've slept with the wolves, and I've become friends with a goblin and fallen in love with an..." Charlie paused, suddenly red-faced, and Dim noticed his eyes flit up towards Ethereal as he let that last sentence fade away. "So dancing around and spitting to ward off a curse does not seem ridiculous to me!" he finished angrily.

Everyone became quiet after the young human's speech. Dim had never really considered how strange this world would be for someone like Charlie. He was so focused on his own agenda and never thought about it from Charlie's view.

Riot stated "We should keep moving." Isabella turned around and started the group moving forward. Riot and Elyclaw, who gave a sniff at Dim in passing, moved by the stout goblin and came up behind

Charlie. Dim noticed that the wolf was moving reluctantly through the trees. He stayed closer to the ground and his tail stayed down. Even the wolf knew the forest was cursed. Isabella was a fool. The hairy green goblin watched as the wolf boy said something to Charlie and smiled. He couldn't hear from behind Elyclaw what he said, but Charlie didn't return the smile.

Ethereal came up next to him and said, "Do what you feel is right for you, Dim. Do not pay any notice to Isabella. She has faith only in what she sees. Sometimes we need to have faith in what we cannot see." She slowed and fell back in line behind Dim.

He didn't want to admit it but he sort of liked Ethereal. He certainly could see what Charlie saw in her. He didn't want to, but he did.

Charlie broke the silence. "So how did this forest become cursed?"

The squat goblin cleared his throat. "It's been said there were dragons that roamed the world. They were feared by all, goblins, Elves, humans even Czar himself. They spoke in tongues and fire and ice flew from their breath. They were on a quest to free a fellow dragon from the frozen caves. A wicked human had trapped a dragon in one of the caves and experimented with spells on him. By the time the other dragons rescued their imprisoned brother and killed the human, the curse had already been cast. They fled together to the forest where they later diminished in size until they were no bigger than a crow. The curse bound them to the forest and is said to seep from their blood into the trees and plants, turning the forest as cursed as they are, so any one within reach of the forest will experience the curse."

"That is an interesting tale, Dim," Ethereal said. "But from what I have heard that is a falsehood. It has been told in Crystal Valley that long ago there was a battle in these woods between a masterful wizard and the Dwarves of Elderby. The wizard had wanted to settle in these woods. He wanted a solitary life where he could master his art and be left in peace. He had fought many battles and taught many humans the use of magic. He was old and tired and ready to settle down and be left alone. But the Dwarves from the East did not want a wizard in these woods. They used the woods for supplies and passage from their underground homes to the waters of Tellbusie. The dwarves feared magic of all kinds and did not want to pass a wizard every day during their travels. They fought and the wizard won cursing the dwarves and changing them to wood nymphs who now live in the trees and poison them with the curse. It's said the wizard still lives somewhere among the forest long since retired to a life of quiet and peace," said Ethereal.

For the second time that day, Isabella laughed. "You both tell wonderful tales, but they are nothing more than tales. Like I said before the forest is not cursed. It's just a rumor."

Riot interjected "Oh the forest is definitely cursed, but not from dragons or wood nymphs, though I understand they are plentiful in the forest. The forest was cursed by the last magic writer."

Isabella stopping walking and the group stopped behind her. "The last magic writer? Why in the world would he want to curse this forest?" she asked incredulously.

"Oh, he didn't want to curse it. No, not at all," Riot answered.

"But you just said the last magic writer cursed it. If he didn't want to curse it, then why did he curse it?" Dim asked sarcastically.

"I'm getting to that! He was young then. He was being mentored by his father who was the current magic writer, so the young magic writer was still in his apprenticeship. During that time he was only supposed to write and practice magic under the supervision of his teacher, but his teacher was his father. And being his father, he didn't allow him to do very much at first and the young magic writer was rebellious as sons can be. The young magic writer told his mentor he wanted to learn to write a curse. His mentor told the young magic writer he was not ready to write such a strong spell and instead had him writing protection spells. The youthful magic writer tired of what he considered boring spells and wandered off one day with the book and pen in hand. He found himself among these trees where he scribbled away in the book writing what he assumed would be a masterful curse spell. But it went wrong and flew from his hands and landed in the woods. Thus the curse!"

Now it was Riot's turn to be subject to the groups open mouthed stare. Isabella was the first to speak. "So you are telling me this forest was cursed...by accident?"

"Yes, that is what I'm saying," Riot said.

"And where exactly did you hear that ridiculumous tale," asked Dim.

"It's not a *ridiculous* tale," Riot firmly corrected the goblin. "What the young magic writer didn't know is his best friend at that time, my father, followed him that day. He saw the whole thing," Riot stated.

The silence settled in as the group tried to determine whether to believe Riot or not. Then Charlie spoke up. "Well, I like Ethereal's tale better. I'm going with what she said." The rest of the group made several comments and Ethereal smiled as they started walking and squeezing their way through the trees.

"Whatever, it's no skin off my nose whether you believe me or not," Riot said. They continued walking as each pondered the three tales they had heard and which one was real.

Chapter Fifteen
The Power of a Curse

Isabella had the group stop for the night. Of course Charlie wasn't sure how she could tell whether it was day or night. The forest seemed to be in permanent nighttime, but he was still glad to rest. The walking in the forest was rough. The stickiness of the ground stuck to his shoes and as they went along his feet became heavier and more difficult to lift. He couldn't tell what the ground was made of, but Charlie was certain it wasn't mud. He looked around wondering where Isabella expected them to sleep for the night. There was no way he was going to sleep on this ground.

Scanning the ground around him Charlie asked, "Where do you intend for us to sleep for the night?"

Isabella answered quickly, "I suppose we'll have to sleep in the trees again."

Charlie's earlier apprehension to sleeping in the trees vanished as he considered the options. He thought of sleeping with Ethereal in his arms again, and he couldn't think of a better way to end a long day of travel.

But these trees were different than the ones in Wolf Country. These were taller and darker and seemed to whisper in the night. It sort of spooked him to think of climbing one of them. Ethereal came up behind him and whispered, "Do you want to share a tree again tonight?"

Looking up at the timber in front of him to determine how far he'd have to climb to reach the first branch, he answered, "Yeah, I do. But do you think we can climb these trees?"

"It will be more difficult with the stickiness on our feet, but we'll manage. I'll stay behind you as you go to make sure you reach that groove in the branches up there. I think it would be the best place to sleep for the night." Charlie just nodded, looking up at the climb in apprehension.

"I think it would be dangerous to start a fire here. We don't know what lives within this forest and fire might attract trouble we don't need. We have plenty of food still in our packs, so we'll all need to make use of it tonight. I'll take this tree," Isabella said pointing to a particularly large tree to the right of the one Charlie and Ethereal had already started climbing. Instead of climbing, Riot had started poking around the base of several of the trees, obviously looking for something. He seemed to find it quickly enough as he stopped and whistled for Elyclaw. The wolf, who had been sitting aside furiously trying to clean the sticky substance from his paws, lumbered up and trotted over to his friend. Charlie paused for a moment in his climbing to watch as first Riot, and then the wolf, seemed to disappear into the base of one of the larger trees. He frowned and then thought they must have found a hollow at the bottom of the timber.

Charlie hadn't realized that Dim had not climbed a tree until the young human boy was already stretched out on a branch with Ethereal. He glanced down below and saw the blurry outlines of the goblin sitting on an old log that had fallen long ago picking the sticky stuff off his hairy feet. "What are you doing, Dim?"

"What does it look like I'm doing, Knucklehead? I'm trying to get the stench of death off me," Dim answered.

"Aren't you planning to sleep up here in a tree?" Charlie yelled down to him.

"I'm not getting in any cursed tree. And if you knew what was good for you, you'd get out of the tree now," Dim said.

"We've been in this forest all day, Dim and nothing has happened to us so far. Don't you think you're being a bit superstitious," Isabella yelled down to the lumpy goblin.

"Call it superstatiousnish or whatever you want to call it, but I'm not sleeping in a cursed tree," Dim stated again.

Charlie chuckled to himself at Dim's faux pas. "No one is going to change Dim's mind. This I've learned about him so far," he said to Ethereal through a laugh.

"And no one should try to change him. He has his convictions and he is sticking to them. It's an admirable trait," Ethereal said seriously.

Charlie stopped laughing. Ethereal saw everyone in such a positive light. He admired that trait and wished he could be a little more like that. Kassie had received the positive, thoughtful trait. He, on the other hand, judged too quickly and he felt ashamed for having laughed at Dim. He looked down again to see what the goblin had planned for the night. He had placed his pack on the ground in front of the log and now sat on it propping his back up against the fallen dead tree. Charlie couldn't imagine how that could even be remotely comfortable, but then again maybe goblins didn't need comfort to sleep.

Ethereal went about tying them to the tree with the rope and Charlie decided Dim's spot was probably as comfortable as his was lying in the crevice of the tree. His only comfort was the warmth of Ethereal's body pressed against him. He had dreamed of having his arms wrapped around Ethereal since the last night they had stayed in a tree. It seemed already so long ago since he had held her. He soaked in her warmth for a while and listened to her heartbeat. Then he slowly let his hand caress her arm and felt the tingle throughout his limbs as the little hairs on her arms brushed his fingers. He loved the softness of her skin. He felt the urge rush through him to touch her more. After a few minutes he got up the courage to lean down and kiss her. She pulled away before their lips met.

"It would not be a good idea to get emotionally invested with each other, Charlie. Our relationship would not be a welcome one among your kind," Ethereal paused before adding "or my kind." He felt the urge to lower his lips to hers again, but he could tell she was serious about what she said. He couldn't understand how anyone would care who he kissed. He stopped caressing her arm.

He considered what she said and couldn't help but wonder if there was more to it. "Why would anyone care about our relationship? It seems crazy to think anyone is even paying any attention to my love life."

Charlie felt a warmth in his heart as Ethereal smiled. She didn't smile often which Charlie thought was a shame since when she did it encased her whole face. "You are the next magic writer and teacher of magic. Everyone's eyes will be on you and following your lead. You will want to seriously consider whether a relationship with a Crystal Elf would be damaging to your calling," Ethereal replied.

"I'm confused, Ethereal. Are you saying in order to be the magic writer I'm not allowed to get close to anyone?" Charlie took his finger and lifted her head up so he could look into those dark pools of her eyes.

"No, you aren't forbidden to get close to others...of your kind. It is unheard of for the Elves and humans to mix. Some would call that *plamic*, or tainted blood. You would have to prepare yourself for much criticism from others if you were to be with me," Ethereal said.

Charlie was appalled that racism was prevalent here in Pulchritude Amity just like back home. "No one will ever tell me who I can and cannot be with," he sternly stated.

"That is easy to say and harder to live by. You will see. We should sleep. Tomorrow could be another long day," Ethereal closed her eyes and lowered her head, commanding the end to the conversation.

Charlie thought about what Ethereal had said. She didn't know him well if she thought he'd allow anyone to tell him who he should be with. Regardless of what anyone here thought, he wanted Ethereal and he knew that. They would all have to accept that or he would not be the magic writer. Was that why Isabella gave him dirty looks any time he touched Ethereal? Did she agree with what the she-Elf believed that races should not mix? Well, she was in for a big surprise if she thought she could control him. No one could control Charlie… or so he believed!

The coughs wracked Riot's body and brought him awake. After a few minutes, he was able to stop hacking and catch his breath. He wondered how long he had been sleeping. His body was weak and he still felt tired, so he determined he had probably only been sleeping a short while. He strained his eyes to try and see Elyclaw next to him, but the darkness was too thick. What he did notice was a flicker of something in front of him. He squinted harder and made out the glowing outlines of wings. They were glowing orange and about the length of his arm. Anyone else would normally have been frightened and cautious of a strange glowing creature, but this was in Riot's wheelhouse.

"Hey, who's there?" Riot cooed soothingly.

The flapping continued and the creature came closer. Riot could now see the form better and he was certain it was a miniature dragon. Dim's tale came back to him and he wondered if perhaps there was some truth to it now that he had a small dragon in front of him. "Hey fella," Riot said softly.

The dragon breathed out and a yellow-red flame issued out of his mouth, coming within inches of Riot's face. The warmth felt good on his chilled body. The small fire breather lowered itself to Riot's leg and slowly relaxed its' wings. Riot sat back stiffly and watched the beast cautiously, wary of the fact that the small dragon could burn him in a matter of seconds if it wanted to.

"What brings a human into our forest?" the dragon demurely asked.

"Well, there is something I didn't expect, a talking dragon," chuckled Riot.

The dragon didn't address Riot's surprise at his being able to speak.

The winged beastie spit out another tongue of flame before speaking. "It's been a long time since there was a human in this forest. Why now?" he asked again.

"I'm...ah...traveling through looking for someone," Riot said, and he couldn't keep himself from reaching out to touch the little dragon. The dragon spit flames at Riot's hands and came within inches of burning them. The young human quickly pulled his hand back, respecting that the dragon obviously did not want to be touched. "What name do you go by," Riot asked.

"I'm known as Listerviere," fluted the small dragon. "I'm not sure who you seek, but you'll only find us dragons and wood nymphs here in this forest. It has not been suitable for other beings for quite some time," continued Listerviere as Riot let out a few more coughs and shivered.

"It sure is cold in this forest," Riot said as he rubbed his hands together and then wrapped his arms around himself, trying to generate warmth.

"The heat throughout our forest is strong. What you are feeling comes from the disease that is raging through your body, causing your chills," Listerviere said.

Riot tried to concentrate on what Listerviere was saying, but his body began to shake and spasm as the chills suddenly grew stronger. The small dragon flew from Riot's leg and hovered just above him, watching as the boy trembled. Eventually the shaking subsided, and the wolf boy let out a sigh as fatigue took over his body. "What's happening to me?" he croaked.

"You are fighting a disease, one that is prevalent in this forest and attacks any warm blooded creature. You were foolish to have come here," Listerviere said.

"Disease? You mean I'm sick?"

"As sure as the sky is blue and grass is green, you are dying. The curse that flows through this forest is now flowing through your blood."

Riot tried to comprehend what the small dragon was saying through the increasing fogginess in his brain. He heard something about a curse and that a curse had found him. His eyes widened as it suddenly occurred to him that if the curse had found him, then what about the others?

He immediately looked around him for Elyclaw and in the soft orange glow coming from the miniature dragon he could see his friend was not with him. Riot stumbled his way out of the tree's hollow. Weakness overtook him before he reached his third step and he let himself drop to the ground. He lay there trying to catch his breath from the exertion and effort it had taken to move even that far. He felt a bit frantic wondering if this disease would also take Elyclaw's life. Before he could stand, Riot heard a whimper next to him and he turned his head to see his pet wolf. It only took him a matter of seconds to see that the wolf was suffering. His eyes were red and oozing a white milky substance and his body shook.

"Elyclaw!" Riot said as he reached out for the softness of his fur. "I'm so sorry! This is my fault. I'm responsible for keeping you safe and I've failed!"

He rubbed the wolf's fur and closed his eyes, comforted by the closeness of his friend. Elyclaw, having fallen weak like Riot, collapsed next to his companion. The trembling wolf lowered his head, placing it on Riot's chest. Listerviere swooped out of the hollow and settled on the log only inches from Dim and watched as Riot and Elyclaw breathed raggedly in sync. He'd seen the curse disease many creatures passing through the forest, but he had never known it to affect a wolf before. Listerviere suspected it had something to do with the wolf's connection to the human. Some of the human's weakness must have passed to the wolf.

Riot moaned as he sat up never letting his hand stray from Elyclaw's gaunt shoulders. From this view he could see Dim slumped forward sleeping. At first glance it appeared as if Dim was

∞ 170 ∞

untouched by the curse. He slept soundly with an occasional snore escaping him. Riot wondered if the silly dance they had made fun of had actually worked and saved Dim. Then the hairy green goblin coughed. Riot cringed at the sound. The young wolf boy heard a noise from behind him. There stood a woozy Isabella. She coughed into her hand and phlegm splattered out of her mouth. She not only sounded sick but she looked terrible. Her face was blotchy and tinted a slight purplish color. Riot wondered if his face looked like Isabella's. He reached up and squeezed his cheeks, forehead and nose.

"You look terrible," Isabella stated.

She answered Riot's question for him. He let his hands slip away from his face and stood up. Dizziness overtook him and he wobbled a little bit and had to place his hands on the tree next to him to keep from falling.

"You don't look so hot yourself," Riot said back.

"I don't understand what is happening. Did we get sick from the meat we've been eating? Do you think it is rank?" Isabella asked shakily. "I know I salted it correctly."

A cackle filled the air. It drew Isabella's attention to the miniature dragon sitting perched on the log. "What..." Isabella stumbled over her words, "What..."

"Hello. I'm Listerviere."

"By gosh, Dim's story is right," Isabella said. "I truly didn't believe any of your tales."

Riot still believed in his father's story of how this forest had become cursed. Seeing Listerviere didn't change his opinion.

"The dragon says we are dying and from the look of you I'd have to agree," Riot said.

Isabella put her hands to her face to see if she could feel what Riot saw. After being able to feel the bumps there, she clasped her hands together. Riot could see she was shocked. It brought a smile to his face to see her disbelief. She truly didn't believe in the curse. He couldn't help but rub it in regardless of how he felt.

"So the know it all doesn't know it all," he chuckled, and then hacked.

Before Isabella could retort back, Charlie and Ethereal made an appearance. The Elf's beauty was tainted by blemishes over her face, neck and arms. She stumbled her way towards Isabella and only remained on foot because of Charlie who held her arm to keep her upright. His face was free of any marks. He stood erect and in full control of his gait. Riot found Charlie's lack of any symptoms more shocking to him than Ethereal's apparent illness. He wasn't sure how it was possible Charlie could be blemish free and his color was his normal pale white. Other than the fear displayed across his face, he looked his normal self.

"How is it...you...you know...fine. How is that?" Riot directed the question to Charlie and then coughed.

Charlie looked around at Isabella, Riot and Dim who all looked sickly lying on the ground. "I...I...don't know," Charlie stuttered as he helped lower Ethereal next to Isabella. "Are you all sick?" He asked.

"Well, obviously not all," Isabella snapped. "If I didn't know better I'd start wondering if you did this to us, Charlie," she spat out between coughs.

"Don't be foolish, Isabella. Where I wouldn't blame him for cursing you, we both know he'd never harm Ethereal," Dim said through wheezes, having just awoken.

"I don't understand," Charlie said. "This is the curse?"

"The forest curses any warm blooded creatures that pass through it," Listerviere stated as he flew over to Charlie and peered into his ears and looked over his face. Charlie jumped back at the sight of a dragon flying so close to him.

"Who...who are you?" Charlie questioned.

"You may call me Listerviere," the small dragon said as he landed on Charlie's shoulder and immediately jumped away after touching him.

"You are him! You are him!" Listerviere shrieked and he flew above Charlie's head and fire flew from his mouth as he spoke. Before Riot could question what Listerviere meant he had flown away up into the trees.

Chapter Sixteen
The Hero of the Cursed Forest

Charlie stood in shock first having watched the small group he traveled with become sick so quickly, then to see a miniature dragon and finally to hear the fear, no not fear, the excitement from Listerviere as he shrieked "You are him!" He stood for a moment looking up into the trees that Listerviere had flown into, but he could no longer see where he had gone. The hoarse cough from Ethereal brought his attention back to the Elf lying so ill on the ground by his feet. He lowered himself and using the sleeve of his shirt he wiped the whitish phlegm from Ethereal's lips. He noticed streaks of blood in the phlegm and without having any training in the medical field he could tell that was not a good sign for Ethereal to be coughing up blood-tinged phlegm.

Charlie sat down on his knees and let Ethereal's head rest on his leg. He let his hands sooth back her hair and felt the dampness from her brow on his fingertips. "How is this curse making everyone ill?" he questioned.

"It must be a disease curse," Riot said. "I've heard of this type of curse from my father. If I remember correctly, as long as we stay within the confines of the forest we will remain cursed until our death. How long that will be I'm not certain. It may be forty-eight hours, it may be twenty-four hours, or it may be two." Riot coughed and bloody phlegm flew from his mouth.

"Then we need to get out of this forest right away," Charlie stated. He knew it would be a challenge to guide two ill humans, a sick goblin twice his weight, a curse weakened Elf and deathly ill wolf out of the forest by himself, but he didn't have a choice. He knew he'd be able to carry Ethereal if need be. He'd improvise the rest.

Before Charlie could encourage the group to travel out of the forest Listerviere reappeared and on his back was a small creature. At closer look Charlie could see the creature's skin had the texture of tree bark. He could see bright green piercing eyes and long sharp claws like nails extending from her fingers. Her hair was black with green streaks pulling upward and outward from her head as if the wind were blowing it back. On her back were the tiniest wings Charlie had ever seen, smaller then even a moths. Charlie couldn't imagine how they would be of any use to her. Perhaps it was why she rode down on the dragon's back rather than fly herself. Charlie recalled the tale Dim had told of the wood nymphs and could only assume he was seeing one in the flesh, so to speak.

Listerviere landed on the ground next to Charlie. "Here he is! Here he is!" the small dragon exclaimed in excitement. The wood nymph fluttered off the back of Listerviere onto Charlie's knee and peered up at him.

"So he is," a seductress voice came from the feminine shaped wood nymph. Charlie felt drawn to the voice and the creature it came from and he stopped caressing Ethereal's midnight locks to reach out and touch the seductress before him.

The wood nymph did not resist as Charlie let his finger touch the rough texture of her skin. He was hypnotized by this seductress and blanked out everyone else around him. After he touched the wood nymph he let his hand drop to his knee in front of her. Her wings fluttered every five seconds and Charlie kept watch and counted between flutters letting his breathing synchronize with the flutter of her wings.

"You are his legacy. You are his blood," she whispered.

Charlie heard what she said but could not comprehend it. He just stared at her as she spoke. The wood nymph fluttered her wings and landed on his arm and from there she climbed her way to Charlie's shoulder. His eyes stayed on her and his face came within inches of the wood nymph's figure. She leaned out and placed her small hands onto Charlie's cheeks. "I'm Flit," she purred. "And you are The One. Your ancestor was responsible for this curse your friends are suffering. For many it has been a death sentence but for us it has been protection and salvation."

Charlie tried to understand what she was saying but he was so soothed by her voice he couldn't turn away or think. Isabella, Ethereal and Riot were staring at Flit as well. Only Dim seemed to be immune to her charms. "Charlie, look at me," Dim coughed out.

Charlie only heard mumbles from Dim as he continued his fascination with the wood nymph. Flit leaned closer to Charlie and let her small cheek press up to a portion of Charlie's face. Charlie closed his eyes and felt her purr her words out. "We have waited for The One to come and continue the work started oh so long ago. We need you," she purred. Flit let her hands caress Charlie's face.

"What do you need Charlie for," Dim spat out. "He is not up for hire."

Flit snapped her head away from Charlie and stared directly at Dim. "What we need from him is of no business to a fat goblin! You are an annoyance to us and nothing more, but you'll be dead soon enough if you don't find your way out of here by dusk. All of you will be dead by then. Minus The One and he will be ours then."

The few minutes Flit had released her grip and eye contact with Charlie was long enough for him to pull himself out of the seductress's trance. "Dead? No, I'll never let that happen," Charlie said as he swatted at Flit to sweep her off his shoulder. Flit tumbled down his arm and landed with a plop onto the ground.

"That's my Charlie! Just don't look at her and you'll be fine," Dim stated.

Listerviere flew over Charlie's head and landed next to Flit who was now wiping sticky black stuff off her bark-like skin. The dragon laid down his wing and Flit hopped onto it and pulled herself to

Listerviere's back. Addressing Dim Flit yelled out, "Soon your grip on him will weaken and eventually you'll be gone. The One will be here alone and we'll be here for him. We are patient. We'll wait. It's been countless years since we have seen a human," Flit chuckled "And then when we do, it's The One. How lucky we are." The miniature dragon flew up into the trees with Flit on his back. Charlie's gaze followed them until they disappeared into the thicker darkness above the forest floor. Somehow he knew they would be back.

Ethereal closed her eyes and tried to concentrate on what the others were thinking, but she found nothing of interest. She then put all her attention on Charlie's thoughts and she felt his confusion as to how he was going to save all of them. She knew if the time came she'd make that decision easier for him. She would not allow herself to be Charlie's downfall. After Listerviere and Flit had made their departure the group had managed to move forward to try and find their way out of the forest. Luckily, Isabella had made marks on the trees as they had moved through the woods. Ethereal should have thought to do that herself.

"I can't believe we are leaving without finding Henrietta," Isabella moaned as she stumbled from tree to tree leaning heavily on them for support. The blotches on her face had doubled and now pockets of pus seeped from them.

"Henrietta is not hidden here," Ethereal wheezed.

"How can you be certain of that?" Isabella asked as she leaned on a tree to take a breather.

"Didn't you hear Flit? Geez, Isabella. Don't you listen to anyone but your own big mouth?" Riot spat. "She said they hadn't seen a human in years. Thus Henrietta is not hiding here. I don't think much gets past Listerviere. He'd have seen her if she was here. Besides I think Henrietta is too smart to have come into these woods."

"So you're saying I'm stupid since I brought us into these woods?" Isabella argued.

"You called it," Riot argued back.

"This is not the time to be arguing. We need to preserve our energy to get out of here," said Ethereal as she leaned heavily on Charlie to keep moving.

"At least I was smart enough to mark the trees so we could find our way out," Isabella stated. At that precise moment the ground under their feet started to shake and the trees appeared to come alive dancing their way around in the forest. Riot and Isabella slipped from the trees they were leaning on and collapsed to the ground as their supports moved and new trees took their place. The thundering shook Charlie and Ethereal as well, but Charlie was able to keep himself and the Elven warrior on their feet, although Dim in his weakened state could not stand any longer and he fell to his knees. Elyclaw, disturbed by the motion, howled weakly.

"What was that?" Charlie asked.

"I think maybe an earthquake," Riot answered.

Isabella let out a weak laugh. "The last I knew earthquakes do not move trees around." Even in her weakened state Ethereal heard the silent "dork" at the end of that sentence.

Ethereal pulled her arm away from Charlie and stumbled to the nearest tree and let her hand run over it. She circled it then stumbled to the next one and circled it. The trees *had* moved. Of course, what better way to keep them trapped in the forest. "The marked trees are gone," Ethereal said.

"Gone? How is that possible?" She asked as she stumbled over to where Ethereal was and circled around the tree. Isabella's hand dropped in a defeated manner. "They're gone."

"Great. Just perfect. Thanks for nothing, Isabella," Riot snapped.

"What? Now it's my fault the trees moved?" Isabella asked incredulously.

"STOP IT!" Ethereal screamed. She placed her hands on either side of her head. The screaming gave her a horrendous headache. She knew better than to lose her cool, but she just couldn't help herself. The constant bickering was driving her insane. At least yelling had quieted everyone. Charlie's thoughts invaded hers and she could hear the shock in them. She'd never lost her temper around him before. It took a lot for that to happen. She had hoped Charlie would never see that side of her.

"This is not helping us. We are dying as I speak. Do you want to die this way?" Ethereal asked. No one answered her. "Charlie, you can lead us out of here."

"No I can't. I wasn't really paying attention when we came here. I have no idea where we are. And...and...I'm terrible with directions. Just ask my dad," Charlie said.

Ethereal put her hand out towards Charlie. He moved the few steps that separated them and took her hand. "You can do this." Ethereal stared into his eyes and pushed her positive feelings onto him. "You know I am right," she said.

Ethereal felt a shift in Charlie's attitude. She watched as he looked around them. "Okay, we are going *that* way," he said, pointing to his right. Without questioning him, Ethereal hooked her arm into Charlie's. As he led them to his right he pulled up Isabella with his other arm. Riot and Dim stayed glued to the trees. Elyclaw crawled along behind. Ethereal didn't think Elyclaw looked well. He was weaker than the rest of them. She couldn't imagine how Riot would carry on if the wolf died. She just hoped Charlie would be able to lead them out of the forest before the curse brought an end to anyone in the group.

Dim's mind started to feel fuzzy. He knew Charlie was speaking but he couldn't make out what he was saying. The trees before him seemed further away and he found himself crashing into them as he walked and cursing at them for jumping up and surprising him that way. His mouth was dry and he kept moving his tongue around trying to find the hidden pouches of saliva but he was never successful. He could feel the cracks in his lips and felt the pain seer through him whenever he moved them. He would surely die today. There wasn't any doubt anymore. It was just a matter of how long before death found him. He couldn't even remember why he was in this forest. Why would he ever have been foolish enough to venture into this god forsaken place? He stumbled over his own feet and fell to the ground where he was certain he saw little wood people wandering through the sticky substance. His hands stuck in the ground as did his knees, and he found himself picking at the substance having forgotten where he was or where he was headed. He felt someone push at him and it lifted him briefly from the fog in his mind. "You need to keep moving Dim. We are close, I can feel it," Charlie said. Dim looked up to Charlie who was now carrying Ethereal and Isabella was leaning heavily onto his back being dragged along. The goblin wasn't sure how Charlie was able to carry so much weight.

He moved forward again, but this time crawling. He tried to envision the end of the forest and the thought kept him moving.

Riot was crawling on the ground next to Elyclaw. Every once in a while he stopped and vomited up a spoonful of blood-tinged phlegm. He felt as if the phlegm in his throat was slowly choking him. His face felt twice its size and from the looks of everyone around he guessed it probably looked that way also. He stayed near the ground to be closer to Elyclaw whose fur was leaking a pus substance that also wept from his eyes. Riot couldn't stand the thought that he had failed Elyclaw. He should have left him in Wolf Country. He'd have stayed safe. Instead he'd dragged the wolf with him into this death trap. Where he blamed himself for not keeping him safe, he also blamed Isabella for taking them into this forest. If they made it out of here alive, he'd make sure to never follow anyone blindly again.

Riot's arms and legs were getting heavy. He figured lifting them from the sticky ground was exhausting what little strength he had left. He collapsed and rolled onto his back and stared up into the darkness above him. This was as good a place to die as any. He let his eyes travel the length of the tall trees and tried to remember what Wolf Country looked like again. The trees there were not as tall and dark as these. He tried to imagine that he was in the beauty of his own woods in Wolf Country. It would be the perfect place to die among the trees and leaves and wolves. Then he saw the flutter of orange wings. They came closer and closer and it occurred to Riot that those wings belonged to Listerviere. Of course, how foolish of them to not realize they were being followed. It was as if the small dragon was taking the place of vultures and coming to tear his carcass apart. He wanted to scream "I'm still alive! I'm still alive!" but he didn't have the energy. The wings got closer until Listerviere landed on Riot's chest. The flapping of his wings brushed against his face and Riot winced at the pain that small touch produced in him. Flit slid down Listerviere's wing and landed silently on Riot's chest. She moved towards Riot's chin and knocked her small fist onto his chin three times. Riot was too exhausted to even flinch from her touch.

"This one is almost gone," Flit said. "And just in time." She slid down Riot's arm and he watched as she jumped from his hand to the paw of Elyclaw. Riot hadn't realized Elyclaw was lying next to him. A tear formed in his eye as he saw the matted fur and still body next to him. The wolf was the only one that ever truly loved him. Even his father was too busy with his own agenda to waste energy on loving Riot. He couldn't help but feel immense sadness at having let Elyclaw down. He closed his eyes and willed himself to die.

"He is almost gone also," Flit said.

Riot tried to block out her voice. He didn't want to hear the moment by moment commentary on Elyclaw's last moments of life.

"Hey, what do you think you are doing," Charlie demanded. "Get off him." Charlie shooed Flit being careful to not look directly at her.

"It's only a matter of time until you are mine," Flit said seductively.

"That will never happen," Charlie insisted.

Riot felt a hand on his shoulder and a voice near his ear. "You can do this. We're almost there, Riot," Charlie whispered.

"I can't. Go without me. Leave me to die in peace."

Riot felt a scuffle over his chest and felt the warmth of Listerviere's breath. He opened his eyes long enough to see Charlie pushing the dragon off Riot and then heard the flapping of his wings moving away into the distance. He closed his eyes with a sigh and willed the end to come. But it didn't come. Instead he felt a tugging and pulling at his collar and his body was dragged across the ground. He felt the stickiness from the forest floor attach to his body. Every muscle hurt as he rolled over bumps and crevices in the ground. He wanted to beg them to stop and leave him, but he was too weak to even speak. Within minutes the bumping stopped and he was still once again. Then he let go and darkness took over.

Chapter Seventeen

Forerunner

Charlie collapsed down to his knees while still holding Ethereal. The Elf had lost consciousness a short while ago. Isabella had held on until they had stepped out of the woods and once there she let loose her grasp on Charlie's back and fell in a heap to the ground. Dim had managed to crawl his way out before collapsing and the true hero in Charlie's mind was Elyclaw who in his weakened state managed to drag Riot the last distance out of the forest before swooning to the ground alongside Riot.

He lowered Ethereal to the ground and gently laid her down. He felt for her pulse for the hundredth time in the last hour and was relieved to find she still had one. He sat down next to her and let the soreness in his body take over. He had managed to get them all out of the forest, but they all still seemed deathly ill. He didn't know if they had made it out fast enough. He had lost track of time in the woods and had no idea if they were in there one day or more. He looked from each of the still bodies and knew he needed to see if they were all still alive, but he needed to rest for just a minute more before getting up again. Carrying Ethereal was a challenge, but doing so with Isabella leaning onto his back was even harder. He didn't know what had possessed him to continue onward, something inside him he had never known existed before.

After a few minutes rest, he got to his feet and decided to see what he could do for everyone. As he stood he felt the ground vibrate. To him it felt like a herd of elephants were headed his way. He turned quickly and looked into the fog, but he couldn't see far enough to see what was causing the vibration. It occurred to him for the first time that with all the others incapacitated it left him the lone fighter. It unnerved him to think he was so vulnerable. He let his hand touch the sword on his belt. He knew he should feel relieved he had it for protection, but honestly he didn't think he'd be able to use it when the time came.

The vibration came to a halt and Charlie could make out figures in the fog. He stepped in front of Ethereal's body and took a stance of protection. "Who is there?"

A figure moved forward and Charlie could see it more clearly. As the fog swirled and cleared a bit, a massive creature was revealed that looked like a mix of a hyena's head on an oversized lion's body and sitting on its back was a huge goblin. Slightly behind them stood an army of goblins. Charlie had considered Dim a stout goblin, but he never realized that he was small compared to these.

Charlie's hand shook as he pulled the sword from its sheath and the blue glow surrounded the sword at his touch. "What...what do you want?"

"Charlie, my boy. Really? You're going to pull a sword on *me*?" said the huge goblin on the strange hyena lion.

"How do you know my name?" Charlie demanded.

The goblin dismounted the hyena lion and moved closer to Charlie. "Of course I know your name. I'm the reason you are here to begin with," the goblin clicked his tongue in exasperation. "I sent Dim to retrieve you! Little did I know that he would be so careless to let you be persuaded to follow these fools," the goblin swept his hands around to indicate those lying unconscious on the ground. The goblin sighed. "Dim has wasted my time traveling the land looking for you. I could have retrieved you myself faster than he did."

"You're Forerunner?" Charlie asked as his hand still shook holding the sword, but he did not lower it. There was something he didn't trust about this Forerunner. This was who Dim had brought him here to see?

"At your service," he said with wickedness in his voice. Charlie raised the sword a little higher.

"What do you want with me?" Charlie asked.

"My boy, please lower that thing. You are bound to hurt yourself rather than me if you aren't careful."

Charlie lowered the sword slightly, but didn't put it away. Honestly, he didn't know why he even held the sword. He wasn't about to use the weapon.

"I've come to help, of course," Forerunner stated.

"Help?"

"I assume your friends are not sleeping," Forerunner stated.

"No, no they aren't. They are very ill."

"Well I can help with that."

Charlie glanced from the limp bodies of his companions back to Forerunner. "How?"

"I've lived here a long time Charlie. You need to trust me."

Charlie just stared at him. The fact was he didn't trust him. There wasn't anything about Forerunner that exuded trust. He kept glancing from Ethereal to Forerunner. The weak Elf's color was still poor and her face was almost unrecognizable. The other fact that hit Charlie was he didn't know how to help them himself. He felt his best chance was Forerunner. He'd have to let go of his distrust and hope he was wrong about the oily-grinning goblin.

"I need help. So I guess I'll take you up on your offer," he said.

"That is wise! Go with Plunto," Forerunner said as he pointed towards a rough looking goblin behind him. "He'll take you to rest."

"I'm...I'm not going anywhere," Charlie stuttered.

"You need to leave me to take care of them. You will just be in the way," Forerunner stated.

Charlie let his gaze sweep one by one over his small group as they lay on the ground, stopping at Ethereal. He wanted to help, but he knew Forerunner was right and he'd just be in the way. And he was tired. He couldn't believe how sore he was. "Okay, I'll go with... Plunto."

Charlie bent down towards Ethereal and let his lips glide across her cheeks and he whispered, "Hang in there. Soon we'll be together again." When he stood up Forerunner's piercing look sent shivers through his body. He sure hoped he was making the right decision in trusting him. He kept reminding himself that Dim trusted Forerunner and Charlie trusted Dim. That had to count for something.

He walked away with Plunto, keeping his eyes on Ethereal. As he vanished into the fog his last view of the Elf was Forerunner bending down towards her and then the fog took her away.

Ethereal's eyes fluttered open and she saw the eerie fog that surrounded her. She smiled as she realized she was finally free of the forest. She never thought she'd be happy to see the fog again. She let her hands touch her face and felt the smoothness of her skin once more. She sat up and felt a wave of dizziness from the effort, but as a whole she seemed almost herself again. She checked her surroundings and saw the edge of the forest and smiled. She looked around for Charlie, but all she saw were Isabella, Riot and Elyclaw a short distance away. There weren't any signs of Charlie or Dim. She closed her eyes and tried to hear Charlie's thoughts but nothing came to her. She had been able to utilize that skill whenever Charlie was near. She was getting the feeling he wasn't in her vicinity and grew concerned he hadn't made it out of the forest. She tried to recall the last few hours, but couldn't. The last thing she remembered was being carried by Charlie. If he hadn't carried her out of the forest, then how did she get here?

Ethereal went over to Isabella and felt for a pulse. It was strong. Her facial lumps had resolved and her color had returned. Ethereal expected her to wake soon. Then she felt for Riot's pulse and his was weaker, but still he was alive. Elyclaw did not fare as well. She could not feel a pulse and he seemed cold, his fur coat matted and dingy. The young warrior

Elf bowed her head and let the sadness take over. It would have been too much to expect they'd all make it out of the woods alive.

Ethereal pulled herself to her feet and looked about again for any signs of Charlie or Dim. She focused her attention on the soft ground below her. There was a trail from the trees to Riot. His body had been dragged and at closer look it appeared the wolf was the one that dragged him. She felt tears well up and she had to block them from falling. A warrior was not supposed to cry. But somehow knowing Elyclaw sacrificed his life to save Riot touched her heart. She placed her hands on the wolf's matted fur and rubbed. "You are a hero, Elyclaw. Braver than many humans and Elves combined."

The she-Elf looked at the trail from the trees to where Isabella laid. There were two prints there. Those were Charlie's. Ethereal was certain of that since they were of those strange shoes he wore. He had allowed them to fit him in more suitable clothing for their land, but he had insisted on keeping his footwear. They had strange tracks on the bottom and they fit those on the ground, first near Isabella and then stepping a few feet away where she had awakened. And then there were the drag marks behind his feet where Ethereal assumed Isabella had dragged behind Charlie having leaned against him as they had made their escape from the forest.

Ethereal looked around further and found more tracks coming from the woods, and could only assume they were Dim's. From their appearance she assumed the goblin had been crawling. A few feet from the forest the tracks stopped and Ethereal could see where Dim's body had lain. The strange part was the two sets of prints going up to and away from his body. They were not human. Ethereal looked at the prints closely and determined they were goblin footprints. Though they were bigger than Dim's they were definitely goblin. Ethereal stood up and followed the tracks into the fog, stopping when they became muddled with what Ethereal could only assume were hundreds of goblin footprints meshed together. A prickle went up and down the warrior Elf's spine. She had a bad feeling about this. So far she couldn't find Charlie or Dim and there were all these goblin footprints around them. She knew Dim had brought Charlie here to take him to someone named Forerunner. Could this Forerunner have gotten tired of waiting for Dim to bring Charlie to him and sought The One out on his own? Before she could further that thought she was brought back to the moment by Isabella.

"They took him. Didn't they?"

The she-Elf turned and considered the shaky young human, who was standing slightly behind her staring at the tracks. It hadn't taken Isabella very long to deduct what had happened here, and it came as no surprise to Ethereal that she had figured it out so quickly. She had after all survived alone in this land for many years. She certainly had come across goblins before, so would likely know what their footprints looked like. "Yes, I believe that is what happened."

"You know what we have to do now, right?" Isabella asked.

"Find him."

Riot felt sore and groggy. He couldn't quite make out where he was at first. The darkness threw him off as to his surroundings. If it wasn't for the flames from the fire, he'd be engulfed in blackness. A fire? Where had that come from? He turned to his side and looked around. No one was near the fire. He turned to his other side and lying next to him was Elyclaw. His wolf had made it! Riot felt relief as he put his hand out to connect with his dear best friend. As soon as he touched him, however, he knew something wasn't right. He struggled to a sitting position and leaned over his friend, trying to detect his breathing. It only took him a few moments to realize Elyclaw was completely still. He felt a panic overcome him and he punched hard on Elyclaw's chest. "Breathe, damn it, breathe!" He felt a hand come down on his arm and he brushed it away. "Breathe!" he screamed through every punch he made to the wolf's chest.

"Stop, Riot. He is gone," Ethereal stated.

Riot ignored her and punched a few more times. "Breathe," he said in a weaker voice. "Breathe." Ethereal's hand touched his arm again.

"He is gone, Riot. He died saving you," she added to try and ease the pain.

Riot stopped pounding on Elyclaw and sat back onto the ground. "Saving me?"

"He dragged you from the forest," Ethereal said gently. "He died a hero. There is not a more noble way to die."

Ethereal's hand slid from Riot's arm to his hand and he felt the strength from her as she squeezed. He still felt confused by the whole ordeal. The last thing he remembered was willing himself to die and then something was dragging him along the sticky forest floor. He had thought Charlie had dragged him from the forest, but now he realized it was Elyclaw. His loyal wolf friend had saved him. He felt guilt swell up in him. He should have been stronger. He should have been the one to save Elyclaw. He'd let him down.

Isabella walked into the camp's firelight, her arms full of wood. She halted when she saw Ethereal holding Riot's hand. "You're awake."

Riot clambered to his feet and surged toward Isabella. His expression of calm changed within seconds at the sight of the young human. "You killed Elyclaw!" He shouted. He went to charge, but the sudden, intense emotion of the moment brought on a bout of dizziness and he stumbled to the ground. "You...you wolf killer!"

Isabella's stance never wavered. "What's he babbling about? I didn't kill anyone."

"You took us into that forest. Ultimately you are responsible for Elyclaw's death! You'll pay. Believe me some day you will pay." Riot put his face in his hands as the tears started to come. He struggled to fight them off, but they came anyway.

"Trust me. You'll pay."

Chapter Eighteen
The Magic Writer's Legacy

Dim's head jerked back and forth and the pounding brought him awake with a start. His body bumped along and he felt the aches and pains from bouncing over a rough surface. He sat up startled. The shock registered on his face as he saw the cage he was sitting in. Then even further shock when he looked outside the cage and saw the cause of the bumping motion, which were three hyenions pulling his cage along. And the rider of the lead hyenion was none other than Forerunner.

Dim shook his head to clear it. He focused his eyes by squinting and looked again, and again he saw Forerunner. How had he gotten here and why would he be caged up? He crawled to the left side of the cage and peering out saw several goblins marching along beside and behind the cage.

"Hey Snotbreath," Dim bantered. "Why am I in this cage and how did I get here?"

"Shut up, Dumb brain," came the banter from the goblin. "You're a prisoner here and prisoners are not allowed to ask questions."

Dim laughed at the goblin's statement, but stopped short when the goblin didn't return the laughter. "Are you serious? Do you know who I am?"

"A traitor," was the answer.

"A traitor? I don't think so. I'm Forerunner's chosen one. I'm his courier. I'm his trusted servant."

"You're his traitor. You've stolen his goods."

"Stolen his goods? I've never stolen anything from Forerunner," Dim answered back.

"Then explain those stolen goods," The goblin stated as he pointed behind Dim to the far back corner of the cage.

Dim turned and looked into the back of the cage. It was darker back there and he hadn't noticed before but there was a figure slumped down in the corner. He crawled backwards to get a better look and stopped when the figure became clear to him. "Charlie?"

Cowering in the corner was Charlie. He was bruised and swollen and he looked timid and scared. Dim wondered how those injuries had happened to him. "Charlie?" he said again.

Charlie backed away from Dim as the goblin moved closer. "What happened to you?"

"I didn't want to go. I didn't want to leave them. He made me."

"What are you talking about? Who made you leave who?" Dim asked. The young human wasn't making sense.

Charlie pointed straight ahead and Dim followed the direction of his gesture. "Forerunner. You mean Forerunner did this to you? Don't be stupid Charlie. Forerunner wouldn't do this to you. He's the one that wanted you. He wants you to help the humans just like Isabella does. Speaking of Isabella, where are the others?"

"He left them. He made me leave them."

Charlie was speaking crazy. Why would Forerunner make him leave the other humans? He wanted to bring the humans together. He sent Dim to find Charlie to set that in motion. He'd never leave the other humans behind.

"You're speaking crazy, Charlie. I think you've received one too many bumps to your noggin."

The boy shook his head and lowered it to his bent knees, covering them with his hands. "Ask him if you don't believe me," he mumbled.

Ask him, he would. Dim moved to the front of the cage and yelled out towards Forerunner. "Chieftain...Chieftain!"

Dim didn't receive a response. The hyenions kept moving forward and the cage kept its jerking motion as they moved. "Chieftain, it's your loyal servant, Dim."

The cage came to a sudden halt and Forerunner dismounted from the hyenion and strode to the mobile prison. In one sudden movement Forerunner shoved Dim away from the gaps in the bars of the cage. Dim fell backwards falling hard.

"Chieftain, I don't understand! It's me, your loyal servant Dim!" The confused goblin said as he sat stunned on the cage floor.

"You are no loyal servant of mine. You are a traitor! A turncoat! A defector! I gave you my trust and you spit on it. You are nothing better than a rodent," Forerunner spat at him. "I sent you on a simple errand, and you never returned. Where do I find you? Among the humans and the Elves. You are a traitor."

Dim sat stunned. How dare Forerunner question his loyalty! He'd been nothing but loyal. If Forerunner only knew what he'd been through these last few weeks. Dim brushed himself off and stood up again.

"I've been nothing but loyal to you! I've done all you asked of me. You did not want Charlie harmed and I did all I could to keep him safe. He wanted to go with the humans and I couldn't stop him without force. I've done all I could to keep him safe and try and find a way to bring him to you without harming him. You wanted him to help the other humans, so I didn't see the harm in being with them. Charlie would need them to bring back magic to the land, so I assumed since that was your plan then it wasn't doing any harm to gather them for you as well."

"My plan has changed. I no longer have use for the other humans. The boy Charlie is all that is needed," Forerunner stated.

"I don't understand. Why do you no longer want the other humans as well?"

"I've had a better offer for Charlie. One that I could not pass up. Soon you'll see. After we have delivered him then I'll take care of you."

Deliver Charlie? Deliver him to whom? Dim couldn't imagine who else wanted the young human. The other humans obviously, but Forerunner had already dismissed them. Who else would know what to do with a magic writer? Then it occurred to Dim. Czar. Of course, Czar. But for him to believe Forerunner was delivering Charlie to Czar then Forerunner was not who Dim had believed he was all along.

"You can't possibly mean you are delivering him to Czar?"

Forerunner slammed forward into the bars and snapped his sharp teeth at Dim. "How dare you question *my* decisions? You are nothing but a gnat that I could squash in a matter of seconds if I so desired," drool seeped down his chin and his teeth gnashed together as he spoke. "I was foolish to think a runt like you could perform this task. But no longer will I need to be shadowed by your dumbness. You will no longer be around to embarrass me." Forerunner pulled himself away from the bars and straightened himself up. "But first I'll take care of the young human. Your time will soon come."

Charlie moved from the shadows at the back of the cage. "Hey, I'm nobody to you. I'm just a simple boy from another land. I'm of no use to anyone here no matter what you've heard."

"Don't be stupid. Do you think I would carelessly pluck you from your life if I didn't have proof that you are the next magic writer? Magic runs through your blood," Forerunner said.

"No, I'm just a simple boy from another land. My blood is my father and mother's blood and they do not know magic. You are mistaken."

Forerunner moved back to the bars of the cage and stuck his face between them again. "I'm never mistaken. Your father's blood is thick with magic. It oozes from him when he bleeds."

Charlie's head shook. "That's not possible. He's just a simple teacher. Nothing more and nothing less."

"A teacher of *magic*. Yes, I see you don't know. Well this should be fun," Forerunner practically growled. Charlie just stared, shock apparent on his face as Forerunner continued. "This world was rich in magic at one time. Whoever controls the magic controls Pulchritude Amity. The magic writer determines who will and won't learn magic. He writes it. He binds it. He teaches it. It's always been a human. No one can explain why. It just is what it is. The grandfather was a wise magic writer beloved by many. His son was stronger and a more capable magic writer, but he unlike his father was selfish. He did not share the magic quite so freely. He was not prepared for Czar's attack on the human race. He did not prepare them well in magic and Czar easily defeated many of your kind. And what did the magic writer do?"

Charlie stood mouth gaping and listened helplessly. Dim had heard some of this story before, but he did not know the full story, so he also stood quiet, listening in shock as Forerunner spun his tale.

"No answer I see. He fled of course. What else would a stupid cowardly human do? He fled with his wife and their two bawling snot-nosed brats."

Forerunner stood silently watching as Charlie and Dim were putting the pieces together. He let his hands slide down the bars of the cage as he watched their expressions change, and he began to smile.

"Ahhh, I see you are processing what I'm saying now. Yes, the coward fled with his family to another world and with him escaped other humans from our land...more cowards. Your kind is dying in Pulchritude Amity because of him. He left them to defend themselves without magic as a weapon, and without a magic writer to write more magic and teach it to others. He left them defenseless."

Dim looked at Charlie with concern. He knew if he figured out who Forerunner was talking about the realization would crush him.

"Personally, that should play right into the hands of the rest of us, but little did we know that without a magic writer our world would start to die as well. Eventually this world will cease to exist. I knew we needed to bring back the magic writer. But he's a coward and would never return. So the next best thing was to bring back his blood. His son." Forerunner stared deeply at Charlie as he spoke and it gave him great pleasure to see the truth sink into the quivering young human.

"Yes…yes…I see you know now. You know who I speak of. The coward is your father."

Chapter Nineteen
Henrietta Finds a Home

H enrietta navigated the tunnels with ease. It was hard to believe that several years ago she had gotten lost so easily among these tunnels. Now she knew them like the back of her hand. Her life had changed so much in the last few years. The war Nefarious had waged on the humans had cost her both her parents and a brother and sister. She was still struggling as to why she was the one that survived. She was fortunate to have had wise, kind, caring parents and a close relationship with her siblings. She missed them every day.

But she was also thankful for the time she had with them. Her mother had been an herbalist and her father had been an inventor. Henrietta had found both so fascinating and had learned as much as possible from both parents. Where she loved learning about herbs and their healing powers, she was fixated on inventing. She spent hour upon hour with her father inventing contraptions. Some worked and some flopped. Henrietta learned as much from the inventions that failed as she did from the ones that succeeded. She had been enamored with her father, and she still felt his loss in her heart deeply.

She crawled through the tunnel to her cubby hole and went about her nightly routine. First she started a fire in the fireplace and then she pulled off her apron, wiping the dust and dirt from her tired hands. She put a kettle over the fire and started her dinner of broth with a dash of nettle and dash of basil. She had taken her mother's herbs when she fled, and they had come in handy. They were one of the few things she had taken besides her father's Clipper Dapper which when used properly could determine the truth in any situation. Henrietta had found much use for that contraption, and it made her feel closer to her father just having it with her. She had also managed to shove several books of her parents into her knapsack before leaving home as well. Most were written by her parents. One was a journal of her father's progress with inventing and Henrietta had found that useful, but a few of the books were just stories her mother's mother had written. Sometimes after a long day of inventing she liked to pull one of those books out of her knapsack and read. It helped her keep connected to her family.

She poured herself a bowl of broth and placed it on her small table in the corner and pulled up the chair and started to eat. While eating she replayed again in her mind how she came to live here with the gnomes...

Henrietta's parents Abdul and Nakima had just called the family for dinner when the minotaurs attacked the village. They became aware of the attack when the wooden home next to them had gone up in flame and Papu and Salma had run screaming from the sudden inferno. Papu had burned to death in front of his family. Salma, who was carrying their one year old baby girl, had watched her husband die a torturous death before she was run through the heart with a spear. The baby girl had fallen and been abandoned by the attackers but was later trampled by the herd of villagers fleeing the minotaurs. Henrietta had stared in fear at the sights she saw through their window. Her parents, on the other hand, who had been prepared for such a day grabbed knapsacks already packed and handed them to her and her siblings. Bruno, her older brother had grabbed his sword from the corner of his room while Kima her younger sister had grabbed her raggedy doll her mother had made for her first birthday. Henrietta had salvaged some books and at the last minute had swiped from her father's bench the Clipper Dapper and shoved it into her knapsack. They had then fled the home through the back way and gotten lost among the herd of people fleeing in panic. The last she had seen of her home were the flames licking hungrily at the walls from a rare fireball thrown from one of the neighbors who had been fortunate enough to have learned magic. Missing its intended target, it had alighted on their home instead.

Henrietta had cried that night as they made camp along with a few other couples that had made it away alive. Akila and Isabella had been among those. They later met up with Riot and Elyclaw who had lost his father during an attack on their farm. They felt lucky to have Akila, Isabella's mother, with them. She and Isabella were the only ones that knew magic in their group. They had moved from camp to camp traveling most of the day. She hated the traveling. She liked staying in one place, but her mother told her not to complain. They were blessed to still be alive when most of their village had died, so she kept the complaints to herself.

Henrietta's little sister had been the first to die. She had never been healthy, and although her mother had tried several different herbs to help Kima's immune system, nothing had seemed to work. Her mother had packed her large array of herbs in her knapsack and when Kima fell ill she had used several combinations of them to ward off the illness. Two days later, however, Kima had still succumbed to death. Henrietta had believed Kima's death was what killed her mother, for she never fully recovered from it. A week later Nakima had been found dead after a particularly long, cold night. Abdul had said it was the sleeping death sickness. Henrietta had said it was a broken heart. She had taken the herbs from her mother's knapsack, not for the healing powers they possessed, but to hold on to something of her mother so she could keep a memory of Nakima with her. She had also found her sister's raggedy doll, and she had stuffed that into her knapsack as well. Her brother would have said she was too old for that doll, but she could still smell her sister's sweetness on the toy and she wanted it close. She had slept with it every night.

They had then continued their flight for several more weeks, traveling through one abandoned town after another. They had eventually stumbled across a troop of minotaurs a month later and had overheard them speaking about Czar the Evil, who had captured any and all humans that had displayed knowledge of magic. According to the beasts, when he couldn't extract the magic from them he had them killed. Now Czar no longer wanted the humans kept alive. He had ordered all humans executed.

After running and hiding for almost a year, they had realized they were the last of the humans left in Pulchritude Amity. They had overheard hints and bits of information from another minotaur troop that some humans had managed to escape Pulchritude Amity, but Czar could not figure out how they had eluded him. He was certain the magic writer had been among those. Akila had rejoiced at this news.

Then one night Akila had awakened with a scream, startling them all from their slumber. She had fearfully told them of her vision. It was a recurring one she had dreamed since she was a child. The One had finally arrived and with him he brought beauty and magic back to the land. But before that could happen something terrible would occur. Something dark and vile would wage a war so evil on the land as to bring much sorrow and much pain, more than had already been wrought on the humans this last year. Isabella had dismissed her mother's dream, but Henrietta had hung on every word. She had believed her. She had feared the evil to come, but with it would be a new day, one that was happy again. Henrietta had anxiously awaited the arrival of The One.

That afternoon they had stumbled upon a squad of hunting minotaurs. They had been ill prepared and her father and brother had been killed while fighting so she and the others could escape. Akila had taken her, Isabella and Riot under her protection and they had found a hidden cave where they stayed for days. Little Henrietta had sat surrounded by the others and frustrated she could not be alone to grieve the loss of her family. But Akila was kind and she had provided

Henrietta the comfort she needed and the space she craved in which to grieve. When Riot and Isabella slept, Akila would sit with her and tell her stories of the magic writer and his family. She had told her he had a young son and magic seeped from him. All you had to do was be in his presence to feel it. Akila had also revealed to Henrietta that she had known the magic writer very well. She had shared with the young girl the feeling in her heart that the magic writer and his family were among those the minotaurs claimed had escaped.

She had then told Henrietta about the Book of Potions and the Book of Truths and the Pen of Knowledge. She had explained how they worked and what was needed to piece them all together. She then had explained how the Pen of Knowledge would glow and magic would surge once again when The One was in Pulchritude Amity.

"The Pen will want to be connected with the magic writer. It will guide you to him when the time comes. I'm telling you this Henrietta because you are vital to the process. You are the keeper of the knowledge. The magic writer will need you. Most might think you are small and weak, but I know differently. You are strong and brave and will help heal this land. You'll help bring our race back to Pulchritude Amity numerous and strong."

That was the last night they had sat and talked. The next day she had given Isabella the Book of Potions and Riot the Book of Truths and Henrietta the Pen of Knowledge and told them to guard them and stay alive. Henrietta had left Akila that day as did Riot and Elyclaw. She had now become truly alone.

She finished her broth and placed her spoon in her bowl, both of which were made from gourds, the bright yellow kind the gnomes loved to work with so much. She rested her head in her hands and continued her remembrance of finding her new home...

At first she had wandered the land mostly staying hidden in small places or living in the trees. Her small stature had helped with her survival. She had seemed to go unnoticed most of the time. But she had grown so tired of traveling from place to place and had longed for somewhere to call home again. One day she had found just that when she noticed a strange creature in a field adjacent to the tree she had used as her sleeping quarters. He, or so she had assumed from the little being's mannerisms, looked like he was actually smaller than her! He had been wearing nondescript brown clothing with a soft, pointy green hat framed by two very large ears. The ears had seemed to match his feet, which were much larger than they should be for a creature this size. He had been fussing with a strange device, apparently trying to make it fly. Henrietta had spent hours watching from her tree and couldn't help but laugh at the tantrums he had displayed when the device had failed to soar into the air. She had wanted to be down on the ground with him helping the poor creature, and she had been fairly certain she knew what was missing to help make the device fly but she hadn't been sure this creature would not harm her. After another hour of watching the failed attempts, Henrietta had made a decision to take a chance with this creature. He certainly had not seemed dangerous.

She had silently climbed down from the tree and had come up behind the little creature that had been very intent on his project. "Do you want some help?"

The small being had jumped higher than Henrietta would ever have thought could have been possible for such a miniature creature and she hadn't been able to stifle a giggle. She had later found out this creature was a gnome.

The gnome's eyes were wide open with fear etched upon his face. "I…I," he had mumbled, backing up towards his thingamajig and darting his head back and forth, looking for a way to escape.

"It's okay! I'm not going to hurt you. I'm an inventor! Like you. I thought you could use my help," she had asserted.

The gnome had kept backing towards the invention that was now just sitting still on the ground a few feet behind him.

"Look...see," Henrietta had stated as she had pulled her father's Clipper Dapper from her knapsack to show the little gnome and reassure him that she meant him no harm.

The gnome had stopped his backward movement and his eyes had squinted as he looked at the contraption in Henrietta's hands. She had been able to sense he was curious about what she held, but he hadn't moved any closer towards her. She had slowly inched her way towards the gnome as she explained, "This is a Clipper Dapper. I invented it a few years ago. Well, actually my father invented it. I just helped him. But still I was part of making it. It's a truth clipper. You clip it on like this," Henrietta had clipped it on each side of her head. "And you push this dapper button here," she had pushed it and lights had glowed from the clippers on her head. "Then you can tell if anyone within a ten foot radius is telling you the truth." Henrietta had managed to get within a few feet of the gnome. His eyes had been fixated on the glowing lights around her head.

"You want to try it?" Henrietta had asked.

The gnome had nodded anxiously. Henrietta had smiled and pulled the clippers from her head and handed the contraption to the gnome. He had eagerly attached the clippers to either side of his head and had then cautiously turned on the dapper button. The lights had glowed from the clippers.

"See now you can ask me anything and you should be able to know if I'm telling the truth," Henrietta had stated.

The gnome had cleared his voice a few times before speaking. "Are you here to harm me?" he had asked.

Henrietta had smiled at the simple question. "No. I'm traveling through looking...well looking for a home."

The gnome had smiled a quick smile and Henrietta had assumed the device had processed her answer and given him the knowledge it was the truth.

"Don't you have a home?" he had asked.

Henrietta's smile had faded as she thought about her answer to the second question. "No. I don't have a home anymore. My home was destroyed as were my family. I've been traveling for so long now and I'm scared and tired and…lonely," she had whispered that last part.

The gnome's smile had vanished as she spoke. They had stood in silence for a few minutes as the gnome looked distinctly uncomfortable. He had then taken the Clipper Dapper off his head and turned the dapper button off and handed the device back to Henrietta. She had taken it and deposited it into her knapsack.

"I can help you with your invention, you know. I wasn't lying."

The gnome had looked behind him at the device sitting on the ground before answering. "That would be nice of you. Thank you."

Henrietta and the gnome, whom Henrietta had learned was known as Dipper, had worked on the device for a few hours and when they were done she had helped him test it again and he had squealed with delight when the contraption flew. It was the best afternoon Henrietta had spent in years. She had been carefree and light again without worry for those few hours. It had been as if she was back in her father's inventing room working on whatever crazy device he had created that day.

When they had finished, Henrietta had gathered her knapsack and stood awkwardly next to the gnome who had still (literally) been glowing from the success of his invention. "Well…ah…It was nice meeting you, but I better move on. It will be dark soon and I need to find a safe place to camp."

The gnome had nodded slowly and put out his hand to Henrietta. She had extended hers and they shook. Then she had turned and headed north and away from the open field. Before she had gone too far, however, she had heard Dipper's voice.

"You could stay with us," Dipper had said. "You could stay with us and call it home."

Henrietta had smiled broadly as she turned quickly to face Dipper again. "I would love that."

She had remained here now for several years and she had never regretted that decision. She lived underground in the tunnels with the gnomes. Her small stature had come in handy here where she found their cramped quarters cozy. She loved the gnomes and their hair-brained ideas. She had learned so much from them and they in turn had learned from her the knowledge she had shared with her father. It was nice to share that knowledge with someone else. It helped keep her father alive in her heart.

But she hadn't forgotten what Akila had told her several years ago. Every night before heading to sleep she took the Pen of Knowledge from the knapsack and tested it, looking for any signs of change, but to this day none had occurred, yet she kept faith that one day it would.

She cleaned up her bowl and stowed it in her cupboard, then went to her knapsack and pulled out a book to read before going to bed. Then she did her nightly check of the Pen of Knowledge. She casually pulled it from the knapsack and stopped short. It was glowing red. A bright red and it tugged in her hand leaning to the left. Then she heard the whisper. "Go North." She stood staring at the tugging pen in her hand and realized it was time.

Chapter Twenty

A Chance Encounter

E thereal stood in the shadows and watched Riot bury Elyclaw. He used a sharp stick he had found to dig up the dirt, and he talked to the wolf as he dug.

"I remember when I first laid eyes on you. I was only eight. I'd known nothing but work and loneliness. Father wouldn't let me join the other kids in combat and warrior school. He never allowed me to be tested for Enchantment Academy. He said it was a waste of my time to do either. He said so few kids made it into Enchantment Academy. Father was bitter about it. He said the current magic writer didn't want to share the magic, so why waste our time having me tested. I believe father was more upset that his friend dismissed his friendship when he took over magic writing. He thought the magic writer grew too big of a head for the small brains he had left in it. I suppose that was father's way of saying the magic writer had outgrown their friendship. Those that didn't make it into Enchantment Academy went to combat and warrior school. Father said that would be a waste of my time and he could teach me all I needed to know about combat. So I stayed home. At first I was terribly lonely, but then I found you. You were so small then, just a pup. I remember your mother had been killed by a hyenion as were the rest of her litter, but you somehow had escaped. It was a rainy day. I remember my father had sent me out to hunt for dinner, but I couldn't bring myself to kill anything. I was heading home trying to think of what I would tell my father when I heard the first whimper. I wasn't sure if it was truly a whimper or not. The raindrops masked most of your sounds. I'm so glad I decided to explore the area. You probably would have died if I hadn't. And there I found you among the bushes shivering and scared. I couldn't leave you there to die, but I knew my father would never agree to keep you. So I brought you back and hid you from him," Riot laughed as Ethereal assumed he was picturing that day in his head. He had almost finished digging the grave by now. "I was so young and foolish. Somehow I thought I'd be able to hide you from my father feeding you scraps from my dinner. It never occurred to me that you'd get so big. I remember waking one morning to the thundering shouts from my father when he found you. I'd never run so fast in my life. I found him standing with his dagger prepared to kill and there you were whimpering in a corner. You could have killed him, Elyclaw," Riot smiled again. "But you didn't. You were too kind a soul to harm another."

Riot had finished digging the grave and he moved over to where Elyclaw laid letting his hand rest on the wolf's paw. "It took a lot for me to convince my father that you weren't a danger. I think what finally sold him was my using guilt on him. I know he felt guilty about not letting me do any schooling and keeping me trapped and lonely at our home out in the middle of nowhere. He finally conceded and let me keep you."

Riot became quiet and let his hand rub back and forth across Elyclaws motionless paw. Ethereal suspected he was fighting back tears and she felt a little like she was invading his privacy, but she couldn't make herself leave.

"Now look where we are. I'm following a human around Pulchritude Amity having forgotten where I came from and you," Riot choked back a sob as he spoke. "And you, you're gone. Why did you save me? Why didn't you just leave me dead in that forest? I'm as good as dead now without you." Riot lowered his head and placed it on Elyclaw's chest. Ethereal could hear the occasional sobs and he lay that way for a while. She was about to leave him to his privacy when he slowly stood up and cleared his throat. He cradled the still form of the wolf in his arms and slowly placed him into the grave. She was surprised how strong Riot was as his muscles flexed while Elyclaw was in his arms.

Riot stood above the grave and looked down at his friend. Taking his hand he placed it over his heart and said, "You are my hero. You'll never be forgotten, Elyclaw. You'll always live in here. Goodbye my friend." Then he covered the grave with dirt.

They had been walking for hours. Isabella was in the lead. Ethereal was behind her and Riot was taking up the rear. He hadn't said anything when he came back from burying Elyclaw. He had just kicked dirt over the fire letting some of the dirt spray onto Isabella who was sitting nearby. Then he picked up his knapsack and said, "Let's go." They were the only words he said all day. Isabella had jumped to her feet immediately. She hadn't been certain whether he would continue with them, so she was thrilled to see he was willing. She didn't want to do anything that would cause any more tension between them.

So they had headed north, the direction Ethereal had determined the goblins had gone, but soon they lost the trail. Isabella stopped to confer with the others to see what they thought might be the best direction to head. After the forest debacle Isabella was slightly shy in making those decisions on her own.

"Do you think we should keep heading north?" Isabella asked.

Riot turned his back on Isabella. She tried to let that go unnoticed, but she was starting to get annoyed with his tantrums.

"If we continue north we'll be heading into Nefarious' territory. It will be almost impossible to avoid his minions there," Isabella continued.

"I sense that north might be the right direction, though," Ethereal answered.

Riot stared into the trees on either side of them and eventually strode away into the tree line to their right. Isabella shook her head as she watched him go.

"I don't know how much longer I can stand being around him, Ethereal. He's acting so childish. After all Elyclaw was only a wolf."

Ethereal bent down and scooped some dirt into her palm and held it out to Isabella. "Is this only dirt?" Then she walked to a tree on her right and let her other hand run down the trunk. "Is this only a tree?" Then she leaned forward until her hand could reach Isabella and she let her hand touch her shoulder. "Is this only a human?"

Isabella just stared at Ethereal trying to understand her point. "This dirt can be used to plant seeds in. This tree relies on the dirt to grow and gives us lush fruit to eat. You pick that fruit to eat to have strength to protect and defend the ones you love," Ethereal tried to let that sink in before continuing. "Elyclaw was a part of this dirt and tree and land and even a part of what we need to exist. He was not only a wolf. At least not to me and certainly not to Riot."

Isabella looked down at her feet as she let that sink in. To her a wolf was nothing more than a meal to eat. She'd never thought of animals as any more than that. It was hard to wrap her brain around the fact that Ethereal and Riot thought of them differently. She decided for the sake of peace she'd try and understand what Ethereal said.

A sudden commotion arose from the trees to their left, and both warriors turned to look, hands on their weapons. Riot came back out from the trees dragging with him a struggling figure that appeared to be none other than a dwarf. Isabella's eyes went wide and she readied her spear, preparing herself for what might come next. She had heard dwarves no longer existed in Pulchritude Amity. She was shocked to see a very small jolly looking creature with a beard down to his knees and only five hairs sticking up from his head. His eyes were a shocking bright green and his ears stuck out abnormally.

"Where did you find this...this thing?" asked Isabella.

Riot addressed Ethereal as he spoke and once again Isabella felt that familiar annoyance creep up in her.

"I heard something in the woods when she," Riot let his head nod towards Isabella to indicate who he was referring to, "was blabbing on about what to do. It's a good thing I went in there since I found this little guy smoking a pipe and listening." Riot shoved the dwarf into their midst and he stumbled but managed to stay on his feet.

"Good day," the dwarf said as he bowed at Isabella and peered strangely at Ethereal. "I was not listening as this one may have you believe. I was having my daily smoke when you happened to come by on the trail. What would you have me do? Cut my ears off so I could not hear you?" the dwarf gave a sneer towards Riot when he said that.

Isabella peered at the strange dwarf as she tried to consider what he said. She looked at his fingers and saw they were dirt and tobacco stained, collaborating his story of smoking. "What are you doing out here all alone?"

"I was out here looking for tobacco. I've been running low and this is the only area left that I know of where tobacco still lives," he answered.

"Do you live near here?" Ethereal questioned him.

"I live here and there where ever I can find a home," he answered. "Why is it any business of yours where I live?" he sneered at Ethereal.

Isabella had heard that dwarves did not have much love for the Elves. The small being confirmed that with his answer. Isabella drew his attention back to her and away from Ethereal. "By chance did you see a troop of goblins come through this way today?" She left out the part about a human being with them. She wasn't sure she was ready to divulge that information to this strange dwarf.

"I don't think you should be asking him that question." Riot snarled.

"I'll ask him any question I want," Isabella snapped back. She was sick of his moping arrogant attitude. If he didn't like what she had to say than he could leave, but she'd make sure he'd leave without the Book of Truths.

"Whoa now, calm down," the dwarf said using his hands in a

shaking motion to indicate calm down. "Hmmm, a troop of goblins. I saw some foxes earlier. Hmmm, and I saw a pickling and her baby go into those woods over there," the dwarf pointed to the woods on their left. "But that is all for today."

"Today? Were you out here yesterday, by chance?" Isabella asked.

"Hmmm, yup, yup...I sure was," the dwarf stated and looked away when Riot gave him a questionable look. "I smoke a lot of tobacco, okay," he answered to try and appease Riot's doubt.

"And did you see anything yesterday?" Riot snapped at him.

"I don't like how you speak to me. I don't think I want to answer you," the dwarf said with hurt feelings.

Isabella gave Riot a dirty look before addressing the dwarf. "Don't mind my friend. He is cranky if he doesn't get enough sleep." Isabella put her hand on the dwarves' arm to get him to look at her and using her sweetest voice possible she asked him. "Did you see any goblins yesterday?"

The dwarf looked at her and she sensed he was weighing whether to answer or not. Then he spoke, "Yup, yup...I sure did. A troop of them came through here. And in the lead was a massive goblin on top of a hyenion pulling some sort of a cage." Then the dwarf leaned his head closer to Isabella, so Isabella leaned in as well. "And you know what he had in that cage? A human," he whispered. "Yup, yup, he sure did. A human alright. I didn't think any of you existed anymore and what do I see in the last day? Not only one human, but," the dwarf turned towards Riot than back to Isabella and she couldn't help but think he was counting, "three humans. Aha, aha. What a strange few days it's been."

"Were they heading north?" Ethereal asked. Isabella nudged her to stop her from speaking. The dwarf didn't acknowledge Ethereal's question, so Isabella repeated it.

"Were they heading north?"

"Hmmm, yup, yup, they sure were," he answered.

Isabella would have to decide one way or another whether to

believe the dwarf. He seemed truthful and she couldn't imagine a reason why he'd want to lie to her. She turned her attention to Ethereal. "What do you think? Should we continue north and hope we can find their trail again?"

"I think the dwarf has no reason to lie to us. We should go north," Ethereal stated.

"Hey doesn't anyone think maybe I should have a say in all this?" Riot retorted.

"I didn't think you cared one way or another what we did. After all a few minutes ago when we were talking you wandered off into the woods. Obviously, you didn't care then," Isabella snapped.

Isabella saw Riot ball his fists up and tension shadowed his face. She tightened her grip on her spear, preparing for a fight.

"Nope, nope...not good. Nope, nope," the dwarf stated.

"What are you babbling about now?" Riot practically yelled at the dwarf.

"You should never fight with your own kind. Nope, nope. That's rule number one."

Isabella couldn't help but smirk at the dwarf. She was beginning to like him against her better judgment. At least he was better company than Riot.

Riot's hands relaxed and Isabella was willing to loosen her grasp on the spear, but she remained wary.

"I agree with you Ethereal. We should go north," Isabella spoke to the Elf, but her eyes stayed on Riot who was now picking his fingernails with a small knife he had pulled from his belt. He seemed bored with the conversation. "We're likely to encounter minotaurs once we enter Nefarious' territory. Do you think we can handle that?"

Before Ethereal could answer the dwarf piped in. "Yup, yup...we will be just fine."

"What do you mean 'we', shorty? You don't think we'd be stupid enough to bring you along with us?" said Riot snidely.

"Yup, yup. I saw them. I know where they went…yup, yup. You need me," the dwarf said.

"Maybe we should bring him with us. He did see them and maybe he could help us find them. Plus four is better than three," Isabella said to Ethereal.

The Elven warrior was nodding obviously weighing the options.

"You can't be serious?" Riot directed that towards Ethereal. "You're not really considering taking this midget with us?"

The dwarf stepped sideways onto Riot's foot and he yelped out in pain pulling his leg up and holding it with his hands as he hopped around. "You stupid midget," he yelled as he stopped his hopping and balled up his hands in a fist and aimed a solid blow at the dwarf's head, who ducked and threw his own punch, hitting Riot low and doubling him over. Isabella stood back and smiled slightly at the dwarves' quickness and precision, actually impressed. And honestly, she just enjoyed Riot getting what he so rightly deserved.

"Stop! Now!" Ethereal said as she intervened between the two. "This is not helping Charlie," she directed towards the angry wolf boy. "We need him Riot. We are short in numbers as it is and we need as much help as we can get." Then she turned her attention to the dwarf. "You need to be tolerant. We are willing to bring you along with us since you said you know where they went, but I will not allow you to stay if you bring discord to the group."

The dwarf nodded his head to that, "Yup, yup…you're right." Then he put out his hand to Riot in peace. Riot stared at it resentfully and rather than shake it he spit towards it missing his palm by inches. Isabella wanted to slap him upside the head, but she held back. Ethereal was handling the situation and she needed to let her take the lead between these two.

The Elf stepped forward and put her hand on Riot's arm and made him face her. "This is not helping, Riot. You cannot be picking fights with everyone. I know you are grieving and you have a right to grieve, but you need to pull it together for now. We need you." Riot kept his gaze on the ground between them as she spoke. "*I* need you," she whispered. Isabella watched Riot's gaze move up to Ethereal's when she said that. Isabella shook her head. She couldn't make out the she-Elf. She seemed smitten with Charlie, but then when she was with Riot she seemed to have a connection there as well. She couldn't respect someone that played two people off on each other. Besides, she was an Elf and Elves were not supposed to be with humans. That was...well that was wrong. Isabella knew how important reviving the human race was going to be and that wasn't going to happen if an Elf came between that. But for now, she'd let it go. Their main focus was Charlie and then finding Henrietta. She'd deal with Ethereal later when the time came.

Riot's jaw unclenched and he stood upright. "If the consensus is to bring this...dwarf with us then I won't fight it. As long as she," Riot pointed at Isabella, "isn't making that decision on her own."

"Then it's decided. He'll join us at least as far as when we find Charlie," Isabella stated. She put her hand out to the dwarf. "Welcome to the group," she paused as she realized she didn't even know his name. "What is your name?"

"Judas," he answered.

What an odd name, Isabella thought. "Well, welcome to the group, Judas."

Chapter Twenty-one
The Glowing Pen

Henrietta decided to wait until the next morning before choosing what to do. She would pull the Pen from her knapsack to see if it was still glowing and if so, she'd have to leave the comfort of her home. She couldn't help but feel sad at the thought. She loved it here. The gnomes had been so kind to her and accepted her as one of their own. She would now have to face the outside world again and she was not looking forward to it.

Sleep, however, didn't come easy for Henrietta. She tossed and turned thinking about traveling again. Once she finally fell asleep, she had images of her mother bending over a pot hanging over a fire and stirring it. "Remember Luv, garlic juice will help it heal as will lavender," her mother kept repeating. Then she disappeared and her father appeared bent over his bench tinkering with some invention. "You see, Little Pickle, inventions can be your enemy or your hero. It's the user that decides that." Then he disappeared and Akila was there sitting by a fire in the cave next to Henrietta. "The Pen of Knowledge will want to be connected with the magic writer. It will guide you to him when the time comes. I'm telling you this Henrietta because you are vital to the process. You are the keeper of the knowledge. The magic writer will need you. Most might think you are small and weak, but I know differently. You are strong and brave. You will help heal this land. You'll help bring our race back to Pulchritude Amity numerous and strong."

Henrietta woke startled from the dream. It had been a long time since she had dreamed of her parents. She wrapped her arms around her and rocked back and forth with her eyes closed trying to keep the comforting feeling of her parents with her as long as she could.

When their image faded from her mind she let go of her arms and opened her eyes. Her vision found her knapsack on the floor near the table and she willed herself to go over to it. Her hands shook as she found the pen and pulled it out. Part of her wanted the pen to be dull and not glowing anymore, but another part of her wanted it to be shining a brilliant crimson. The bright red glow lit up the room as she pulled the pen from the safety of her knapsack and it wiggled in her hand leaning to the left. The whisper "north" emanated from the pen. Henrietta closed her eyes and said a silent prayer for safety as she knew she would now be leaving her home.

She carefully packed the pen back into her knapsack. She busied herself with breakfast and then went about preparing what little she owned for a journey. She crawled through the tunnel to the main chamber in the underground gnome city where she found several dear friends of hers gathered discussing some sort of invention they were currently working on.

"Henrietta, tell Imbode that a pulley system on the Sinker Pullinko will just not work." Her friend Lens stopped short when he saw the grave look on Henrietta's face. He immediately turned his attention to her, wobbling over and taking ahold of her hands. "What's the matter child?" he asked.

"Remember when I first arrived here I told you there would be a day I would need to leave?" she said as she tried to swallow a sob.

"But, my child, why? Have we not provided for you well enough?" he asked.

"You've all provided for me more than anyone could ever have expected. You are," she cleared her throat and choked on the sob that stayed stuck in her throat, "You are my family now."

"Then I don't understand why you must leave us," he said wiping the tear that had fallen down Henrietta's face.

"I know you don't. There is someone I need to help. Someone I need to find. And now is the time to find him," she said.

The gnome looked behind him at the others gathered in the room and felt certain he could speak for them when he said, "Then we'll go with you to find this someone."

Henrietta's eyes got wide with surprise that he would offer up such help. "I...I could not ask that of you. It would be too much to expect."

"Is it too much to expect your family to help you? What sort of family would we be if we left you to fend for yourself in this dangerous world?" The gnomes behind him nodded in agreement.

More tears fell from Henrietta's eyes as she was overwhelmed by the gnome's kindness, and she stared down at her feet in an excess of emotions. "It might be dangerous to find who I'm looking for. It wouldn't be right for me to ask you to sacrifice your life for a cause that does not affect you."

The gnome lifted her face until her eyes met his. "What affects you, affects us. And the last I knew we have never shied away from danger. After all we do have our inventions to protect us!" he said smiling at her.

"Are you sure?" she asked.

The gnome looked back at the other gnomes behind him again and they all nodded. Looking back at Henrietta he smiled and stated, "Yes we are sure."

Chapter Twenty-two
Bubbles in the Night

Charlie's stomach growled as he sat in the dark corner of the cage with his head resting on his bent knees. He heard the crackling of the fire in the distance and the goblins constant bickering. Occasionally, the bickering would evolve into a blown out fight and one of the goblins would end up unconscious on the ground.

He smelled some sort of meat roasting and hoped it wasn't one of the unconscious goblins being cooked. The smell made saliva pool in his mouth.

"Do you want some Whickle weed?" Dim offered up to Charlie.

The goblins had found it amusing during the days travel to throw patches of dirt with Whickle weed attached at Dim. They seemed to enjoy calling him traitor and Dirt Pile and so many other cruel names. The smack of the dirt hitting the caged goblin on various parts of his body drew laughter from their captors. Charlie found them despicable and felt partly to blame for what was happening to Dim. If he had gone with him to see Forerunner to begin with, none of this would have happened. But his hairy goblin friend had the last laugh. Whickle weed was edible and he'd been munching on it all night. It had a foul smell and a bitter taste, but at least it was something to eat.

Charlie on the other hand hadn't been able to concentrate on food. He had spent the day and now most of the night in the back corner of the cage mulling over what Forerunner had told him. How could it be possible his dad was the magic writer? He just couldn't believe it. He knew his father well. He was a kind generous man who worked hard every day to help provide for the family. He didn't show any signs of knowing magic. What those signs would be, Charlie didn't really know, but it still just seemed crazy that his own dad would be the magic writer. He was also hard pressed to believe his father had been lying to him all these years about where they came from. But then again, there were the boxes in the basement. The mysterious boxes that Charlie had always wanted to get a peek at. The boxes his father said held the past. Could he have been talking about this past?

He didn't want to believe his father was the magic writer. To believe that he also had to believe his father was a coward. How else could you describe what the magic writer had done? He had fled his people and left them here to die a terrible death. His father was not a coward!

But in his heart of hearts he suspected what Forerunner had told him was true. How else could he explain why he was to be the next magic writer? Of course, they could have the wrong person. After all he hadn't written any magic so far. That was likely, Charlie thought, but deep down he suspected they were right and he was the next magic writer. He could not really explain so many feeling the magic in him in any other way.

Charlie let out a trembling sigh. He was going to have to face what his father had done. He just wasn't ready to do that right now. At this moment he needed to face the situation he and Dim were in and try to think of a way out. But when it came down to it, he had no idea how to get out of a cage in the middle of who knows where.

"You can't beat yourself up over this, Charlie. You are not to blame for the decisions your father made," Dim said, attempting to console him. "Moping now isn't going to help our situation. What I do know about Forerunner is he keeps his word. If he says I'll be executed then I'll be executed. And if he plans to feed you to Czar, you can guarantee that will happen."

Charlie didn't lift his head from his knees and tried to ignore what Dim was saying. He didn't want to face the fact his hairy green friend would be dead soon and he'd be a prisoner of this Czar person before long. He wished this nightmare was over and he was home with his family. But then again, could he ever be relaxed and comfortable with his father now?

"Hey, Knucklehead. I've been betrayed by my own kind and about to be put to death. You don't see me pouting." Dim slapped the side of Charlie's head lightly to get his attention. "Snap out of it already."

Charlie snapped his head up to face Dim. "You've been betrayed by your own kind? Are you kidding me? My father is supposedly a coward of a magic writer. I've been living with him my whole life and wouldn't you think I'd know that by now? I'm the one that has been betrayed!"

"Oh boo hoo hoo. Get over it already! Just because your father didn't tell you everything about him doesn't mean he's betrayed you. Have you ever thought that maybe he ran to save you? To save your mother and sister? You might think that is cowardly, but others would find that heroic."

"Heroic? He left hundreds if not thousands of humans to die! And for what? To save me and my family? How can I ever live with that knowledge?"

"You'll live just fine. Trust me. You're being dramatica," Dim stated.

"Dramatica? You mean dramatic. Gosh, say it right or don't say it at all," Charlie said snidely.

Dim turned his back on him and sat staring out the cage. Charlie felt a bit ashamed he had ridiculed his goblin friend. He hadn't meant to. Dim after all had only been trying to help. He stared through the flickering firelight at the back of the hairy green goblin and felt guilty.

"Hey, Dim, I'm sorry. I didn't mean to…"

Charlie never finished his apology. A big bang shook the ground under them and Charlie slid backwards in the cage slamming into the opposite wall next to Dim who also flew forward face first into the cage bars.

"Wha…what was that?" Charlie stammered.

The goblins started shouting and pointing to the woods behind them and some of them went storming off in that direction. Forerunner could be heard shouting commands. "You five head that way! Bring back what you find! The rest of you stand guard in case anyone makes an appearance!"

Another big bang shook the ground again and this time Forerunner had a hard time keeping on his feet. The hyenions made a mournful growl as the noise agitated them. Charlie hooked his hands around the bars to keep from sliding around the cage and stared out into the darkness to see what was causing the commotion. Dim took a stance next to him doing the same. "I've never felt anything like that before," the goblin stated. "But if Forerunner is shaken than it must be something big."

A third bang snuffed the fire out and they were engulfed in darkness. Charlie tried to adjust his eyes to the sudden blackness to see what was out there. The first sign of anything out of the ordinary showed up around the group of goblins standing guard around the encampment. Flowing out of the darkness appeared a round, white object, roughly the size of a giants head, hovering around the guards. It glowed eerily in the dark night. At first he thought there was only one, but soon he could vaguely see hundreds of the floating white spheres. They wafted and hovered in the air, wavering ghostly in front of the goblins, who were mesmerized by them, as were the two caged captives. They reminded Charlie of bubbles, and he smiled at them as they floated over their captors. Dim reached out through the bars of the cage to touch them, but they were too far away from their mobile prison. A few goblins reached out towards them as well, and they popped, spraying liquid around and on the goblins, who screamed in pain as the liquid hit them in the face and burned holes in their skin. A mist appeared where the popped bubbles had been, making the night murky and decreasing what little visibility there had been.

"Don't touch them," Forerunner screamed at the goblins. "Guard the prisoners!"

A few of the goblins tried to stumble back towards the cage, but they collided into more bubbles as they staggered and the screams could be heard from all directions as the liquid sprayed onto their faces. The fog grew bigger as more bubbles collided into the goblins and soon all the area was covered in a ghostly vapor, including the cage. Charlie could no longer see Dim, but his goblin friend grabbed his arm and forced him to the floor so they could avoid any bubbles above their heads.

Then came the buzzing and snapping near Charlie's head and he let his hands go up to his ears to cover them from the noise. He felt fear creep over him as he realized whatever was causing this deadly-sounding disturbance could be worse than the goblins.

The buzzing and snapping continued for a few more moments as Charlie tried to block out the screaming and commotion of the goblins as they were attacked by the spray. He no longer heard Forerunner making commands and he could only hope the bubbles had gotten to him as well.

After the buzzing and snapping ended he felt hands take hold of his arms, trying to lift him. He struggled, fighting them off. "Knucklehead, what are you doing!?" shouted Dim, reaching towards the boy. His gnarled hands came into contact instead with a small leg, and Dim knew instantly this wasn't Charlie. With a snarl he grabbed tightly to the leg and yanked. He was rewarded with a shrill yelp. The grin on his face was wiped away suddenly when he felt a very hard thump on the back of his skull, and stars floated in front of his eyes. A second whack caused him to release the small leg and he groaned as he fell back to the floor of the cage. Charlie, still struggling with something on his other arm yelled. "Dim! Dim, what's happening!? Are you okay?" But the din and noise of panic was far too loud, and he could barely hear himself. Well, they weren't going to get him that easily, and he prepared himself to start swinging. From slightly behind him and to his left he heard muffled voices. "Stop struggling. We're here to help you." Then he felt something being shoved over his head and onto his face and he panicked. The panic faded within moments as the item covered his face and Charlie realized he could see. And standing in front of him were the strangest little old people he'd ever seen. And next to them stood a single small girl with a small club in her hand. They all wore the same strange contraption over their faces. Obviously it was some sort of night mask that could see through the fog. The girl smiled through the contraption as she realized Charlie could now see her.

"We need to go before the Blisters are gone and the fog lifts," she said to Charlie.

He looked to his right and stood shocked as he realized that the bars had been cut away to leave an opening. He couldn't believe his luck that this girl and her friends had come to save him. She reached out to grab his hand and step out of the cage. Charlie stopped mid step.

"My friend Dim...we can't leave him," he said.

The girl stopped and looked down at the dazed goblin lying near Charlie's feet. "Are you speaking of this beast?" She asked stunned.

"Yes, I won't leave him," Charlie said stubbornly.

The gnomes and the girl looked at each other and she shrugged her shoulders at them and they shrugged theirs back. "We did not bring another mask. You'll need to guide him if you want to bring him along. It won't be easy to bring a cumbersome goblin with us, but if you insist, then he must come with."

"I insist," Charlie stated. He could never leave Dim to the fates of the goblins. He leaned down to his hairy friend and said, "Take my arm, Dim and don't let go. I'm getting you out of here." The goblin grasped his arm and didn't ask any questions as they followed the girl and her friends out through the fog and into the forest leaving the chaos of the goblins behind.

Chapter Twenty-three

Deluded and Concluded

E thereal took the lead for a while. Isabella took up the second position followed by Judas with Riot bringing up the rear. Ethereal wanted to get away from the bickering. Riot and Judas bickered and Riot and Isabella bickered. She felt like she was supervising a bunch of children. She was tired of dealing with it. Leading the group gave her the opportunity to concentrate on finding Charlie. He was the only reason she remained with these crazy humans. And besides, in normal circumstances she'd never travel with a dwarf. Her mother would be surprised with her allowing the dwarf to come along. Ethereal knew it was unlikely that Judas could be trustworthy. In her opinion, dwarves as a whole couldn't be trusted. They looked out only for themselves. She had only decided to allow him to come with them because she wanted to keep an eye on him, and of course there was the small chance he knew where the goblins had taken Charlie, but so far he hadn't helped much. He spent the majority of his energy fighting with Riot. Ethereal could hear them now bickering over whether Bamble seed was edible.

"Yup, yup, I'm telling you I ate a whole seed and as you can see I'm still here walking and talking," Judas argued.

"You probably only *think* it was a Bamble seed. I'll guarantee it wasn't. My father's friend ate one and a small tree sprouted from his head and slowly leaked a poison from the roots killing him within a week. There is no way you ate that Bamble seed and lived to tell about it," Riot stated sarcastically.

"Well maybe your father was loopy on the brain...yup, yup... there is no way a tree would sprout from anyone's head, nope, nope," Judas said.

Riot reached out and gripped Judas by the arm. "Are you calling my father crazy?"

"If he is seeing trees sprout from people's heads then yup, yup," Judas said making a stance.

"Stop already," Isabella said sweeping Riot's hand from Judas' arm. "Bamble seeds and trees sprouting from heads. I think you two are the crazy ones!"

Ethereal stopped in her tracks and looked back at the three. They certainly found the most inane subjects to fight about. "Shhhh...," she said. "I think I hear something up ahead. We do not need to draw attention to ourselves."

Riot shoved Judas who let his hands slap in the air in a continuous rolling slapping motion towards Riot as Isabella tried to separate them. Ethereal turned away from them and rolled her eyes. She was traveling with a group of infants. She leaned forward and listened intently. Riot, who had obviously stopped his childish fight with Judas, came up behind her and leaned forward as well.

"You heard something?" Riot whispered.

Judas came up on her other side. "Yup, yup, I hear it too." Ethereal tried to pretend they weren't there and continued to listen.

Isabella moved in next to Judas. "I don't hear anything," she said.

Ethereal sighed. "Maybe we would have better luck if all of you ceased talking."

She listened again. This time she heard the swish of splashing in the distance. There was some sort of body of water to their left and from the sound of it there was someone in the water.

"Do you hear that?" She whispered towards Riot.

"Yeah. It's water."

They looked at each other and Riot smiled for the first time in a long time. "It's water," he said louder this time and before Ethereal could stop him Riot took off towards the sound.

"No, stop Riot! It might not be safe!"

Riot continued on towards the sound and whooped, pumping his fist as he went. "Water, yeah!"

Judas starting running after, and with his small legs ran faster than Ethereal would ever have imagined possible. "Water?" he questioned.

Ethereal closed her eyes and longed for Charlie to be here and make it worth her having to deal with these three. Isabella touched her shoulder. "Shouldn't we go after them?" she asked.

"Yes, I think we better."

Henrietta immediately liked Charlie. All she had to do was look into his face to know that he was a kind soul. And Akila was right, just being in his presence she could feel an air of magic exuding from him. He was what they needed to bring back magic and humanity to Pulchritude Amity. She was also delighted her gnome friends had successfully used their Blister Begetter to help rescue the magic writer. They hadn't successfully experimented with the contraption before, so none of them knew whether it would be successful or not. She was concerned the acid bubbles would endanger Charlie, but the gnomes had figured out the dimensions beforehand while they spied on the goblins earlier that evening from the trees and were able to direct the acid bubbles away from where Charlie was jailed.

Three gnomes, Tripsel, Whikered and Lens, were leading them back home. Henrietta walked along side Charlie chatting while Dim followed closely behind. The rest of the gnomes brought up the rear. Henrietta noticed Dim was eyeing the gnomes behind him as if he expected them to pull out a sword and stab him. She found it amusing.

"So how did you find yourself in the company of a goblin?" Henrietta asked.

"The name is Dim," the hairy green goblin interjected.

Henrietta looked back at Dim and smiled. "Sorry, I didn't mean to offend you…Dim. So how did you find yourself in the company of…Dim?" Henrietta asked Charlie again as she eyed the goblin and smiled. Dim grumpily frowned back at her.

"Dim is the one who brought me to Pulchritude Amity," Charlie stated.

"Ah, so we have him to thank for your wonderful arrival," Henrietta looked back at the goblin again. "Thank you, Dim! We are in your debt," she said through a smile.

Dim tried frowning again, but instead his mouth got twisted in an awkward way, halfway between a smile and a frown, and Henrietta had to suppress a laugh. Dim sure was cute! She never could believe a goblin could be cute.

"I didn't do it for you," Dim grumbled. Henrietta chose to ignore that comment.

"Where are you taking us?" Charlie asked.

"Home," was Henrietta's simple response.

"Oh no," Dim practically yelled. "Do you know what I had to go through to get him here? I'm not about to let you take him back home."

"Not his home, silly. My home," Henrietta let her hands extend over the gnomes walking with them. "Our home."

"Your home? So you live with these…with these…people?" Charlie asked.

"Yes," Henrietta said as she skipped around Charlie with delight. "I live with these *people*. They are gnomes! I can't wait to show our home to you. Wait until you see their inventions! They're amazing." Henrietta stopped walking and leaned in close to Charlie and whispered, "But I'm not sure if that one will fit into the tunnels. It will be difficult for him, I'm afraid," she said as she nodded her head towards Dim.

"I'm not deaf," Dim growled. "So are you saying I'm too fat for these…these odd little creature's home?"

Henrietta giggled at his description of the gnomes. "They're gnomes, silly. And I'm not saying you are fat. I'd say stout and strong and maybe too stout and strong for the tunnels!" Henrietta started walking again and Charlie and Dim followed suit.

"You know I'd love to see your home," Charlie said. "But, you see, I have friends out there," he let his hand sweep the horizon. "And they are looking for me. Or at least I'm pretty sure they are." He looked at Henrietta. "I believe they were looking for you as well before the goblins found me. You're Henrietta, aren't you?"

"Hmm, what friends are you talking about?" Henrietta asked slyly.

"I believe they are friends you may know. Isabella, Riot and Elyclaw and then of course Ethereal."

Somehow it didn't surprise her that he mentioned Isabella, Riot and Elyclaw. They had the other items the magic writer needed, but she didn't know anyone named Ethereal. "Ethereal? Who is this Ethereal?"

"She's a Crystal Elf that pushed her way into joining us," Dim said.

It didn't get past Henrietta that Charlie gave Dim a dirty look. "She didn't push herself into joining us. She came along to help protect us."

Henrietta looked from the goblin to the human with curiosity. Dim just scowled at Charlie. She sensed there was more to the Ethereal story, but for now she'd let it go. She figured she'd never get the full story with Dim hanging around.

"Well, that's actually awe inspiring that she was willing to risk her life to protect you. You'll have to tell me how that came about when we have more time! Yes, I am Henrietta, pleased to meet you! So you said they are out searching for you and for me? Do you know where you last saw them?" She asked.

"We had just gotten out of the Cursed Forest," Charlie said.

Henrietta stopped walking immediately as did the gnomes and they all turned and stared at Charlie. "You went into the Cursed Forest and made it out alive?" She asked.

Charlie looked from one gnome to the next until he stopped at Henrietta. He fidgeted and she could see how uncomfortable he was with being stared at. "Ummm, yeah."

Henrietta was speechless. She had never known anyone to come out alive from the Cursed Forest.

"What? Why are you all staring at me?" Charlie stuttered.

Dim touched Charlie on the shoulder. "I think they are all surprised we are still alive," he stated.

When Henrietta found her voice again, she stepped forward and let herself grasp Charlie on both arms. She felt a tingling in her fingers at that mere touch and that brought a smile to her face. "I'm so amazed and thankful you are alive," she said. "I'm not sure how that is possible, but nonetheless I am amazed! Are you certain the others fared so well? Perhaps they did not survive like you and Dim."

"They were alive when I left them, but I suppose they may not have survived," Charlie said. Henrietta saw the worry skirt across his face at the thought of the possibility. She looked around at her gnome friends, who had gathered into a group around the two humans and the goblin. They smiled and nodded at her encouragingly.

"Well, I suppose we need to find them then. Whether dead or alive, we need to know," said Henrietta.

Charlie nodded. "I couldn't possibility go back with you without knowing that."

She let go of Charlie and looked at Dim. "Do you agree?" She asked.

Dim grunted and kicked at the dirt before answering. "Whatever Knucklehead wants to do is what I'll do."

"Okay, then it's decided! We'll find your friends!"

Chapter Twenty-four

Intimate Things

Isabella and Ethereal came bursting through the trees to find a water-fall crashing down into a small pond. They hadn't seen a big body of water since they had left Crystal Valley. The small group had managed to quench their thirst from the few narrow streams that still flowed through Pulchritude Amity. There were few big bodies of water that had not dried up, so seeing this pond was a treat. Riot had already stripped down and jumped into the water. Judas stayed on the edge of the pond and splashed in it like a child. Isabella and Ethereal took stances at the edge of the water and looked around. The human warrior trusted Ethereal's instincts, and if she thought there was someone who had been in the water earlier, then she felt certain there must have been.

"Do you see anything?" Isabella asked as she readied her spear and scanned the area.

Ethereal did the same, readying her bow with a nocked arrow. After a few moments the she-Elf answered her. "No, but I'm sure I heard splashing coming from this area."

Isabella stayed ready for battle as Ethereal lowered her bow and started to scan the ground near the water banks. The she-Elf stopped about twenty feet away and lowered herself to the ground letting her fingers play over the wet surface. "Isabella, over here," she said as she motioned the young human warrior over to join her.

Isabella kept her spear readied and walked sideways to where Ethereal crouched, never letting her eyes leave the tree line. "Did you find something?" She heard Riot splashing around and knew he was stripped down to his skivvies and she didn't want to see any of that, so she turned her eyes to the ground where Ethereal crouched.

"You see these tracks?" she asked Isabella. "I believe they are dwarf tracks."

"Dwarves?" She let herself glance over towards Judas for a quick look to see if he was listening, but all she saw was Judas now sitting in the shallow water letting the mud and water sweep over his legs. She looked from Judas to the tracks Ethereal was pointing out. "How can you tell?" She asked.

"See the size of the boot tip and the strange oblong curve in the middle? Those match Judas' print almost perfectly."

Isabella looked closer and saw the shapes Ethereal was pointing out. She was surprised that the elven warrior had noticed Judas' boots. Isabella hadn't paid any attention to them, but then again she had spent too much time refereeing Riot and Judas to notice such a small detail.

She lowered her voice as she spoke to Ethereal, "Do you think these are friends of Judas or do you think they might be of danger to us?" She had already become fond of Judas and didn't want to see that relationship strained.

Ethereal whispered back, "It's hard to tell. All I know is dwarves are rarely what they seem to be." She stood and scanned the tree line again before letting her gaze settle on Judas. "We need to keep this to ourselves for now. They could have been dwarves that just found this water for bathing and drinking like we are or this could be something more. We can't blame Judas for what hasn't happened. For now we stay alert."

Isabella nodded. She could feel the adrenaline rush through her body at the thought of a fight. But Ethereal was right. They could easily have just been dwarves that were wandering through here and found this body of water and like Riot and Judas they had enjoyed a bath and drink before moving on. But she couldn't chase the feeling it was more than that.

Riot slowly walked out of the water leaving Isabella shocked at his lack of modesty as he walked by both her and Ethereal not the least bit concerned if they stared or not. She couldn't help but notice that Ethereal watched unperturbed by Riot's lack of clothes. Isabella however felt heat rise to her face as she watched his lean body glistening with water as he walked by her.

"We should camp here for the evening. It's late and we'd be fortunate to have a water source tonight as well as in the morning," Riot said, shaking excess water from his long hair.

Judas stomped over towards them filthy with mud stuck to his clothes and feet, his boots in his hands. "Yup, yup, I agree."

Isabella couldn't believe Judas agreed with something Riot said. She looked towards Ethereal to see what her opinion was on staying here for the night. She wasn't certain it was a good idea if the Elven warrior thought dwarves were lurking in the woods nearby.

"If that is the consensus, then we should camp here," Ethereal said as she gave Isabella a quick glance. "I will take first watch."

"No, I will," Isabella said. Riot and Judas looked from one to the other and Isabella could feel Riot's watchful eyes staying on her longer than normal.

"Is there something we need to know?" he asked.

"Ummm, well," Isabella started.

"No. Everything is fine. I just think we need extra protection tonight since I would assume a body of water such as this would attract many predators," Ethereal stated.

Isabella took Ethereal's cue and let the subject drop. She hoped Riot's gaze would leave her face though. She was getting the feeling he didn't believe anything they were saying.

"Yup, yup. I have no troubles with you two taking watch. I'm bushed." Judas plopped down on the ground and pulling out his pipe, filled it with tobacco and started to smoke.

"Perhaps you could collect some firewood," Ethereal said to Riot. He pulled his gaze from Isabella to the she-Elf. "Sure," Riot said hesitantly as he turned and walked to the tree line.

"Hey, aren't you going to get dressed?" Isabella looked perplexedly at the young wolf boy as he continued to walk over towards the woods.

"I'm just collecting firewood! Give me a break," Riot yelled over his shoulder. "Besides, I like to air dry," he added to himself.

"Shouldn't one of us go with him?" whispered Isabella, shaking her head at Riot's behavior.

"I suppose you are right. I think it should be me since you two cannot seem to talk without fighting." Ethereal trotted off after Riot leaving Isabella with the dwarf.

She stood behind Judas for a while watching the smoke billow from his pipe. She wondered where he came from and if there were many more dwarves like him.

"Why don't you just ask me already," Judas said.

"W-What?" Isabella stammered.

"About the footprints and whether or not I know anything about them."

Isabella walked over next to Judas, but didn't sit down with him. She wanted to keep her spear ready just in case. "Footprints?" She wasn't sure how he knew about the footprints.

"Yup, yup, do you not think I would recognize the footprints of my brothers?" Judas asked.

Isabella felt stunned that Judas was admitting he knew about the tracks. She squinted down at him, trying to determine if he was serious. "So the footprints are from your brothers?"

"Yup, yup...well actually not my real brothers. But they are dwarf footprints. You think I wouldn't notice them when I came down to the pond?"

Isabella didn't think Judas was observant enough to recognize anything let alone footprints, but she didn't want to tell him that. "If you noticed them right away, then why didn't you tell us about them?"

"Isn't that what I'm doing now?"

He was telling her now, but she suspected that he would have hidden this information from them if possible. "You noticed Ethereal looking at them and that's why you mentioned it, right?"

"Nope, nope. I waited until the others left because I wanted to tell you. I trust you. Yup, yup."

"Tell me what?" Isabella asked.

Judas waved for Isabella to sit down with him. She looked around uneasily before deciding to join Judas on the ground, but she still kept the spear ready. Judas whispered, "I know these dwarves that once were here, yup, yup. They are evil dwarves. They no longer side with what is good in this world. Nope, nope." Judas paused for a moment before continuing and his voice got lower as if he was certain he could be overheard. "They side with Czar."

Isabella searched his eyes, looking for falsehood. What she saw seemed sincere. "Are you telling me the dwarves are now siding with Nefarious?"

"Yup, yup."

"Then why aren't you with them?" Isabella suspiciously asked.

"I stayed here. I won't side with a...human killer," Judas whispered the last few words. "The other dwarves were persuaded with gold and silver to do Czar's dirty work."

Isabella stood up and backed a few feet away from Judas. She positioned her spear towards the pipe smoking dwarf. "How do we know you aren't with Nefarious as well?" She asked.

Judas raised his hands up to his face to ward off Isabella's spear tip. "Why would I tell you this if I was with Czar? I'd run. There is nothing that is holding me back. I despise my brothers for turning their backs on the rest of us for gold and silver! Please don't kill me, nope nope."

Isabella watched as his hands in front of his face shook. He didn't seem like he was lying. And he was right, he could have run rather than stay and tell her about the other dwarves. Isabella lowered her weapon and put her hand out to help him up. Judas accepted the hand and stood up next to her.

"I believe you," Isabella said. "I believe you."

Before Judas could speak, Riot and Ethereal came storming out of the trees running at breakneck speed. Riot tossed an armful of wood he was carrying to the side and yelled "Prepare for battle...prepare for battle!"

Fear took over Judas' face and Isabella had to nudge him and say, "Get your sword ready," before he would move. His shaking hands grasped his sword and Isabella readied her spear and looked around them for the enemies. Night was falling quickly and she was hoping she'd be able to see what was coming before the darkness took over everything.

Riot skidded to a stop a few feet from Isabella, but Ethereal stopped closer to the trees and pulled out her bow. Riot, no longer dripping wet in his skivvies, reached down and grabbed his sword out of its scabbard, and Isabella could see the fear in his face as well. "Bet you wish you put your clothes on now," she taunted. Riot gave her an evil glance. Ethereal on the other hand was steady and sure of herself and Isabella felt a bond with the she-Elf in their need to fight. She felt confident in her skills in combat, but she suspected Riot and Judas would be of little help. She was happy for the first time since Ethereal joined them that the Elven warrior was with them.

Isabella anticipated hyenions or minotaurs, but what came crashing through the trees was a large group of dwarves all wearing the red and yellow band of unity that Czar Nefarious' minions wore. These must be the dwarves Judas had spoken about. She quickly glanced towards the dwarf and saw the look of recognition in his face, and his shaking became almost uncontrollable.

The dwarves came through the trees screaming Czar's name. Ethereal took aim and fired, her arrow piercing the chest of an axe waving dwarf. She quickly nocked another arrow and let it fly, sending another dwarf to the ground. The Elven warrior quickly fired a third time and the arrow hit its target, putting another dwarf out of commission.

The dwarves were small but fast, and Isabella realized the Elven warrior would not be able to get another shot off before the dwarves were upon them, so she moved up next to Ethereal and assumed her stance, crouched slightly with her spear lightly balanced on her right thigh. She steadied herself as the dwarves approached and felt the excitement of battle course through her veins. She whispered to no one in particular as the first dwarf attacked. "Time to die, little minions." And she weaved her spear towards her target.

Chapter Twenty-five
The Magic Is Revealed

Henrietta never stopped talking. Charlie wasn't sure if she had been lacking for human contact all this time or if she naturally talked a lot. He could tell she annoyed Dim, but Charlie found listening to her comforting. There was something about her that reminded him of Kassie and he really missed his sister. After having spent the last several weeks with Riot and Isabella, Henrietta was a refreshing treat. But Charlie's heart ached for Ethereal. He could feel her presence in every beat of his heart, so he never felt totally without her, but he longed for her touch. He tried not to think about the possibility of her not having survived the Cursed Forest. He needed her. He felt certain, however, that if she were no longer alive, he somehow would have known deep down inside.

The first part of the day was spent getting as far away from the goblins as possible though Tripsel was certain the goblins would be in too much pain for the next few days to follow them. Dipper however wanted to make as much headway as possible from the goblins just in case a few of them had not been sprayed with the painful Blisters.

Then they had to change directions after Charlie had told them he needed to find Isabella, Riot, Elyclaw and Ethereal. They had been moving southwest, but after Charlie had mentioned he'd last seen them coming out of the Cursed Forest, Henrietta had redirected southeast. She was the only one in the group that knew where the Cursed Forest was. The gnomes rarely ventured from their home. They were not adventurous creatures, so they were willing to follow the directions Henrietta gave them. The gnomes seemed to adore her. Charlie could feel the connection between the girl and the small

creatures. She cared for them dearly as if they were family. He blink-
ed away the sudden moisture in his eyes, and they stung from the salty
tears that were forming. He missed his own family very much right
now. Then he thought of his father and he wiped his eyes in disappointment. He knew some day he'd have to face what he had learned
about his dad. He looked over the trees of the forest as the last of the
daylight faded from view.

"Henrietta," Charlie said.

The young lass twirled around when she heard her name, "What
Charlie?" she said enthusiastically.

"Do you know anything about my father?"

Dim shot a quick warning look towards him, but Charlie ignored
it.

"Your father? Ummm, I don't think so? Should I know your father?" She asked.

Charlie looked at Dim and saw him wrinkling his hairy eyebrows
and pursing his lips as he slightly shook his head, trying to quiet him and
Charlie could tell the goblin obviously didn't think he should be telling
her too much about his father. The hairy gremlin turned his back to
the girl as he mock stretched his hands over his head. "Tread carefully,"
Dim whispered to him. "You don't know if you can trust her."

Henrietta looked from Charlie to Dim and back to Charlie. He
couldn't tell if she had heard Dim or not. If she had, she didn't let on.
Somehow looking into her eyes he was drawn back to the last time he
had seen Kassie and he couldn't help but trust her. "I understand he
was the last magic writer," Charlie said.

Dim's shoulders slumped and he shook his head, looking down at
the ground in front of him as he mumbled "Knucklehead."

"Ahhh," Henrietta said. "No, I didn't know him, but I knew of
him!" Charlie's disappointment must have been evident on his face
since Henrietta stopped walking and reached out to touch his arm.
"Why do you ask?"

"I just…I just found out things about him that I didn't know and I was hoping someone could help me put those pieces together," he said.

"I'm sorry, Charlie," Henrietta said as she let her hands soothingly rub his arms. "I wish I could do that for you, but I don't think what I know of him would help much." There was a pause in the conversation and then she added, "But I know where you could find out more about him!"

Charlie brightened up hearing that information. "Where?"

Before she could answer, they heard crashing sounds to their left in the woods. A few moments later an eerie shrilling shout echoed out of the trees, and Charlie froze at the unmistakable sound. A warrior's battle cry. Ethereal.

Without thinking Charlie turned towards the din and started running. "Ethereal!" he shouted. He quickly plunged into the darkening tree line and disappeared into the forest.

"Wait! Stop!" Henrietta yelled at Charlie. The moon was not out yet but the stars were already burning bright, and she could still make out the boy's form as he worked into the trees. But Charlie kept running. He ran as fast as his feet could carry him and when he suddenly crashed through the trees into a clearing, he gripped the pommel of the sword at his hip. He was thankful Henrietta had grabbed it from the ground near one of the goblins when she had saved him. He didn't know if he could use it but he knew he'd have to try. He couldn't leave Ethereal in danger. As he glanced around the clearing and took in the scene in front him, he heard Dim blast through the trees behind him and out of the corner of his eyes saw the goblin take up a spot to his left holding his axe. Charlie did not see Henrietta and the gnomes. The clearing looked surreal in the growing starlight, and the figures struggling within took on a ghostly look.

In front of him he saw what he thought could be dwarves fighting none other than Isabella, Riot and Ethereal. Charlie didn't see Elyclaw anywhere in sight. He stopped to catch his breath and steady his shaky nerves. Could he really kill someone? Somehow he doubted it, but he couldn't just sit back and watch his friends die.

"Come on Knucklehead," Dim shouted to him as he ran forward yelling his warrior call. Dim raised his axe and moved in on the two dwarves fighting Riot. Charlie stood frozen with his hand still on the hilt of his sword. He felt like a coward. He was no better than his father who had run from danger. He watched his friends battle and heard the sickening sounds as weapons met flesh, and yet he remained frozen. Even the movement to his left and right as the gnomes moved closer all holding some sort of square metal box didn't free him from his sudden paralysis. As the little gnomes closed to within about fifteen feet of the battle, they started shooting some sort of glowing round pellets from these strange boxes, and a few that hit their target made a sound like a 'splat' and a sticky-looking substance clung to the area. Yet he still stood frozen watching the battle as if he were standing in his living room watching it on television.

Henrietta ran up behind him. "Charlie, you can't just stand here. You'll be killed," she screamed into his ears as she pulled out her club and stood next to him, ready if any of the dwarves made their move on him.

"I can't do this, Henrietta," Charlie said as he let his hand fall from the pommel of his sword. "This is not me. I can't kill anyone."

"You don't have to. Use magic, Charlie," She yelled to him over the noises from the battle.

"I don't know magic," Charlie shouted.

"Yes, you do. You're Charlie the magic writer, son of Daubier the former magic writer. Magic is fading, but not gone from this world yet. You could melt those weapons they hold with magic."

Charlie just shook his head. "I don't know how to do that."

"Close your eyes and concentrate, Charlie. Deep down the spell is within you. You just need to look for it," Henrietta was practically yelling to be heard over the battle din.

Charlie just stood there shaking his head. "Come on, Charlie! Trust me," Henrietta said again.

Charlie closed his eyes and tried to feel any possible magic within him, but the noise of blood flowing and cries of death invaded his concentration and then in the midst of the commotion he heard Ethereal in his thoughts. "Stay calm. Stay safe. You can do this, Charlie." He wasn't sure how he was hearing Ethereal, but he was certain it was her inside him talking. His nerves vanished and the noise around him disappeared. And there it was floating around his brain. Magic. His hands moved forward with fingers extended and he uttered "*Olonso Elipto Guensa Mult.*" He felt a surge flow from his chest to his arms and out his fingers and he shuddered, collapsing weakly to the ground, shutting out the sounds around him.

Chapter Twenty-six
An Odd Assortment

Riot watched stunned as the axe of the dwarf in front of him suddenly wilted and then melted, and the dwarf screamed as the
scalding metal burned his hands. Riot had never witnessed such an
event before. He lowered his sword with his mouth agape as the dwarf
fell to his knees in pain. Before he could process what had happened,
Dim sliced through the dwarf from behind ending his agony. "No," he
yelled. "He was defenseless!" Then he gaped at the hairy goblin just
realizing who he was.

"He's the enemy, defenseless or not," Dim flatly stated as he moved
away into the melee.

Riot shook his head at the goblin then watched bemused as weapons
melted away from the other dwarves, and he noticed Isabella also taking
advantage of their foes to pierce the weaponless dwarves in front of her
leading to their death. Where Riot could fight for his life when needed,
he could not kill a defenseless creature. Riot heard another voice scream
"No," as well and Ethereal heeded the cry and lowered her weapon as
the dwarf in front of her screamed in pain on his knees. He was the lone
survivor of the squad of dwarves that had attacked them. Judas, who
had spent the majority of the fight swinging his sword at dead air, was
now shaking his hand in front of him, no sword in sight. He stood next
to the Elven warrior. Riot focused on the poker-faced dwarf and wondered if Judas had even broken skin let alone killed another dwarf. It just
fueled Riot's dislike of him. They were all sweating and bloodied from
battle, but not Judas. The suspicious dwarf stood refreshed and clean.

Isabella had scurried over next to Ethereal and raised her spear
towards the kneeling dwarf. "Beg for mercy," she screamed at him.

Riot was sickened by her thirst for blood that she would kill this defenseless dwarf. Before he could stop her Ethereal put her hand out and pushed Isabella's spear away from the prisoner. "Enough," she said. "He cannot hurt us now. We are not barbarians. We will not kill a weaponless dwarf."

"Then what do you intend to do with him? You can't let him go. If these dwarves were truly minions of Nefarious then this dwarf will just inform him as to where we are," Isabella said.

Ethereal snapped her head towards Isabella. "Minions of Nefarious? You are saying that these dwarves serve Czar Nefarious?"

Isabella fidgeted uncomfortably as she realized she had given away something Judas had told her in confidence. Riot caught the glance between her and Judas. "Well, ah I'm just saying what if they are then it would be dangerous to let him go," she stammered.

Riot kept his eyes on Judas. He wanted to catch his reaction to what Isabella was saying. Judas kept his gaze on the ground towards his feet and his toes twitched. The dwarf appeared to Riot like someone keeping a secret. Then it dawned on him. The dwarf knows. Riot was certain he knew about these dwarves and where they came from. But for whatever reason he wasn't saying anything to them about the dwarves. But Isabella knew also. Riot was sure of it. Judas must have told her about them when he and Ethereal had gone into the woods looking for firewood. So Isabella was probably right. These dwarves were Czar's minions. And if that were the case then why was Judas not with them?

Ethereal turned her attention back to the dwarf in front of her. She pulled a torch from her pack and using a flint struck a spark into the end, blowing the flame to life. As the torch began to burn brighter she handed it to Isabella. The captive dwarf was no longer screaming from the pain the melted metal had seared into his skin. He now cradled his burned hand and rocked back and forth moaning. Ethereal took her sword and let the tip reach under the dwarves hairy chin and let the blade guide his head upwards until his eyes were looking into her eyes. "Is what she is saying correct? Are you working for Czar Nefarious?"

The dwarves' defiant eyes made a quick glance from Ethereal to Judas. Riot didn't think the she-Elf noticed, but he had. "Why don't you ask…" before he could finish his statement, Judas kicked dirt into the dwarves' face and spit upon him.

"You and your friends make me sick. YOU'RE TRAITORS, yup, yup," Judas said. "My human friends and I will bring you all down, yup, yup!" The animated dwarf whirled around, waving his hands angrily in the air. "Yup, yup, bring you down." He started jumping backwards as he repeated the words again and again. All eyes in the group were on Judas as he jumped around backwards in the circle of light from the torch, repeating "Yup, yup, bring you down." On his fifth jump his feet became tangled together and his hands went up into the air flailing around trying to keep himself from falling. As he went down his waving hands banged into the contraption held by one of the gnomes, who had moved forward entranced by the scene, and it set off a dart. The dart flew forward and landed with a smack into the center of the lone surviving dwarf's forehead. The dwarf's eyes widened and he muttered a groan as his eyes rolled backwards in their socket and he fell backward with a plop.

Not one of them made a sound as they all stared at the dwarf lying wide eyed on the ground. Riot was the first to speak up. "You stupid fool! Look what you did." Judas pulled himself up to his elbows and looked with a shocked expression on his face at the dead dwarf. "I didn't mean it, nope, nope," Judas said quietly.

"What was that?" asked Isabella as she bent over the dwarf and inspected the dart sticking out of his forehead.

"It's a poison dart," Henrietta said as she moved forward from behind the group into the circle of firelight towards them. All their attention went from the dwarf with the dart sticking out of his forehead to the girl who approached them.

"Henrietta?" Isabella said. "Is that you?"

Henrietta smiled at Isabella and said. "Yes, it's me!"

The gnomes who were situated loosely around the group also moved forward into the light to make a semicircle behind Henrietta. Isabella reached for her sword having just noticed the gnomes.

"No, don't! The gnomes are with me," Henrietta said. Isabella let her hand release its grip on her sword. "It was their gadget that the dart came from!"

"How did you find us?" Riot asked.

"It was a power beyond ours that led us here at the precise time you were battling! We were fortunate to find you when we did," Henrietta said.

"So it was you who provided the dart that killed this dwarf with that…thing," Isabella waved towards the contraptions the gnomes held. "And was it you that melted the weapons?"

Ethereal answered for Henrietta. "No it was not Henrietta or the gnomes that did that." She stepped over the dead dwarf and moved passed Henrietta disappearing into the darkness. Riot lost sight of her as she went. But seconds later she reemerged from the darkness holding the hand of none other than Charlie.

"It was Charlie," Ethereal revealed. "Charlie melted the weapons."

Ethereal had sensed Charlie's presence as soon as he had entered the meadow. It had only pushed her to fight harder. She had connected to his thoughts immediately and had felt his doubt and fear. She had passed on her best encouragement to him to believe in himself and he had listened. She knew some of the old magic would still be within him.

"Charlie?" Isabella practically whispered. "You're alive! We thought the goblins had taken you." Isabella moved forward quickly, handing the torch to a suddenly outraged Riot who exclaimed "hey I don't want this," as she walked past him to Charlie and embraced him. Ethereal had never seen that type of emotion from Isabella before. Charlie stood stiff with shock himself at the human warrior's affection.

Isabella pulled back and her brow furrowed as she said, "Was it Henrietta that stole you away from us rather than the goblins?"

"No, it was Forerunner and his troop," Charlie said.

Isabella looked around the group standing in the torchlight until she found the goblin, and she turned an accusatory look on Dim. "So your master stole Charlie!"

"He's no longer my master," Dim grumbled darkly. "And yes he took us."

"How did you get away?" Riot questioned. "Did he let you go?"

Charlie looked from the group to Henrietta and the gnomes and his face softened when he looked at her and her friends. "Henrietta and her..." Charlie let his hand expand over the group of gnomes behind her "...family saved us," Charlie hesitated only for a second before referring to the gnomes as her family.

Henrietta's smile reached from ear to ear as Charlie described the gnomes as her family. The gnomes just nodded with smiles on their faces, affirming what he said. A few of them, Dipper and Whikered among them, moved forward and laced their arms into Henrietta's as a signal they were indeed her family.

Ethereal was curious about the obvious connection between Charlie and Henrietta. They had obviously bonded and she reminded herself she'd have to find time to explore Henrietta's thoughts to see what that connection was.

"Then you are all our family as well. Anyone that would risk their lives to save Charlie is family to us," Ethereal said as she laced her arm in Charlie's to make it clear who he belonged to. Riot snorted at Ethereal's statement and Dim muttered, "Whatever." But Isabella stepped forward and put her hand on Henrietta's shoulder and said "I agree," and she smiled an awkward smile.

Judas piped in, "Yup, yup, we are all family, yup, yup."

It didn't get past Ethereal that Riot glared at Judas when he spoke. It was obvious the wolf boy didn't like the dwarf, but there was a deeper meaning behind his look this time. Before she could explore his thoughts, Henrietta piped up.

"We should camp here tonight and tomorrow we can head home." She looked at her gnome family as she spoke and they all nodded in agreement and she smiled.

"Home?" Isabella asked. "We don't have a home anymore Henrietta."

"Yes you do," Dipper said. "Our home is your home." Dipper gripped Henrietta's hand and squeezed. Ethereal wondered if the gnomes would become a hindrance eventually, but for now she was glad she'd have a place to call home for a while and hopefully a place to keep Charlie safe.

"You expect us to live with some gnomes," Riot sneered. "How safe could that be? They…they are…well…"

"Go ahead. Say it," Dipper said.

"Fine. They are small and weak and I'm guessing defenseless." Riot finished.

"Is that not what you said about Henrietta when you thought she might not be alive? Somehow she is still alive and standing right before you," Ethereal said. "I would say wherever they live must be safe as they have kept her safe all this time. I vote we go with them."

Charlie smiled and let his gaze fall on the she-Elf. "I vote with Ethereal."

Riot rolled his eyes. "No surprise there."

"Wherever Charlie goes, I go," said Dim.

Ethereal looked to Isabella next to see what she thought. The young human warrior sighed. "I don't know if holing up with gnomes is a great idea. Nefarious has an army of minotaurs and now I guess dwarves as well. What do we have? A bunch of gnomes?" The gathered gnomes muttered in indignation and she snorted at the thought.

"But I guess it will be nice to get Charlie out of the open and now that we are all together we can concentrate on having him write magic finally. After all, that is what this all was about. So I vote we go."

"Well, I guess I'm the only one that thinks this is a bad idea," Riot spat.

"I haven't had a vote, nope, nope," Judas said.

"*You* don't get a vote. You're lucky we haven't killed you and left you for the wolves to eat," Riot said. Judas pursed his lips together and he formed fists with his hands, rolling them in front of him trying to hit Riot.

"You fart breath," he said to Riot as he advanced closer to the young human.

Riot stepped forward and shoved Judas. "You liar!"

"Riot stop," Isabella said as she pushed him away from the dwarf.

Riot stabbed a finger at Judas in anger. "He lied to us about the dwarves and you knew about it," Riot said. "He can't be trusted. And neither can you!"

"He didn't lie to us! He told me about the dwarves when you were getting the firewood. We were going to tell you about it when you came back. How could we know the dwarves would attack us?"

"I don't believe you," Riot said as he let his gaze encompass the group. "And you shouldn't either. He can't be trusted. Look at him!" Riot said as he waved the torch at Judas. "He's clean. If he were fighting with us and helping us, he'd be bloodied like us."

Ethereal looked from Riot to the sullen-looking dwarf. He had a point. Judas was clean. And the more she thought about it, she couldn't recall Judas killing let alone harming any of the dwarves they had just fought.

"Just because he is a bad fighter does not mean anything," Isabella defended.

"Yup, yup, I'm a bad fighter. I'm a lover, not a fighter," Judas said.

Ethereal looked the dwarf over. She couldn't tell if he was being honest or not. She felt this was as good a time as any to explore his thoughts. She closed her eyes for a moment and let herself in, but a pain seared through her and she felt like she had run into a wall. She looked at Judas closer and tried again, but again she hit some kind of force that stopped her. Being new to using this magic she'd never tried listening to the thoughts of a dwarf before. Perhaps they had a way to block one from entering their thoughts. Just then Judas' gaze passed over her and she noted a glimpse of sparkle in his eyes, but then it was gone. She wondered if he knew she was trying to read his mind. She'd need to keep a close eye on this one. There was more to him than what she was seeing. Yet to cut him loose now would be worse than taking him in, and if he really was lying, then he could tell others too much about their plans now.

"Perhaps he really is just a bad fighter," Ethereal sided with Isabella. "It is not cause enough to label him a liar." She looked into Riot's eyes and tried to persuade him to see her side. He just grunted and brought up his arm without the torch and let it fall down to his side in exasperation.

"Fine, don't listen to me, but you'll regret it," Riot said.

"So does that mean I'm going with?" Judas asked.

Ethereal looked from Riot back to the dwarf. "Yes, you are going with us." The group fell silent as they absorbed this decision.

The silence was broken as Charlie piped up. "I have a question." The group's eyes turned as one towards the young magic writer. "Why is Riot in his underwear?"

Chapter Twenty-seven

A New Home

The next few days of travel passed without any surprising events. On the morning of the third day, Dipper and Lens had taken the lead while Henrietta walked alongside Riot chattering. The wolf boy's eyes were vacant. Dim had determined Riot was shutting out Henrietta's chatter. He was just glad Riot was the target of the blathering human's endless conversation rather than himself. Isabella walked behind him along with Judas. Occasionally Isabella would comment on something but for the most part Judas just hopped along looking at the weeds and plants they passed, searching for tobacco, only nodding occasionally. Dim waddled alongside Charlie who walked next to Ethereal. The squat goblin wanted a chance to talk alone with Charlie. They had not been alone since the cage and Dim wanted to ask the young human where he stood in this new group.

He had followed orders to bring Charlie back to Pulchritude Amity. He had risked his life and almost died from poison. He had gone with Charlie when the boy chose Isabella over him, almost being eaten by a cannibal along the way. He'd been threatened by Elves, cursed by a forest and then captured by his own kind. He had been caged and betrayed by Forerunner, and he'd found out the master he had followed was a traitor and liar. Now he was traipsing around Pulchritude Amity with some gnomes, an Elf, a dwarf and four humans. Where did a goblin fit with this group? His only purpose now was Charlie's safety. He actually wasn't sure why that was of any concern to him anymore, but somewhere between the portal and here, Dim had become fond of the boy. He'd never admit that if anyone asked him, but he knew Charlie had crept into his heart. This young human was unlike the others. He wasn't bossy like Isabella or rude like Riot. He didn't talk nonstop like Henrietta. He was a different breed according to Dim. Somehow the goblin had found a new master.

"We're here," Henrietta said as they walked into a clearing. Dim didn't see anything but brown grass and bambleweed scattered throughout. He obviously wasn't the only one who couldn't see where "here" was.

"I don't get it," Isabella said. "I don't see anything. Are you saying the gnomes live in this meadow? How could that be a safe place to live?"

"No, silly," Henrietta said as she giggled. "They live there." The small girl stepped over to a large oak tree at the edge of the clearing and pulled down on a stubby branch that projected from the rough bark. There was a hollow 'snik' and up a piece of the thatched ground flipped, revealing a hole underneath.

"Underground?" Riot asked. "Cool." Riot nodded to himself as if he had misjudged the gnomes and their situation. He crouched down next to the hole and peered in.

Dipper tapped Riot on the shoulder. "We'll go first," the diminutive gnome intoned, "Otherwise, our peoples might think we are under attack." Riot moved aside as Dipper stepped up to the hole and without warning dropped in. There were several gasps from the group and Riot quickly leaned back over, peering into the hole again. "Dipper is fine," giggled Henrietta. "It is just quicker to drop in than to use the ladder, but you may use it to climb down if you wish. The drop is only about six feet."

The others followed Dipper's lead until the only ones left were Charlie, Dim and Lens. Charlie slipped in easily and yelled up to Dim, "Clear! Now it's your turn, Dim." Lens pushed his hands forward to indicate the squat goblin should go next.

Dim looked at the hole and wondered what he'd find in there. He didn't like the idea of being confined underground. Something seemed unnatural about it. But he knew if he wanted to stay with Charlie, he'd have to deal with it. He leaned forward and stuck his head into the hole and saw a small tunnel leading into a large room. Down below he could see Charlie and the group all staring up through the tunnel at him. He knew immediately that he'd never fit through that hole. His head had barely made it through. But before he could pull himself back out he felt Lens pushing him from behind and his wide waist scraped against the edges of the hole.

"Hey mini man, stop pushing," Dim yelled, but his voice only echoed in the tunnel. Lens kept pushing, but the squat goblin didn't budge any farther, not even a little bit. His wide body had gone as far as was possible in the smallish hole. If only he could move a few inches more and he'd get himself into the tunnel. The tunnel seemed larger than the hole, so he was certain once he made it past the entrance, he'd be able to maneuver the rest of the way through the tunnel.

Dim heard Charlie laugh as he said, "Hey, he's Winnie the Pooh." The group all turned and looked stone faced at Charlie's comment. "You know, Winnie the Pooh when he got stuck in the hole after eating Rabbit's honey." Charlie looked around stunned that no one commented. "Winnie the Pooh, the bear..." Charlie tried one more time.

"I saw a bear once," Riot said. "He was searching for fish in old Harper's pond. I don't know if his name was Winnie, but perhaps it was."

Charlie's mouth dropped open for a minute at Riot's response. Then he mumbled "Oh never mind."

"Hey Knucklehead, can't you tell I'm stuck? Rather than tell tales of a bear named Winnered, you could perhaps give me a hand before this freaky gnome behind me gives up on pushing me and decides to use a branch or something worse to shove me through!"

"Give me a hand, Riot," Charlie said. The wolf boy gave a boost to Charlie so he could reach up into the tunnel and grasp Dim's hands. "And its Winnie, not Winnered," Charlie added.

Dim grunted, "Whatever!"

Riot wrapped his hands around Charlie's ankles and Ethereal grabbed Riot by the waist and Charlie said, "At the count of three everyone pull." Charlie looked down at Riot. "And please try not to yank my ankles off my legs."

Riot smirked at Charlie. "Sure bud, whatever you say."

On the count of three they all pulled and Dim grunted as his body moved a few centimeters forward. The group stopped, panting at the exertion, leaving Charlie hanging from Dim's hands. Once again Riot grabbed Charlie's ankles and Ethereal grabbed Riot around the waist. This time Isabella came forward and placed her hands above Riot's onto Charlie's legs. Riot snorted at Isabella, but didn't protest her help. On three they all pulled again and this time Dim came loose and fell face first into the group. The groans and complaints brought a slightly embarrassed look to the goblin's face.

"Geez I'm not that fat," muttered the goblin as he stumbled to his feet and helped the others up making sure they weren't hurt. He took extra care looking Charlie over. The young magic writer swatted his hands away.

"I'm fine, Dim," he said as his cheeks flushed red with embarrassment. Dim hadn't realized the rest of them were all staring at them.

Lens dropped into the hole and reaching up, pulled down on a lever cleverly concealed on the tunnel wall. The patch of ground up above dropped into place and covered the hole from the outside world.

Henrietta leaned close to Charlie and whispered, "I told you that one would have a hard time getting through the hole."

Dim sent a scowl Henrietta's way, and she backed up from Charlie and smiled awkwardly at the plump goblin. "You might need to stay here in this room Dim. I'm not sure if you'll fit through some of the other tunnels. Except that one," she said pointing towards a tunnel to the far right. "That one leads to the food hall. The hole is a little bigger, so I think you'd be able to use that one." The goblin noted there were four tunnels total leading from the room they were in.

"He might want to avoid that way then," Riot snorted.

"I'm getting sick of fat jokes," Dim said clenching his hands into fists as he directed the statement towards Riot. "The next one that makes a fat joke will be sorry."

Riot's smirk left his face. Dim was twice his size weight wise. The hairy goblin figured the young human didn't want to find out what his fist felt like.

"I'll show you all where you can stay," said Dipper. He went through the tunnel to the far left and the others followed.

"Hey Knucklehead. You mind staying back for a minute?"

Charlie nodded. "Sure." He walked over to Dim, who was wiping dirt and debris from his clothes as he watched the others file into the tunnel.

"Charlie," hummed Henrietta appealingly, "I really need to show you where you're staying and also the writing room," she said.

"I'll meet you through there in a minute," Charlie said gesturing towards the tunnel to the far left.

"Okay," Henrietta said with a smile. "I'll be waiting for you."

Ethereal touched Charlie's hand for a minute before she followed Henrietta through the tunnel and Dim was finally alone with Charlie.

"What's up?"

"What are we doing here, Charlie?" The goblin questioned.

"I don't understand what you mean."

"I guess what I really mean is what am I doing here. I was supposed to bring you to Forerunner. I failed at that and now I've been labeled a traitor and outcast from my own kind. You know Forerunner will be out for blood and he won't rest until I'm dead and you are handed over to Czar. He's not the giving up kind."

Charlie stepped forward and let his hand come down onto Dim's shoulder. "You're here because if it wasn't for you I wouldn't be here. I'm finally figuring out my place in this world. I understand why you brought me here. Sure Forerunner played you, but your reasons for bringing me here are still pure regardless if Forerunners weren't. I guess it's possible that Forerunner may find us. I am finding out there isn't anything definite in this world. All of us are just trying to find our way. I believe this is my way. When I pulled that magic out from within me during the battle with the dwarves, I felt for the first time that I had a purpose here and if I can do that better than my father did, then I'll feel good about it. I need to try. You asked what you are doing here. You are here because I need you. You are here because we," Charlie pointed from himself to Dim, "are a team. No one can change that. You are here by my side as a teammate…as a friend. And I hope that is where you'll always be."

Dim felt moved by Charlie's speech and looked around the room at anywhere but Charlie, slightly embarrassed as well. He hadn't expected the human to say those things. He'd just hoped for the young magic writer to say he belonged there.

The goblin cleared his throat a few times. "Okay, Knucklehead," he said gruffly, trying to hide how touched he was by what Charlie had just said. "All you had to say was this is where I belong. You didn't have to get all mushy on me."

Charlie smiled as he pulled Dim in for a hug. The goblin stood stiff and awkward as the human hugged him and then let go. "Sleep well in here," Charlie said as he glanced around the stark lobby-like area. "I'll meet you in the food hall tomorrow morning." Then he turned and disappeared into the tunnel. Dim sat down and contemplated what Charlie had just said.

Chapter Twenty-eight
A Council of Humans

After showing the companions one by one where they would stay, Henrietta led the last two travelers, Ethereal and Charlie through a small tunnel which came out to a small room with a fire burning in one corner. In the corner across from the fireplace were a makeshift bed of feathers and some sort of material that looked like cotton balls. The room also had a small table and chair. After weeks sleeping on the hard ground and worrying about what one might encounter at every move, this room looked luxurious to Charlie.

"This is where you'll sleep," Henrietta smiled at Charlie.

Charlie smiled back. "It's nice. So where will Ethereal be?"

Henrietta looked at the she-Elf. "Well I was going to put her with Isabella, but Isabella insisted that she needed the room to herself. Something about not being able to share a room because she might wake up and forget who she is with and might hurt them!"

Charlie nodded. "Okay, so where does that leave Ethereal?"

"It is okay Charlie. I think Henrietta is saying they do not have any rooms left."

"Well, I was thinking you could have mine," Henrietta said.

"I could not take your room," the Elven warrior stated.

"Why doesn't Ethereal stay in here with me?"

Henrietta and Ethereal both stared at Charlie. "Umm, well if it were up to me, that would be fine, but I think...uh...I know the others wouldn't be okay with that," said the petite human girl.

Ethereal put her hands out and touched Charlie. "We both know that is not a good idea. I do not need a bed or a fire to sleep." Ethereal said.

"Why don't you share my room?" Henrietta asked.

"I would not want to invade your space."

Henrietta looked at Charlie again before answering. "Don't be silly! I'd be honored to have you share my room!"

The young magic writer smiled at Henrietta. "Then it's decided. Ethereal will stay with you."

"Yes, she'll stay with me!" And Henrietta giggled.

Ethereal and Charlie had spent the rest of the day exploring the gnome's home. Charlie thought it appeared more like an underground city than a home. He was amazed how anyone could have created such a safe haven underground. They strolled through a garden. Since coming to Pulchritude Amity, Charlie had not come across anything quite so green and beautiful, even the garden with the Iron Gate had not been this impressive.

"How do you suppose they keep everything green and alive down here?" He asked.

"The underground does not seem to have been affected as much by the loss of magic as above ground. The gnomes are quite intelligent. They have set up their home so they do not have to rely on anyone but themselves." Ethereal bent down and let her hands glide over the purple blooms on a bush. "Crystal Valley was once this beautiful. These blooms make me homesick."

Charlie's hand reached down and touched Ethereal's and he squeezed. "I know what you mean about homesick," he said. "Though nothing here reminds me of home. Well...actually Henrietta does."

Ethereal looked into the young human's eyes. Charlie couldn't help but wonder what was behind them. She kept her emotions and thoughts well hidden from him.

"You have become fond of Henrietta," Ethereal stated.

"Well yeah, I suppose I have. She reminds me a lot of my sister."

"I sense you are extremely close to your sister."

"She is my conscious, my kind side. Without her it is hard to know what is the right and wrong thing to do. I've never met anyone who knows how to take charge and do the right thing like she does. I've always been more of a follower...I know I know, that's not a good thing. My mom tells me that all the time. But Kassie, she's not a follower. She's a leader. I could use her leadership about now."

Ethereal released Charlie's grip on her hand and glided them up over his arms and shoulders until they reached his face and there she let her hands rest one on each side. "Somehow I do not think it will be long before you see her again."

Charlie smiled down at Ethereal. "I want to see her again so much, but I don't want to leave here and leave you." He reached up to where her hands were on his face and placed them over hers. His thumb rubbed along the curve of her hand and then he grasped them and moved them to the nape of his neck. He went to lower his lips to hers and she pulled away. "Now is not the time," she said. "There is much to be determined for you in the next few days. Getting too close to me will just muddy what needs to be done."

"Are you still concerned about what others think of us?" He moved away from her as he spoke. "I don't care what they think! I know my own mind. If Kassie were here she'd agree. She'd be right next to me encouraging me to fight for you! She's a fighter." He let his hands run through his hair as he spoke to her. "Speaking of Kassie makes me homesick. I don't want to leave here...or you, but I want to be home with Kassie as well."

She moved towards Charlie and let her hands touch his arms. "It is not as easy as you making a choice. I doubt the others will give you a choice in who you can be with and who you cannot. And as for your sister you will not have to choose between seeing her or being here," she said a little breathless. "She will find you *here*, Charlie."

He straightened up and let his hand rub his face to steady his nerves. He tried to process what she said through the fog in his brain.

His arm still tingled from where she touched his skin. He wiped across them with his hands hoping to remove her sweetness from them so he could think straight again.

"I don't understand what you're saying."

"Where we need you here to bring magic back to this world, we also need a leader. Someone who is kind and can be the conscience of those that live here in this world. I know you must know who fits those qualities," she said as she stared at him waiting for it all to click.

"You can't possibly mean Kassie," Charlie said shocked.

"Kassie is the obvious choice. She comes from powerful blood as do you. You yourself said she is a leader. We have not had a great leader in this world for many an age and the time has now come for such an individual."

Charlie stepped further back from Ethereal. "There is no way I'm allowing Kassie to come here. Are you crazy? I would never allow her to be put into such a dangerous position."

"I do not think you will have a choice in that matter," Ethereal stated.

"Of course I'll have a choice. I'll fight anyone that even suggests such a thing!"

"Charlie, fate will have its way. You can fight all you want, but if destiny has determined Kassie belongs here, then she will come here one way or another. Whatever you do will not change that. It might just delay it, but it will not change it."

He shook his head at her. "You're wrong. You must be wrong." He turned and walked away from Ethereal. "I'll never allow it," he said as he left the she-Elf standing alone in the garden.

The four humans sat at a large wooden table which was centered in the middle of the gnome's conference chambers. It was the first time they had been alone since Charlie had come to them. Dim had grumbled when he found out they would be meeting without him.

Ethereal had just nodded and said she understood their wish to talk alone. Judas, who had become Isabella's shadow, had said nothing about being excluded from the meeting. Perhaps he realized how lucky he was to have been allowed to come with them in the first place and knew complaining about the meeting would just give a reason to rethink him being there at all.

They had been staying with the gnomes for a few days now. They were well rested and had eaten more in the last few days than they had in weeks roaming the countryside. Isabella couldn't remember the last time she had eaten fresh greens such as those that their guests provided. The gnome's vast garden offered them a large variety of food to choose from and they all splurged as if they had never seen food before.

Isabella had organized the meeting, so she felt it was only right that she lead the conversation. Riot, on the other hand, obviously did not agree. They hadn't been seated for more than a few moments before he started.

"If you think you are going to start bossing us around again then I'm going to get up right now and leave," Riot threatened.

Isabella took great care not to raise her voice since she knew that would only egg Riot on. "I have no idea what you are talking about. I'm just here to try and help us put together an agenda for what needs to be done now that we are all finally together."

"Well, as long as you don't start acting like you are in charge," Riot said with a bit of a pout.

"Its okay, Riot! She really is just trying to get us moving in the right direction," Henrietta said as she smiled at him. Riot didn't smile back. He just looked down at the table in front of him.

"So, we need to get Charlie acquainted with the book and pen," Isabella said. She fidgeted for a few minutes as she suspected the next request was going to cause an issue with Riot. "And I think I'm probably the best suited to do that."

Riot's head snapped up as he ranted, "No way. I don't agree with that. You are many things, none of which I can say here without offending the others, but you are not a teacher."

"I'm best suited for the job Riot even if you don't agree. After all I am the only one sitting at this table that made it into Enchantment Academy, so I'm the only one that knows anything about magic," Isabella said with a raised voice.

"Oh, I see. You think you're better than us because your mother pulled rank to get you into Enchantment Academy. Well, if I remember right, you almost flunked out," Riot stated.

"I didn't flunk. I just chose to move to the combat and warrior class after a year. That had nothing to do with how well I knew magic and more about where I belonged. I certainly know more about magic than you do!"

Riot snorted. "And that makes you an expert?"

"Can we stop with the arguing already?" Charlie said with exasperation.

Riot ignored him as he continued his rant. "Who says Charlie needs a teacher anyways? From what I saw the other night, he knows more about magic than any of us and he did that all on his own."

"I agree! I don't think he needs a teacher. I think he needs more of a...guiding hand," Henrietta interjected.

Isabella overlooked Henrietta's statement and addressed the wolf boy. "He got lucky, Riot. He's clueless about magic. You have to see that just by looking at him."

Charlie sat back in his chair and crossed his arms and pursed his lips together.

"Oh, so now you're calling Charlie stupid?" Riot said.

Henrietta pounded her hand on the table to distract them from their bickering. "I think I should step in and be his guide into magic," she said with the loudest voice she could muster.

"Just because he needs a teacher does not mean I'm calling him stupid...stupid," Isabella spat.

Riot jumped up to his feet knocking his chair over. "Now you're calling me stupid?"

"I'm calling it as I see it," Isabella said even though her inner voice told her not to.

Charlie stood up as well and banged his fist on the table making a much bigger impact then Henrietta's small fist had. Isabella and Riot both stopped arguing and looked with shock at Charlie. "Enough already!" Yelled the angry young man. Isabella and Riot crossed their arms and turned and glared at each other. "I think you both have forgotten that I am right here. You're so busy arguing that you're not even listening to the rest of us!"

Henrietta nodded and smiled, obviously pleased with Charlie taking charge. "I also think I have the right to choose who...guides me in magic writing," Charlie said as he smiled at Henrietta when he used the word guide. "And I want Henrietta's help."

"Henrietta!?" Isabella questioned. "Henrietta knows nothing about magic!"

"Perhaps you're right. But I think Riot's on target about the magic being deep inside me and I just need to channel it and I think Henrietta is the one that can help me do that."

Riot smiled smugly at Isabella, who wanted to wipe the smile off his face with her fist. "*I* think we should vote on it," Riot said never letting his eyes leave Isabella's.

"I think that is a good idea, Riot," Charlie said.

"Fine," said Isabella. She hated Riot at that moment, yet she knew she didn't have a choice but to call for a vote now. "Who votes for Henrietta?" she asked. Riot, Charlie and Henrietta's hand went up. It took all her will to keep from spitting in Riot's face. He had won this one, but she'd be blasted if she let him win the next issue up for a vote. "Then it will be Henrietta who teaches...*guides* Charlie in magic writing. Now we need to discuss who will take on the leadership role," Isabella continued as she let her gaze stray away from Riot's smug look.

"Well, it's not going to be you," Riot started again.

"We're not going down that path again," Charlie stated before Isabella could retort an answer.

"None of us are equipped to be in charge," stated Henrietta with a smile.

"Well, I personally think I'm equipped to handle it," Isabella retorted.

Henrietta reached out to Riot, who was seated on her left, and grabbed his arm to stop him from answering back. "I think you have wonderful qualities, Isabella, but you are needed to keep us safe and that will take up too much of your time to be dealing with leading us as well."

The young human warrior knew Henrietta was right and that she'd be needed more for protection, but she couldn't help but want to take on a leadership role. Yet she knew fighting over it right now would be futile. Perhaps she could wait until a better time when she could persuade the others to her side. "What are you suggesting then? Are you expecting us to go without a leader?"

"For now, perchance," she said. Henrietta looked at Charlie as she continued. "I've had a persistent dream that there is another. One that comes from Charlie's world who will come to lead us. I think we need to wait for her to come to us."

"Why don't we go after her and bring her here ourselves if you are certain there is another somewhere that can lead us? After all isn't that how Charlie got here. Dim went to get him," said Riot.

"That is a possibility," Henrietta stated.

"If you are talking about who I think you are talking about, there is no way I'm allowing you to bring my sister Kassie here."

"Your sister?" Isabella asked. "I didn't know Charlie had a sister."

"I think she is the one that will lead us, Charlie," said Henrietta.

"No," Charlie said in a raised voice. "I'm not allowing you to bring Kassie to this...this dangerous place!"

"I don't think that is your choice," Isabella said. "I think we need to vote on something like that."

"I said no," Charlie yelled. "If you want me to be your magic writer than you'll leave my sister out of this!"

"Okay, okay," Henrietta said. "We don't have to talk about this anymore today!"

"No I suppose you're right. We can talk about this later. Today was really about Charlie," said Isabella. "We'll discuss leadership on another day."

"Nothing is going to change my mind. My sister stays where she is…period. End of conversation."

Chapter Twenty-nine
Of Magic and Messages

er long blonde hair flowed behind her as she ran across the
meadow. Her bare feet glistened from the dew that coated the
grass. She stopped a few feet from him and her piercing pale blue
eyes looked up into his and he saw them sparkle as she smiled at him.
He reached out and brushed the swoop of her hair that lay across her
forehead, so that he could see her eyes better. The touch sent a tingle
through the tips of his fingers that slowly coursed down his arms and
into the rest of his body. He felt his heart beating and was certain
she could hear it for it seemed so loud to his ears. He wanted to ask
her who she was, but before he could speak she turned from him
and looked to his right and her smile broadened and she exclaimed,
"Charlie!" Riot turned as well and his eyes saw Charlie running towards them and he heard Charlie yell back at the girl, "Kassie!"

Riot woke with a start and he knew. The blonde girl from his
dreams was Charlie's sister...the leader.

The room only held a desk, table and a fire burning in the fireplace. It was small, but cozy. Only he and Henrietta were in the room,
but Isabella and Ethereal stood at the other end of the tunnel keeping watch. The human warrior had wanted that job by herself, but
Ethereal had insisted she be there as well. Isabella had conceded when
Riot had insisted also. Charlie suspected the wolf boy was wearing
on Isabella. If only they could stop arguing. Their constant fighting
was wearing Charlie down. He couldn't see a future for humans in
Pulchritude Amity if the few humans left couldn't get along.

Henrietta pulled two books from her knapsack and Charlie fixated on them. "This book is the Book of Potions!" Henrietta started as she held out the smaller book. "Isabella was keeping this book safe. It won't be the first book you'll work with. It will take time to understand potions!"

Henrietta flipped the books around so the bigger book was on top. "This book is the Book of Truth! It's where you'll start. It's where all magic is written." Henrietta placed the Book of Truth onto the desk in front of the novice magic writer and put the smaller book back into her knapsack. Charlie looked at the book curiously. She smiled at him. "Go ahead! Open it!"

Charlie let his fingers touch the leather that covered the book and sighed. It had been a long time since he had touched a book, and he realized now how much he missed the feel of the cover, the texture of the pages. He let his fingers trace the letters engraved on the cover. *Onso Thaumaturgico* and below it was *Daubier Kayne, magic writer.*

"Daubier Kayne magic writer? I thought my father was the magic writer," he said.

"He is...was," she said.

"Then why does it say Daubier Kayne?" Charlie asked.

"That's his name."

Charlie looked up at Henrietta confused. "That's not his name. His name is Dabney Kane."

"I can only assume he changed his name when he took you to the other world."

He considered what she said. It was possible he supposed. He let his hand glide to the edge of the book and slowly opened it. Charlie wasn't certain what he expected, but what he saw was definitely not it. He flipped through the pages and they were all the same. "They're blank," he said.

"Well, not quite." Henrietta reached around Charlie and flipped the pages back to the first page. "If you look closely you can see faint writing," she said.

Charlie looked closer and he saw the faint writing Henrietta pointed out, but he couldn't read it. He flipped a few more pages and by the fourth page the faint writing was gone. "Yeah, I can see it for a few pages, but then the rest is blank."

"Yes, they are! I assumed someone told you that magic is fading here in our world," she said.

"Well, yes, but I didn't know that meant the book would be blank."

"It's why we need you Charlie. All of the magic your father wrote has faded. Most is gone. Without it our world is dying! We need you to write new magic in this book. It's what you were born to do Charlie!"

He let his hand glide over the faint words his father had written on the first page, and he couldn't help but feel his father's presence course through him. He pulled his fingers away from the words. "Okay, how do I start?"

Henrietta pulled a pen from her pouch. "This is the Pen of Knowledge! You'll need this to write."

Charlie looked at the pen in Henrietta's hand. It was glowing red and a pulling force seemed to be angling it towards him. She held it out to him. He hesitated for a moment before letting his fingers grasp the pen. It hummed under his fingers and he felt as if it were speaking to him inside his head. Before Henrietta could say any more, he opened the book back to the first page, leaned forward and placed the point of the pen to the paper and started to write, but nothing appeared on the page.

"Ummm," Charlie said as he looked at Henrietta, "It's not working." Charlie felt a panic swell up inside him. What if after all this they were wrong and he wasn't the magic writer.

"Of course not, silly," Henrietta said. She pulled out a container of ink and placed it on the desk above the book. "You need ink to write," she giggled.

Charlie blushed as he realized this wasn't a ball point pen, but one of those old ink well pens. "I don't know how to write with one of these," he said.

"You dip the pen in the ink and then you write! It's not hard. You do know how to write, I assume?"

Charlie gave Henrietta an exasperated look. "Of course I can write, but where I come from the ink is already in the pen."

"In the pen? Wow, I never thought of that! I'll have to tell Dipper! He loves any new inventions."

"It's not new. It's been around for a long time...oh never mind," Charlie said as he put the pen into the ink. He took a deep breath and began to write.

Judas had been left to his own accord for a few days now. He had found that the best way to gather information was to wander around as if you belonged everywhere and eventually, others would believe it. He had gone unnoticed outside the tunnel leading to the conference hall where the humans met. The tunnels channeled sound and everything said could be heard from his end of the tunnel. He'd gone unnoticed when he'd sat in the tunnel to the right of where Isabella and Ethereal stood guard. He had heard their conversation. They mentioned how Henrietta had Charlie writing magic in the room they guarded and wondered how it was going. So, he figured he'd go unnoticed if he slipped out when Whikered left the tunnels for the outside world. Once a week the gnomes sent someone out to experiment with their latest inventions.

Judas timed it down to the minute and when Whikered told the guards at the exit tunnel he was going outside to try out some of their inventions he waited until the gnome was let out and he made an appearance. "Hey there," Judas said.

"Hey there, yourself," the guard said.

"I'm with Whikered," Judas said as he held out some widgets. "He sent me back to get these. I need to take them out to him, yup, yup."

The guard looked down at what Judas held in his hands and then looked into his eyes, scrutinizing them. Judas waited as the silence became uncomfortable. Finally the guard said, "Be careful now and stay with Whikered!" And he pulled the lever to open the dirt cover off the tunnel and let Judas out.

Judas wasted no time as he darted to the left and stayed within the tree line and away from the meadow where he assumed Whikered was playing with his inventions. He got about five minutes away from the gnomes home and once there he whistled a high pitched tweet four times and then two low pitched tweets. Then he planted himself on a rock behind a bush and waited.

Five minutes went by and then ten. Judas started to fidget and he hopped off the rock and paced. He didn't know how long he had before Whikered finished his experiments. He couldn't wait much longer or he might get left out here and that would ruin everything. Just when he thought he'd have to give up the wait, he heard the caws in the distance. Within minutes a Raptor Soarer glided down and landed in front of him. Judas jumped back startled. He'd been working with Raptor Soarers for the last year now, but he still became nervous whenever he was in their presence. He knew the Raptor could swallow him whole if it wanted to. He pulled out of his big pocket in the front of his vest a piece of parchment paper and held it out to the Raptor.

"Take to Czar…now, yup, yup," he said in his most authoritative voice.

The Raptor Soarer snapped up with his beak the parchment paper from Judas' hand. The dwarf yanked his hand back to keep it from going into the beak along with the parchment. He watched quietly as the Raptor turned and flew off.

It was done. He couldn't undo it. He watched until the Raptor disappeared into the sky and then he scurried back to the edge of the clearing and hoped upon hope that Whikered had not already returned. It took him a few minutes to find the stubby branch that opened the door to the tunnels. He pulled it down when he found it and heard the '*snik*', bringing the door up from the ground. Judas ran over and leaped down into the tunnel landing before the guard. The guard looked surprise when he saw the dwarf there. "Where is Whikered?" he asked.

Judas was relieved to find he had made it back before Whikered. "He sent me back. He said he didn't need me anymore, nope, nope."

The guard scrutinized him again before reaching up and pulling the lever to close the opening. "Well, go on then," he said to Judas.

The dwarf turned and scuttled away.

Chapter Thirty
The Evil Burns Deep

Wisps of flame emanated from his red and yellow body as he walked. His head was devoid of hair, with flames licking from the top of his scalp. His eyes were black as midnight and his nose was missing leaving only two small holes in the middle of his face. His lips were wide and long and the color of the sun, and he continually licked them, as if they were constantly dry. Behind him he dragged a tail with a barbed tip as sharp as a knife. He used it as a weapon as well as another arm often using it to point to various locations when talking. It had been said he had stabbed clean through a man with his tail, spearing his heart and ripping it from his body in one vicious motion. Others said he used it as a constrictor to strangle those that annoyed him. Perhaps both were right. He could not touch another without causing pain for the heat that came from his body no one could withstand.

He stood in the once dark room now glowing with the light from his body. "How did you lose them?" his booming voice spat flames as he spoke.

The tall-for-his-race goblin cowered and raised his scarred face up to the flaming one. "We...we were attacked by acid," Forerunner stuttered. The other goblins with Forerunner remained on their knees, hands over their eyes in fear.

"Acid...bah! What a fool you are. I should have known better than to rely on an incompetent moronic goblin like you," he hissed.

He stalked towards Forerunner and his tail lifted. The cowering goblin pulled his hands up to his face and whimpered, "No, please...I can make this right," he said.

The flaming one let his tail lower slightly. "And how do you plan to do that?"

"I can find them! One of my own is still with them. He trusts me. I'm his master! Please give me another chance, Lord Czar," Forerunner begged.

Czar stood still with his tail poised and threatening, regarding the quivering goblin malevolently. "Hmmm…perhaps…," muttered the flaming figure. In a single motion Czar Nefarious's tail speared through the goblin next to Forerunner, protruding from his back, the unlucky goblin's heart stuck to the sharp end. The goblin slumped over onto the tail. The figure of flame puffed up and flames licked across his tail and engulfed the goblin's listless body, burning it fiercely to ash around his tail, leaving only the heart on the end. The sinuous weapon weaved a path over to Forerunner, waving the dead soldier's heart in front of the cowering goblin. Sweat broke out on the scarred goblin's forehead, and he abstractly found himself wondering how long Czar had practiced to be able to do something that horrific. Czar Nefarious flicked his tail and the heart dropped with a sickening splat to the ground at Forerunner's feet.

"You have a fortnight to find him. If not, your heart will join your comrades," and he turned with a wave of heat and flame, singeing Forerunner's face as he moved away.

Forerunner shook as he hurried off and out of the dungeons, mopping at the sweat that was stinging his acid-scarred and now burned face. He shoved the fleeing goblins ahead of him out of his way as he cleared the stairs out of the tunnel into the courtyard. He needed to find Dim. He needed to make it right, and quick.

The nightmare began as soon as Charlie closed his eyes. In the nightmare he was looking for his father, who was lost among flames, only to become lost himself in the fire. He covered his mouth to avoid choking on the smoke that surrounded him. He only removed his hands long enough to cry out for his dad, and then replace his hands over his mouth. Out of nowhere three tunnels appeared. He couldn't decide which way to take. None of them looked safe. Flames came from all three passages. He yelled out for his father again, but was greeted only by the noise of a roaring fire. Then something red, long and sharp came into his vision out of the smoke and it pointed to the tunnel on his right. He crouched down and tried to look into the tunnel, but the heat pushed him back. He'd have to take a chance and enter and hope it was the right way. He crawled through the tunnel. He felt the sweat dripping from his face as the heat in the tunnel almost took his breath away. After what seemed like days, he finally came out the other end to find his father standing in the distance. Flames surrounded him and he stood there trapped. Charlie reached out towards him. "I'm coming Father," he said. His father screamed in pain and the flames licked at his body. Charlie stood up and ran forward, but no matter how much he ran he never came any closer to his father. He stopped running, sure that he had been running for hours, and dropped to his hands and knees, trying to catch his breath. Sweat dripped off his body and he felt faint. He looked up at his father. "Dad," he said. "I can't reach you." Just then the red sharp object that had pointed him down this tunnel appeared next to his father and ripped into him and his father's screams intensified and then disappeared. Charlie screamed as his father's body vanished in the fire and all that was left was his heart that rolled to Charlie's feet. Then Charlie woke up.

Czar Nefarious stood on the balcony and watched the hundreds of dwarves as they went through their military drills. The minotaurs had already had their time for drills and now Czar had the horned beasts delving into the mountain so he'd be able to build a city of slaves and keep it well hidden. He was prepared to demolish the last few humans once his scouts found them, but he was running out of patience. They should have found something by now. Since it was clear that the magic writer was gone from this world, he no longer was worried about the art of magic. Once he killed the last of the humans, the threat of magic would be gone and he'd be the most powerful being in Pulchritude Amity. The food source would soon die and then the others would fight each other for survival. Once they were starving and destitute, they would have to come crawling to him for help. They would need him for food and shelter and survival. He'd become their leader by necessity, taking his rightful place as the ruler of this world. They would have to bow to him and worship him.

The cawing brought Czar's attention to the sky. The fog covered a large area around his stronghold and even his jet black eyes could not penetrate too far into the distance, but his senses were strong and he could hear for miles. The Raptor Soarer he heard was to his left, and he watched, waiting for the Raptor to break through the fog. Suddenly the Soarer appeared, and flew in directly towards Czar Nefarious with his caw echoing through the field below. The dwarves stopped their drills to look up at the incoming creature. Czar's voice boomed through the area as he demanded the dwarves continue their work.

"Death awaits those who stand idle," Czar's voice vibrated loudly.

The dwarves started back to work immediately ignoring the incoming visitor. The Raptor landed several feet from Czar and deposited the parchment paper on the ground. Czar clapped his hands together and fire sparked in every direction. The dwarf guard to his right picked up a rodent and flipped it into the air directly in front of Czar. Czar clapped his hands again and the flames roasted the rodent in a matter of seconds. The scorched carcass fell to the ground in front of the flamed one, and the Raptor bent down and grabbed the rodent with his sharp beak, swallowing it whole.

Czar's tail snaked towards the parchment paper and the tipped point jabbed towards it as he demanded, "Guard, read the message."

The minotaur guard to his left skirted around the flames emanating from Czar and bent down to retrieve the message.

"Ahumm," he cleared his throat before speaking. "Found the three remaining humans. All together living with the gnomes to the West. Special news I have for you. The magic writer is with them. Come immediately, yup, yup. Judas."

Czar's head snapped around as he heard the last part of the message. The magic writer was back? How could that be? He snatched the parchment from the guard's hands to see for himself the words Judas had written, but the heat disintegrated the paper within seconds of his touch. Curse his heat! He'd have to move fast. He could not allow magic to regenerate!

His booming voice halted the dwarves work below. "The time has come! We must strike and take this world! You must do as you have been trained! Kill the humans that live with the gnomes and bring the magic writer to me...alive. The end of the human race happens now," Czar commanded.

He turned and went back to his mansions to await the death of the humans and the capture of the magic writer. The time had finally come.

Epilogue

Adelaide Kane yelled up the stairs for her daughter Kassie once again. "Kassie, could you please do another load of laundry now?" Kassie rolled her eyes. She didn't have a clue where Charlie had disappeared to today, but she was getting tired of doing his chores. Once again he was being irresponsible and leaving the work to her.

Kassie swooped down the stairs to the basement and moved the basket to the front of the dryer to ready it for the clothes. She pulled them from the dryer, scooping them into the basket. With the dryer nearly empty, pushing the basket of clothes aside, she leaned in to see if she had them all. Up in the right hand part of the tumbler she found a sock stuck to the wall. It was stuffed into a hole in the dryer. She yanked on the sock to pull it from the hole and it freed itself. She squinted to see how the sock had become stuck. Behind where it had been sticking out was a heart shaped hole. Hmmm. Kassie wondered if it had always been there or if a piece had broken off.

She let her fingers trace the hole and realized the shape seemed familiar. She let her other hand dip into her pocket and searched around until she found the blue stone she had collected earlier from the dryer. She looked from the stone to the hole. It was the right shape and size. She leaned deeper into the dryer until all that stuck out were her calves and feet. She shoved the stone into the heart shaped hole and it fit perfectly! She smiled as she felt she had discovered something important when the rumble started and she lost her balance and fell forward, banging her head on the inside wall of the dryer. Her feet flipped up in the air and the dryer door bashed into her calves. With a yelp Kassie instinctively pulled her legs inwards to keep the dryer door from crashing into them again and the door slammed shut. The dryer started spinning and she let out a scream hoping her mom would hear her cries. She tumbled around screaming and yelling until her head hit hard against the dryer wall and she saw black.

She awoke slowly and felt the pain searing through her head. She reached up and touched it to find a bump the size of a walnut stemming from her left temple. "Ouch," she said as she touched the sore spot. She put her hands on the ground and felt the coldness of the dirt as she lifted herself to her feet, wincing at the pain in her calves. Darn dryer door! She gazed around her confused at her surroundings. She bent down and scooped up the dirt in her hands and let it sift through her fingers. Where was she? She slapped her hands together as she wiped the dirt off. She didn't know where this was, but she knew one thing. It wasn't home.

CPSIA information can be obtained at www.ICGtesting.com
Printed in the USA
LVOW07s0758221114

415001LV00002B/10/P